Never Tell Chloe

Diana L. Forsberg

CKBooks Publishing

This is a work of fiction. Names, characters, places, and incidents either are the products of the author's imagination or are used factitiously. Any resemblance to actual persons, living or dead, business establishments, events, or locales is entirely coincidental.

All rights reserved. No part of this book may be reproduced, distributed, or transmitted in any form or by any means, including photocopying, recording, or other electronic or mechanical methods, without the prior written approval of the author, except in the case of brief quotations in a book review and certain other noncommercial uses permitted by copyright law. Contact author at authorforsberg@gmail.com.

Publisher's Cataloging-in-Publication Data
Names: Forsberg, Diana L., author.
Title: Never tell Chloe / Diana L. Forsberg.
Description: Edition. | New Glarus, WI : CKBooks Publishing, 2021.
Identifiers: LCCN 2021913994 (print) | ISBN 978-1-949085-48-8 (paperback) | ISBN 978-1-949085-49-5 (ebook)
Subjects: LCSH: Demoniac possession--Fiction. | Forgiveness--Fiction. | Family secrets--Fiction. | Paranormal fiction. | Suspense fiction. | BISAC: FICTION / Occult & Supernatural. | FICTION / Thrillers / Supernatural. | FICTION / Thrillers / Suspense. | GSAFD: Occult fiction. | Suspense fiction.
Classification: LCC PS3606.O77 N48 2021 (print) | LCC PS3606.O77 (ebook) | DDC 813/.6--dc23.

LCCN: 2021913994
Copyright © 2021 Diana L. Forsberg
Front cover photograph by Diana L. Forsberg
All Rights Reserved by Diana L. Forsberg

CKBooks Publishing
PO Box 214
New Glarus, WI 53574
CKBooksPublishing.com

I dedicate this book in the memory of my parents, Leon and Dorothy Forsberg, who are long-gone but not forgotten.

♥

I also dedicate this book to my sister, Julie. Without her encouragement, my dream of writing a book would have stayed only a dream. Her encouragement was the push that I needed to start this journey, and she has my endless thanks.

Chapter 1

"Aren't you supposed to be dead, Joan?" Frank asked, staring at the woman who had just knocked on his condo door.

"Aren't you supposed to be surprised that I'm alive?" she replied.

Frank stood silently for a few seconds. Yes, he thought, the word *surprised* fit the occasion. He *was* surprised that his supposedly dead wife was standing at his door and equally surprised that he didn't immediately slam the door shut.

After giving her a not-so-subtle glance over, Frank was also surprised she no longer looked like the woman he once loved. She was now make-up-free and well-tanned, a natural tan—not a spray-on boutique tan. And her seemingly blond hair had reverted back to its natural mousy brown. She was also sporting a faded t-shirt, sturdy jeans, and scuffed up hiking boots, making it clear that her fashion sense had also changed—from expensive and stylish *to* thrifty and outdoorsy.

Outdoorsy—very surprising indeed, he thought. Joan fancied herself as an environmentalist back when she was in his life. Frank grinned slightly, remembering that she had actually preferred the tamed, manicured *wilderness* of city parks and the safe, well-worn paths near their weekend cabin.

However, he approved of the changes, thinking that Joan looked better in her forties than when they first met over twenty years ago.

Frank slowly turned his scrutiny to the older woman standing next to Joan. He recognized her as well, guessing that she had to be somewhere in her sixties by now. He decided, however, that the older woman hadn't changed much over the last twelve years. Clad in a colorful bohemian blouse and matching skirt, she still looked every inch the eccentric artist that she was.

Frank looked back at Joan for a moment, wondering why she and her Aunt Edith were standing at his door. Wanting to know the answer to that was the only reason he hadn't yet slammed the door shut.

His gaze turned downward at an old dog that was standing between the two women. Frank bent down and petted the dog, briefly running his hands over its soft, silky fur. Although he hadn't seen the dog in twelve years either, Frank sensed that the old dog remained the gentle soul he remembered. As the dog looked up at him, Frank knew it recognized him as well. The dog sat and lifted up his paw, offering it up for a handshake. Frank smiled and gently shook the dog's leathery paw.

"Hello, Molly," Frank quietly said to the dog. "You were always very smart."

Frank looked at the two women. "You better come in. No need to let the neighbors hear anything more."

"Why a condo? What happened to your house?" Edith asked as they all entered.

"Chloe is off to college now, and the house was too big for only me. And it held too many sad memories," Frank admitted, staring at Joan. He wished that the last part hadn't slipped out.

"I hope that there were some good memories too," Edith said.

Frank didn't respond.

"Why aren't you surprised that I am alive?" Joan asked.

"I saw you once when I was attending a conference in downtown Denver," Frank answered. "You were on the other side of the street—just *strolling* along on the sidewalk. I yelled over to you, but the traffic noise was too loud. By the time I got across, you were gone."

Frank took a deep breath before continuing. "I ran up and down the streets in the area, but I never caught sight of you again. However, I was sure that it was you. I put up posters in the area with your photo, asking for help in finding you. But no one came forward with any info."

As his eyes locked on Joan, he asked, "Did you see me?"

The intensity in Frank's eyes unsettled Joan, but she held his stare and answered, "No."

Frank believed her. The woman he remembered wouldn't have been able to look directly at him and lie.

"Since that day," Frank said, "what really upset me . . . hurt me . . . was that I couldn't fathom why you let your family think you were dead. Why not call me . . . or call someone? Only one answer made sense to me; you wanted nothing to do with us."

Joan looked away, silently confirming his suspicion.

"Why are you here, Joan?" Frank's voice lacked emotion, but the hurt showed in his eyes.

"Did you tell Chloe that you saw me?"

"No, I did *not*. You wanted to be dead; so, I let you be dead. Chloe thinks you were cremated and your ashes sprinkled in the park."

"I'm sorry, Frank."

"Too late for that, isn't it? Why are you and your aunt here?"

"Harriet's back in Wisconsin," Edith blurted out.

Frank's jaw tightened. "How's that possible, Edith? You told me that Harriet died."

"I know that you're probably surprised," Edith replied. "But Harriet *is* back."

"No, shocked is the word, not surprised," Frank mumbled. "I thought that Harriet had a heart attack and died twelve years ago."

"I only told you that because of Harriet's mental state," Edith said. "Maybe it was wrong of me, but I thought it was best to cut ties with you and Chloe. It was less complicated that way for all of us. I convinced Harriet to commit herself to a mental institution. I assumed that she would *never* be well enough to be discharged from that place."

"So, how is it that she's back in Wisconsin?" Frank asked.

"She was a voluntary patient," Edith explained. "She was also a very compliant patient. Because of that, I suppose, the doctors didn't categorize her as a danger to herself or others. So, they couldn't hold her against her will, and she was able to just walk out."

"Is our daughter in danger?" Frank asked, looking at Joan.

Joan nodded a quick yes.

Frank sat down before he fell. For a second, he felt as if he had been hit by a bullet. He motioned for his two guests to sit as well.

"We aren't sure if Chloe is in danger, but there's a good chance that she might be," Edith said. "Harriet told one of her caregivers that she was going to Wisconsin to see her granddaughter. And I tracked down the taxi driver who drove her to the airport, and Harriet had told him the same story. But we have a plan to handle this situation."

Frank stared at his guests, willing himself to quickly digest the words that he was hearing.

"Wait a minute—to the airport? How in the world could someone who just walked out of a mental institution afford to buy an airplane ticket?" Frank asked.

"I had established an account at the institution for her. I wanted her to have the funds to buy whatever she wanted or needed: clothes, treats, books, or whatever. She never really used much of it. But before she left there, Harriet drained all of the funds from the account. She had enough for a ticket but not much more than that," Edith explained. "But I have no doubt that when she needs more cash, she'll find a way to obtain it."

"Is all of this concern really warranted? You just said that she had been a very compliant patient. Anyhow, how dangerous can an old woman pushing seventy years old really be?" Frank asked.

Edith raised her eyebrows, sat a little straighter in her chair, and answered. "Yes, she *is* an old woman. But let me tell you, old women should never be underestimated. We have decades of life experiences to draw on. That knowledge makes us wiser, craftier, and probably more dangerous than someone half our age."

"You're probably right," Frank answered, looking down to hide a slight grin. "Harriet was always a formidable woman, and I suppose that she still is. What's your plan?"

"First, I think that we need to tell you what really happened twelve years ago," Joan stated.

Frank watched as Joan pulled her hair back, tying it in a loose ponytail knot. As it quickly fell free, he was surprised once again. Joan seemed unbothered by its unruliness. He wondered what other surprises were about to be revealed.

With a slight nod, Frank signaled his willingness to listen.

Afterwards, Frank found it difficult to speak. His only response after several minutes of silence was short. "I don't want Chloe to know that."

"Agreed," both women said in unison.

"Did either of you contact the police about Harriet?" Frank asked.

"And tell them what? That an old woman wants to visit her granddaughter?" Edith snapped.

Regretting her tone, Edith quietly added, "They wouldn't understand the seriousness of the situation."

"Okay, then what's *your* plan?" Frank asked.

"The two of us are going to follow Chloe. And when Harriet shows up, we will . . . Well, I should say when Harriet is alone—remember we don't want to involve Chloe," Edith stammered, taking several deep breaths before finishing. "We will *try* to convince her to return to New Mexico with me."

"Shouldn't I warn Chloe about the danger?" Frank asked. "Or maybe have her stay with me for a while?"

"No, that wouldn't solve anything. You can't hide Chloe at home forever, and she would undoubtedly ask a lot of questions about what's going on," Edith said.

"And we've just all agreed to never tell Chloe anything. It's best that she never finds out what really happened all those years ago," Joan added.

"Okay, but I have a question. What if she refuses to return to New Mexico?" Frank asked.

"Then we'll come up with another plan," Edith said. "We can't let Harriet stick around here. She needs to be dealt with in some fashion; otherwise, Chloe's going to spend her life always looking over her shoulder."

"But we will *not* let Chloe get hurt," Joan said. "That's something both Edith and I promise."

Frank looked over at Joan, gauging her commitment to the plan. She looked directly back at him, and for a moment, Frank was startled. It was a strong woman who stared back at him. Joan had changed—of this, he was certain.

"Harriet's your mother, Joan. Do you *truly* feel that she's still dangerous?" Frank asked.

Joan replied with only one word, "Yes."

Lines slowly burrowed into Frank's forehead, and he grew very still. Joan stared at him. She had seen this before. Frank was weighing the options.

"Okay, I'll go along with the plan for now," Frank said in a slow and even voice. "But if I believe that Chloe is in danger, then I'll put an end to all of the secrets. It would be better for Chloe to know the truth than be dead."

"Agreed," both women said in unison again.

After they left, Frank sat quietly, wishing that he had taken the situation more seriously twelve years ago.

∼

Harriet stood by the window in the apartment, waiting for her young neighbor to return from work. As she waited, she wiped the sweat from her forehead. She had been wiping sweat from her forehead since Sunday evening when she first took up residence in the second-floor apartment, and it was now Wednesday.

When she fled Albuquerque a week or so ago, she didn't realize how much she would miss the dry heat of the Southwest. Unfortunately, July in Wisconsin means hot and humid, and Harriet wasn't happy about that.

Regrettably, the apartment that she was holed up in didn't have central air—only a small air conditioner perched perilously in one of the windows. And since it was so annoyingly loud, Harriet avoided using it. It prevented her from hearing every little noise, and her inner voice told her to be vigilant: to listen, to watch, and to wait for the right moment.

Since she was a young child, Harriet obeyed her inner voice. It had been twelve years or so since she was last in Wisconsin, and it was her inner voice that told her to return.

Everything comes full circle, she thought—everything.

However, she was becoming impatient. She wanted to proceed with her plan, and it was the waiting that was driving her crazy. She smiled at that thought. Though others might disagree, she knew that she wasn't crazy.

In fact, Harriet felt that resourceful was the best word to describe her. It had always been easy for her to coax people into doing things for her—for example, letting her into a locked apartment. And it was even easier now. People instinctively want to help an old woman. Harriet laughed and slowly looked around the apartment until her eyes settled on a slightly ajar closet door. She then laughed again, and said, "After all, how dangerous can an old woman really be?"

So far, Harriet felt that her plan was going smoothly. This wasn't unexpected, she knew, as her plan only had two steps in it. And the first step was already completed—to find Chloe. Harriet laughed once again, mumbling to herself, "The first step was so easy. Everyone's on the internet these days."

However, the second step was proving somewhat more complicated. Harriet hadn't foreseen one thing, and that was a cat—an old, grumpy cat who lived across the hallway with Chloe. She had tried striking up a conversation with Chloe on the previous day but failed. As Harriet had started to speak, the cat loudly and persistently hissed. Before more than just a few words were exchanged, Chloe closed her door, apologizing for the cat's rudeness.

"That awful cat hissed at me!" Harriet complained to herself, annoyed at the missed opportunity.

Harriet wanted to *rid the world* of the grumpy cat. But the voice in her head, her inner voice, told her to be patient; the cat is old, just wait.

So, she waited, believing that her inner voice possessed knowledge that most did not.

Chapter 2

"What a god-awful hot day," Chloe mumbled to no one in particular as she stepped off the city bus at her stop.

It was one of those sweltering July days that happen so often in Wisconsin. The thick, humid air wrapped around Chloe, almost immobilizing her. Chloe forcibly pushed her way, step by step, through the nearly impenetrable air. As soon as she got to her apartment and sat in the cooled air, Chloe knew she would slowly recuperate from the brutal summer heat.

She wished, however, it was as easy to recuperate from the last four years of studying and part-time jobs. She had recently graduated from college and landed a coveted summer internship at a local Madison law firm. But this left her with no break between classwork and an office cubicle.

Unfortunately, Chloe also disliked her internship. Although she was fully proficient at the tasks assigned to her, she felt out of place there. Too often, she stared blankly out the window next to her cubicle, wishing that she was somewhere, or really anywhere else. Although her father was an attorney, Chloe wasn't sure that she wanted to be one. She didn't dislike attorneys.

Chloe believed that most attorneys were like her father—trusted advisors rather than the vultures of modern-day myth.

But if not an attorney, then what? That was a question that she was unable to answer.

When Chloe finally reached her apartment and unlocked the door, she was met with life-renewing cool air. Not every apartment in her building had been retrofitted with central air, but Chloe felt the extra rent she paid was worth it. Or, as Chloe liked to say, her cat was worth the extra rent. Since the deaths of her mother and grandmother twelve years ago, Chloe loved only two things in the world: her father and her cat.

Chloe closed the door quickly to prevent the cool air from escaping, and as usual, her cat ran over to greet her. As the cat started to purr, Chloe picked her up and hugged her.

"You're such a sweet cat, Lulu," Chloe whispered into her cat's ear. "Why did you hiss at that old woman yesterday? You've never hissed at anyone before."

Chloe was worried about her cat. It was more than only the hissing. Her cat had been acting strangely the last few days, jumping at the slightest noises and racing off to hide. The cat wiggled out of Chloe's arms and hurried over to the couch. Within seconds, the cat curled up in her favorite spot, anticipating her usual routine of snoozing while Chloe ate supper in front of the TV.

Just like her cat, Chloe felt more anxious than usual over the last few days. Inside her small apartment, with her cat and a locked door, Chloe had always felt safe before. Wishing that she knew what had changed, Chloe popped a frozen dinner into her microwave and unexpectedly shuddered.

Chloe was only ten years old when her mother and grandmother unexpectedly died. Initially overpowered by the tragedy and the grief that came with it, she withdrew into herself, avoiding life outside of her bedroom as much as possible.

However, it was fear that kept her isolated—that truly imprisoned her. Even in the sanctuary of her bedroom, fear hovered in the background. And each night, she felt compelled to look under her bed before turning off the light, always expecting to find *something*—but what, she never knew.

With her father's support, Chloe worked hard to heal after the pain of her losses. He promised her that in time both her pain and fears would fade. Just as her father had promised, as each day, month, and year passed by, she slowly healed and started to venture out more freely. And attending college in nearby Madison was an accomplishment that both Chloe and her father were very proud of.

However, Chloe kept a secret from her father. Although it had been twelve years since her family's tragic losses, she still dealt with a vague sense of fear as well as emptiness. And she still looked under her bed every night.

Carrying her steaming meal over to the couch, Chloe sat next to her cat and turned on the local evening news. As was the custom, Chloe gave her cat several treats to nibble on. Normally, Chloe enjoyed their simple evening routine, but today something was gnawing at the edges of her consciousness. Wanting to hear her father's comforting voice, she decided to call him.

"Hello, Dad. I hope that you weren't already asleep in front of the TV!" Chloe said teasingly.

"No, wiseguy," Frank laughed. "What's up, sweetheart? You don't usually call mid-week."

"I just feel a little anxious and wanted to hear your voice."

"Anything, in particular, causing you concern?" The worry in his voice made Chloe regret calling her father. She knew that it had been a rough twelve years for him too.

"Nothing that I can put my finger on. It's just a feeling that something is off. It's probably only me trying to decide what to do with my life."

"Sweetheart, don't twist yourself up over that. You don't have to be an attorney. Maybe we can brainstorm some ideas this weekend?"

"Okay, that sounds great, Dad. I only wish that I had a glimmer about what I really want to do."

Neither spoke for a few seconds.

"Dad, please don't think that I am crazy. But I started a meditation class a couple of weeks ago. And before you ask, the class is really cheap. You know that I save almost every cent that I make." Chloe laughed as she pictured her father's eyeroll.

"I wasn't going to ask that, sweetie. You're an adult. You can take a meditation class if you want. People swear about the benefits of meditating these days—good for stress relief or whatever."

"Hmm. That sounds very *enlightened* for you. Anyhow, when I was meditating the other day, a thought came out of the blue to me: *You can have many interests but only one true calling.* Do you think that's true?"

"Wow, you come up with a lot of deep questions, sweetheart. Too many philosophy classes, maybe." Frank hoped that his voice sounded lighthearted.

"Sorry, Dad. I know that I'm a nerd."

"You aren't a *nerd*. You are a smart and insightful young woman."

"Insightful—I like that. But you haven't answered my question."

"I don't have an answer for you. Unfortunately, I don't believe that many people actually know or try to pursue *a true calling.*"

"Is being an attorney your true calling, Dad?"

"Probably not. I came from a working-class family and wanted to make something of myself. Being an attorney was a good way to accomplish that."

"If not an attorney, what would you have wanted to do?"

Never Tell Chloe

"I don't really know. I love to cook, so maybe that. Not any fancy cuisine. Just good food—the type that an everyday family likes to eat—chicken dinners, pizza, brats, burgers, and Friday night fish fries."

"Wow, it sounds like you have thought about it."

"Only in my daydreams, sweetheart. Now try not to worry about your career options anymore tonight. We'll talk more this weekend. Sleep tight and stay safe."

"Okay, Dad. Good night," Chloe said, hanging up the phone. Stay safe? What an odd thing for him to say, she thought.

Chloe felt a gentle coolness briefly wrap around her. An invisible hug is what she called it as a child. The hugs, or more precisely, the strange visitations started shortly after her mother's death, slowly decreasing over the years, until now—and she wondered why.

Never sure if her visitor was an angel, ghost, or merely her imagination, Chloe sensed only gentle and loving feelings radiating from it. However, even as a child, she instinctively knew that others would doubt her sanity if she spoke of it. So she kept it a secret from everyone, except Lulu. Her cat didn't judge.

After giving Lulu a few more treats to crunch on, Chloe turned in early. As usual, her cat snuggled closed to Chloe in bed and purred, almost vibrating with love and contentment. Both felt safe and loved in their little world.

However, at the end of a hot, humid day, Harriet didn't feel safe in the little apartment across the hall. Sitting at the window and straining to see through the darkness, she felt tired. It was the type of tired only the old understand; a tiredness accumulated though many, many years. She peered into the darkness outside of her window, certain that someone in the shadows was watching her. She could feel it deep in her bones; a stalker lurked outside. Harriet knew that she needed to remain vigilant.

Cloaked in the darkness, two women sat in an old, rusty

pickup truck, looking up at the windows in the apartment building across the street. Both wondered if Harriet was looking back. With the old dog asleep between them, they watched in silence.

Breaking the silence, Edith asked, "Were you ever happy in your life back then, Joan?"

Slightly startled by the question, Joan answered, "Yes, there were times when I was happy. But usually, I felt empty. Why do you ask?"

"Have you been happy during the last twelve years? After you left here?" Edith asked, avoiding Joan's question.

"That's a harder question. When I left, I was searching for something. I couldn't really define what back then. I still can't. You know how people used to say that they needed to *go find themselves*. It was kind of like that for me. But finding yourself is really hard for those of us who are truly lost."

Edith nodded in agreement.

After a short silence, Joan continued, "I tried a little of everything. I searched out the guidance of preachers and mystics alike. I meditated, hiked in the mountains, and swam in crystal clear lakes. I camped in the wilderness just so that I could look up at the night sky and see the breathtaking beauty of the stars. In time, I found some peace, if not happiness."

"What do you mean that you found *some* peace?"

"I was at a campground in Oregon a few months ago, and just by chance, I started talking to an old man. He said that he was from Northern Wisconsin and that he took care of an old historic church. I had already guessed that he was from Wisconsin, though. His t-shirt had the word *bubbler* blazed across the front of it. It's funny. From time to time, I still ask people *where's the bubbler—not where's the drinking fountain?*"

"Bubbler?"

"It's a Wisconsin thing," Joan smiled. "Anyhow, his church sounded charming, and I got caught up in his storytelling about it and about his favorite fishing creek. He was so easy to talk to. And for some reason that I cannot explain, I confessed that I had left my old life behind in Wisconsin and that I was finding it hard to start my next chapter in life."

Joan closed her eyes for a moment, remembering the old man's advice and then continued. "He told me I was having trouble starting a new chapter in my life because I still needed to finish the current chapter. He then just disappeared."

"Disappeared?"

"Yes. I reached over to take a sip of my coffee, and when I turned back, he was gone. It gave me the chills, but I haven't been able to get his advice out of my mind. He was a really sweet old man. He wore one of those floppy brim fishing hats, and the hat had so many silver fishing lures that when the sun hit it, it looked like he had a halo. Swear to God, it really did. So anyhow, I decided that maybe I should heed his advice and take care of some stuff. You know, wrap things up and find closure. Or something like that so that I could start fresh."

"He sounds like someone you were destined to meet."

They sat in silence again for a few minutes.

"I know that I sound like a crazy old hippie or maybe a New Age nut, but I believe that sometimes fate kicks in. It did for me," Edith said.

"Wow, that's funny. Not the fate stuff; I believe that also. But all of those years ago, Frank thought that you were some sort of crazy artist hippie. That's why he didn't believe you when you tried to warn us."

"He believes me now. I hope."

"Yes, I think so."

Neither spoke again for a few moments.

"Years ago and quite by accident, I met a kindly old artist who helped me get my art studio off the ground. You know how horrible my childhood was. You can also guess that I was as lost and damaged as any soul could be," Edith said. "Without her, I would be just another starving artist or worse. Her advice saved me."

"Unfortunately, heeding that old man's advice led to all of this." Joan's voice was barely a whisper.

"Sometimes, we don't have a choice in life, Joan. The past catches up with us. It always does."

Joan nodded in agreement.

"I have a question, Joan, and you don't have to answer if you don't want. Why didn't you let Frank know that you were alive?"

Joan stared into the night but didn't answer.

"I should get back to the van that I rented," Edith said. "Why don't you head back to the hotel and get some rest? You've been watching Chloe virtually nonstop for a few days. I'll take over for tonight. Anyhow, Frank just texted, saying that Chloe had turned in. It's unlikely that anything more will happen tonight."

"Okay, thanks. But I have a question first," Joan said, looking at the white cargo van parked behind her. "Why did you rent a van instead of a car?"

"A van is best for this situation."

"Why? Are you planning on kidnapping Harriet?"

"First, I'm going to try to convince her to return with me to Albuquerque."

"And if she doesn't go with you willingly, then are you going to kidnap her?"

Edith didn't answer the question.

"Here are some clothes that I picked up for you at a thrift store earlier today," Joan said, handing a bag to Edith. "I think it would be best if you dressed a little less . . . um, artsy."

"Okay, I understand," Edith laughed. "I will try to blend in more with the locals."

"Just so you know, my pickup is running really rough, and

I made an early appointment at a garage. I don't know exactly when I'll be able to meet up with you tomorrow."

"Don't worry about that. I'll be fine alone, and text me the garage's phone number. I'll call and give them my credit card number," Edith said. "And please don't refuse my help. I can afford it. You wouldn't believe how much money art collectors pay for my sculptures."

After a moment, Edith quietly added, "And that kindly old artist that I mentioned left me a fortune in her will many years ago. She was my mentor and friend. No, actually, that's not true. She was more like a sweet older sister to me. I miss her so very much. Cancer is a despicable thing. Unfortunately, life has taught me that there are many despicable things in the world."

Joan allowed a few moments of silence to pass before softly saying, "I'm really sorry that you lost someone so dear to you. And thank you for the help with paying the repair bill."

"Sure, it's best that we have two vehicles available anyhow, and it's good that your pickup has the camper on the back. That might prove helpful also."

Joan nodded in response, silently agreeing with the potential kidnapping. "The repairs might take the whole day but hopefully not more than that."

"Okay, don't worry. I'll follow Chloe tomorrow. You need a break anyhow." Edith got out of Joan's truck and walked to her van.

As Joan drove off, Edith looked up at the dark windows in the apartment building and whispered into the darkness, "Are you there? Can you feel me watching you?"

∼

When Chloe woke the next morning, she was surprised that her cat had not pestered her for breakfast yet. Chloe never needed an alarm clock to wake her. She joked that Lulu was part cat—part alarm clock.

Chloe turned over to pet her cat, expecting to see her cat doing early morning yawns and stretches. However, the cat was eerily motionless as if frozen in place. Shocked, Chloe stared in silence. She read once that after a soul departs, the energy changes in a room, and she could feel the cold, shifting energy as her cat's essence departed.

The eerie quiet in the room pierced through Chloe's shock, and she started to cry. After a while, she stopped and wiped her tears away. She then inhaled deeply, forcing herself to accept that it was her cat's time to depart. She took some comfort in knowing that her cat had lived a very long life—for a cat, at least.

Despite this, Chloe would miss her cat. Her cat was much more than merely a pet. The cat was her loyal friend and confidant. Only with her, Chloe felt safe sharing her tears, her fears, and her secrets. Now, like her mother, her cat was gone too. And Chloe felt the pain of loss once again. She gently petted her cat's soft fur, keenly aware of its new coldness. Chloe whispered, "I love you."

After she composed herself, Chloe called her office to explain that she would not be in. She then gently put her cat into a shoebox and drove over to the veterinary clinic. The vet assured Chloe that her cat's death was likely peaceful.

Comforted by the vet's assurances, Chloe stopped at the reception desk prior to leaving the clinic and paid the young receptionist, who emotionlessly explained that the cat's ashes could be picked up in about a week. Chloe cringed at the coldness of the words.

After Chloe returned to her car, she called her father. "Dad, something awful happened. Lulu passed away last night."

"I'm so sorry, Chloe," Frank said. "Is there anything that I can do?"

"No. I already took her to the vet, and I can pick up her ashes in a week," Chloe softly answered. "But I took the day off. I don't feel up to working today."

"Of course, I understand. Please let me know if you need anything, okay?"

"Okay," Chloe whispered, fighting back the tears as she ended the phone call.

Frank sat quietly for a few moments after the call ended, aware that his daughter was deeply upset by the death of her cat. He could hear it in her voice. Frank understood how much the cat had helped Chloe survive the last twelve years.

Frank also hoped that its death wouldn't undermine his daughter's hard-won wellbeing. While he had been uncomfortable with Edith and Joan's plan, he now silently and fully committed himself to it. Frank felt that it was best to shield Chloe from the ugliness of the past.

~

Harriet watched Chloe return to the apartment building, listened to Chloe's slow walk up the stairs to the second floor, and heard Chloe's apartment door open and shut. She had overheard Chloe's earlier crying but wasn't sure what had happened.

Donning a look of concern, she crossed the hall to knock on Chloe's door and ask if anything was wrong.

Chloe looked closely at the old woman, wondering why her sweet cat had hissed at her. Was there something that she was missing, Chloe wondered? The only surprising thing to her was that someone older lived in the building. Most tenants were either college students or recent grads.

There certainly was nothing scary about her that Chloe could see. Her gray hair was cut very short, almost a buzz cut. A very *cutting-edge* hairstyle for an old woman, Chloe thought, finding it endearing. However, the old woman's blouse and slacks were faded and baggy. And rather than endearing, Chloe felt her clothing seemed drab and lifeless. Even with her taste in clothing, she seemed quite ordinary and harmless to Chloe

As Chloe's eyes securitized her, Harriet doubted she was recognizable. After all, she barely recognized herself anymore. The expensive clothes, spiked heels, plump collagen-filled lips, contact lenses, and peroxide blonde hair were all gone. Gone too were forty pounds and her curves. Harriet smirked to herself—*the bland institutional food was the best diet she had ever been on.*

"Do you *live* in this building?" Chloe asked.

"Yes, I'm right across the hall from you," Harriet said, shoving her simple, plastic frame glasses back into place.

Chloe looked toward the apartment, wondering when the grad student who lived there moved out, and this older woman moved in. However, she decided against asking that question. She did not feel like having a long conversation with a stranger.

"My cat, Lulu, died overnight," Chloe finally said.

Harriet offered her condolences and turned away before smiling. *The cat was out of the way, and she felt that was miraculous—a word that she seldom used.*

However, once inside her apartment, Harriet shuddered. Staring at Chloe had frightened her—but just for a moment.

Chapter 3

After her new neighbor left, Chloe sat down on the closest chair and stared at nothing. Normally, she considered her apartment a sanctuary of sorts—like being wrapped safely in a cocoon. However, the apartment seemed too quiet, too empty, and too lifeless without her cat. But she knew it was more than just the quietness that was bothering her. Without her cat, Chloe's own emptiness was more apparent.

"Dammit, Lulu. Why did you leave me? I'm going to miss you," Chloe said out loud. Her words lingered in the quietness, reinforcing the sense of emptiness that she felt.

There had been an uncomplicated bond between Chloe and her cat. The cat brought love and companionship (mixed with a measure of chaos) into her otherwise solitary world. The cat was often relentlessly demanding in her quest for treats. At other times, she was aloof, avoiding even a glance in Chloe's direction. The cat jumped up on countertops searching for trouble; she attacked paper bags with a vengeance, and she frequently knocked her toys under the couch with a swift and purposeful whack of her paw.

However, Chloe refused to scold her cat, feeling that Lulu was merely acting like the cat that she was. Chloe simply had no desire to try to mold her cat into something it was not.

Chloe felt a chill as she suddenly remembered her mother's often-spoken advice to her: *It's always best to just be yourself.*

A sudden urge to be among the living seized hold of Chloe, and she grabbed her purse, escaping her empty, lifeless apartment. Hurrying to the nearby bus stop, she caught a bus to State Street in downtown Madison. Distracted by her grief, Chloe stared out the window, not noticing that her new neighbor had also boarded the bus and sat several seats behind her.

Chloe loved downtown Madison, especially State Street—an eclectic blend of bars, shops, and eateries, running from the State Capitol building to the local university.

As a student, she had walked State Street every day between her classes. And since her law firm was downtown as well, she continued the same routine as an intern. Chloe enjoyed looking into the windows of the little shops, fascinated by the variety of items displayed—art, books, comics, mystical trinkets, and endless souvenirs.

She also enjoyed the mixture of people that walked the street with her—university students, pan handlers, tourists, government employees, and street vendors. Although she always strove to remain invisible to those she passed by, she craved the heartbeat of State Street. Chloe had always understood a simple truth: State Street was a safe haven from which to *watch* life.

Lately, however, Chloe started to notice a change on State Street and the downtown area, and it made her cringe. In almost every direction, Chloe saw a crane at work as the old buildings were replaced by cold towering structures, whose signs boasted of high-rent apartments, over-priced retail space, and costly hotel rooms. Her *haven* was vanishing.

Getting off the bus near the Capitol building, Chloe strolled down State Street, only vaguely aware of her surroundings. Like most days, Chloe felt more like a shadow than a person, still fighting to heal after the deaths of her mother and grandmother, still hiding behind a facade.

As she walked, Chloe suddenly remembered her puppy, Molly. The puppy had died alongside Chloe's mother. Now, her cat was also gone. Her eyes teared up, revealing the sadness that always hovered just below the surface.

Lost in her thoughts, Chloe failed to notice that Harriet was following closely—very closely. As Chloe wiped her tears, Harriet suddenly brushed by her, and Chloe stumbled off the curb in front of an oncoming city bus. Trying to catch her balance, she screamed as the bus headed toward her. A good Samaritan snatched Chloe back to the safety of the sidewalk.

Glancing over her shoulder as she hurried away, Harriet stole a look at the good Samaritan, recognizing her immediately.

"Oh shit. So it's Edith who has been following me—stalking me," Harriet mumbled as she quickened her pace.

Now back safely on the sidewalk, Chloe steadied herself and thanked her good Samaritan.

"Are you okay?" the good Samaritan asked.

"Yes, I guess so," Chloe responded as she looked into the dark green eyes of the good Samaritan. "Wow, your eyes remind me of my mother's. She also had beautiful green eyes."

"Thanks, but please be more careful, young lady. Keep your wits about you at all times," the good Samaritan advised. Her tone left little doubt to the seriousness of the advice.

"Um, okay," Chloe answered.

"Be careful," the good Samaritan said as she walked away.

As her good Samaritan disappeared into the noontime crowd on the sidewalk, Chloe noticed something else about her. They shared the same hair color—what her grandmother mockingly called *dishwater blonde*. She shrugged off the strange similarities, grateful to be unharmed.

Edith hurried in the direction that Harriet went but soon lost sight of her. She texted Joan, *"Where are you?"*

"Still at garage—waiting. Something wrong?"

"I'm downtown. Saw Harriet but lost her. I'm following Chloe now."

"What can I do?"

"Take a taxi to Chloe's apartment. Maybe Harriet will show up there."

"Okay."

∼

Sitting on a nearby bench, Chloe sensed a familiar gentle, cool presence wrap around her. A faint floral scent lingered in the air as she heard a soft whisper, "You are loved."

Chloe glanced around; no one was nearby. She wasn't sure if what she was experiencing was real. She had felt the presence many times over the years but had never heard anything. However, she felt comforted by the words nonetheless and let her tears freely run down her face. After a few minutes, Chloe inhaled, closed her eyes, and tried to regain some composure.

The first thought that came to her was simple: It had been a terrible day—first Lulu's death and then nearly getting hit by a bus. The next thought was also simple: The good Samaritan's green eyes had conjured up memories of her mother, and she wished that she was still ten years old. With that thought, childhood memories started to drift freely through her mind.

First came memories of the family's fishing cabin. The cabin sat nestled in what, as a child, she called an enchanted forest, and it seemed like most of her happiest memories had happened there.

Chloe remembered hiking in the *enchanted* forest with her mother. Chloe could almost hear her own innocent laughter as she made countless discoveries on these hikes—wildflowers, colorful pebbles, and whatnot.

Chloe suddenly put her hand over her heart as she remembered her puppy, Molly, again. The puppy loved to chase the butterflies and birds by the cabin. Such a sweet pup, Chloe smiled. As with her cat, Chloe loved the pup with the fullest of her heart.

Other memories fluttered by as well, such as her mother on the cabin's front porch, sitting at her easel, fully immersed in her art—and fully detached from the world around her. Despite feeling invisible to her mother at these times, Chloe loved watching the whimsical paintings take form. Eventually, her mother's paintbrush would be put down, and she would emerge from her art, giving Chloe a quick kiss on the forehead.

It was much the same with her father and fishing, she thought. As he fished in the nearby creek, he drifted away into his own thoughts, only vaguely aware of the activities around him. Chloe remembered patiently sitting next to him, waiting for him to emerge from his thoughts. When he did, her father always smiled at her and said that he loved her.

Chloe remembered one other thing—a silent tension between her mother and grandmother. The tension was so strong that even as a child, she recognized it.

She also fondly remembered how close she and her parents were back then. Their daily routines, words, and emotions were intertwined. She ached, remembering what it felt like to be so close, so loved that you felt a part of each other. At least that was how Chloe remembered it, and she was afraid that she would never feel that again.

Sadly, Chloe also remembered the pain she felt when her mother and puppy were torn from her life. She felt like a part of her heart had been ripped out. Mourning is the word for it, of course, Chloe knew. However, she never knew how to explain how deep her pain went. To her, it felt like part of her was still missing—like a book with pages ripped out.

When it was late at night, and neither her father nor she could sleep, he would say that their shared loss left a real wound—not just a scratch, but a deep wound. A wound, he told her, takes as long as it takes to heal. Her father reassured Chloe that she was strong and would heal in time. He also said that someday she would recall more happy memories than sad ones.

Sitting on the bench, still wrapped warmly in her memories, a quiet revelation came to Chloe. Her wound was healing. It was leaving a scar behind, to be sure. However, the scar was knitting her back together, and Chloe was grateful for its toughness.

Chloe stood up—she made a decision. She was going to stop hiding from life. She needed to start acting like a living person.

She quietly asked herself, "But how do I start? Quit my internship?"

The gentle, cool presence wrapped around her again and whispered, "Yes."

Chloe looked around again. No one was nearby. However, she heard the whispered answer. She was certain of it.

Nervously biting her lip, she decided to quit her internship.

Although the law firm was located across from the State Capitol building and within a short walk, Chloe needed to marshal the courage to carry out her decision. She walked slowly toward the Capitol building and then around the four blocks that formed the grassy square on which the Capitol building sat. She then walked around the square again, then again, and then again—passing by the law firm each time.

Chloe was not changing her mind. She knew that it was the right decision. The seemingly endless legal research, paper-pushing, client coddling, long hours, and the stale air in her cramped cubicle had a numbing effect on her. If she stayed too long, Chloe feared that she would never escape. She feared being lulled into a safe, robotic life.

To be fair, the law firm was highly respected, and the attorneys were good at their jobs. Chloe had sincerely tried to be part of that world, always completing the tasks assigned and always at the highest level of competence.

When Chloe finally entered her supervisor's office and resigned, it surprised those whom she worked for and with. Profusely apologizing, Chloe gathered up her few personal items and quickly dashed out, knowing it was highly unprofessional to resign without any sort of notice. As she burst out of the door and back onto the sidewalk, she felt much like an animal that just escaped a trap.

Walking toward her bus stop, Chloe sheepishly phoned her father, dutifully explaining her actions. Much to his credit, her father understood.

"It's always best to admit that something is not right for you, Chloe. Part of becoming an adult is finding the right path or at least the best option to pursue in life. Maybe that's what a true calling is. Some people know from birth what the right path is for them—to be a firefighter, a soldier, a teacher, or whatever. But most of us," her father calmly explained, "must search to find our place in the world."

After a few moments, he added, "Don't spend a lifetime trying to mold yourself into someone that you aren't. It'll just eat away at your soul. If it doesn't feel right to you, then it's not right for you. Go home and stay safe."

"Dad, thank you for understanding," Chloe said, wondering if her father would have been happier as a fry cook.

Chloe also wondered about his advice to stay safe but quickly put those words out of her mind. She was too happy to be free of the internship to focus on much else right then.

As she boarded the city bus to go back to her apartment,

Chloe felt exhausted. Grateful to find an empty seat on the crowded bus, she collapsed into it and quietly watched the rush hour traffic through her window as the bus moved along its route.

Surprisingly, however, Chloe still felt vaguely uneasy. And she asked under her breath, "What is the right path for me? How can I fill the emptiness inside and feel more alive? But mostly, why am I always so afraid?"

Back at her apartment, Chloe flopped onto her bed. The day had drained her, and as soon as her eyes closed, she fell asleep. However, nightmares came to her as quickly as did sleep. And her nightmares remained unchanged over the last twelve years—the fishing cabin, fierce rain, swirling fog, and a terrifying scream that always pierced the veil of sleep, forcing her awake with a lingering fear that she was in danger. The nightmares were another secret that she did not share.

Edith arrived shortly after Chloe and parked her van just down the street from Chloe's apartment. Joan hurried over, and as she leaned into the van's open window, Edith asked, "Did Harriet show up here?"

"Yes, a little while ago. I saw her enter the apartment building just as I got here, but I couldn't get inside. The building's locked," Joan said. "Oh, and Chloe just got home too."

"Yes, I know. I was following Chloe's bus, and let me tell you, that's not easy in rush hour. It's like following a lunatic who speeds up and then suddenly stops and then crawls along and then suddenly speeds up again. Well, you get the point."

After briefing Joan on the details of the day's events, Edith took a deep breath and said, "I kept Chloe safe today, but we'll need to keep a close eye on things. Today proved that."

"I agree, and I'm sorry that I didn't get here in time to nab . . . I mean . . . confront Harriet."

"We can't worry about missed opportunities."

"Yes, I guess that's true."

"I don't mean to be rude, but you need to leave and get back to the garage before they close. We'll need your truck."

∼

As she stood vigil, looking out of the apartment window, Harriet's thoughts drifted to the countless shrinks that she had encountered in her life. Each had tried to change her, trying to silence her inner voice. And indeed, occasionally, the voice would go silent for a moment or a day or maybe two, and she admitted that she felt a little happier whenever that occurred. However, her inner voice always returned, and she always felt compelled to listen.

Damn, she cursed to herself, upon hearing Chloe's apartment door shut. She had missed Chloe's arrival. She looked out the window, wondering if her stalker had returned also.

After a short while, Harriet decided that it was time to move forward with her plan. She crossed the hallway and repeatedly knocked on Chloe's door. Finally, the door opened.

"Do you want to take a road trip?" Harriet asked.

"Um . . . I don't understand? Us? I mean . . . I don't even know your name?" Confused, Chloe stared at the older woman standing in front of her.

"My name is Hetty," Harriet lied. She felt it best to use her childhood nickname: a name she had not been called in over sixty years, a name that Chloe would not recognize.

As questions swirled in her mind, Chloe silently asked herself: *Go on a road trip? With an old woman? With a stranger? Sure, we exchanged a few words, but we just met yesterday. This is very odd, isn't it?*

However, she found it even odder that she didn't immediately reject the idea. Even before her cat's death, it had been a difficult, gloomy week. Images of the dreadful night that ended her mother's life had been invading her daytime thoughts and her nighttime dreams more and more lately. She was feeling a growing uneasiness and didn't know why.

So, the idea of a road trip intrigued Chloe. Even if it was with an old woman that she didn't know, the lure of an escape was very tempting. She had grown up in a little town about 40 minutes west of Madison, where her father still lived, and leaving for college was the boldest thing she had ever done. Not that it was really all that bold, she thought. Maybe doing something spontaneous, maybe even foolish, for once was a good idea. It wasn't like her, but then that was a large part of the appeal.

"Hetty, I don't mean to be rude, but are you sure? I mean, you don't really know me. Do you even know my name?"

"You're Chloe." Realizing that Chloe might question how she knew, Harriet quickly lied, "One of the other tenants told me your name."

"Even so, Hetty, we don't know each other."

"I'm sure that *I am* in no danger from you."

Chloe smiled and said, "Of course not! But an old woman should be more careful about going off with a stranger. Oh geez, I'm sorry. I didn't mean to call you an *old* woman."

"No offense taken. I am an old woman. So why can't you call me that? I earned the right to be called old. Life is rough, and I managed to survive a very long time. And that is nothing to be ashamed of. I certainly am not going to pretend that I am a young broad."

Chloe grinned, slightly flushed after Harriet's none-too-subtle rebuke. "Okay, Hetty, then let's go on a road trip!"

Wow, Chloe thought, she just agreed to go on the road trip, and her decision made her feel—well, alive.

"I'm so happy that you agreed, Chloe."

"We can leave first thing tomorrow morning, okay?"

"Can we go right now? It's only 7 pm, and there's still plenty of daylight."

"Sure, what the heck," Chloe slowly said as a realization came to her. If they waited until morning, she would chicken out. "I'll throw a few things in a tote and meet you by my car. I drive the little yellow car in the parking lot."

"Fantastic!" Harriet said. She quickly returned to her apartment, grabbing a billfold off the table and her already-packed tote bag. After one last glance around, she was confident that there was nothing left that she had any use for, and she hurried off to the parking lot.

As Harriet waited by Chloe's car, she flipped through the cash and credit cards in the billfold. Her eyes turned up toward the apartment she had been occupying. She smirked and whispered, "The interest rates on these credit cards should, frankly, be a crime."

With one hand on her doorknob and the other holding her packed tote, Chloe froze. A faint jingling sound caught her attention, and a thought forced its way into her conscious mind: *Don't go.* However, the idea of an escape was too tempting. She took a deep breath, summoned her courage, and walked out of her apartment.

∽

Shit, Edith thought. She had nearly reached Harriet before Chloe came outside. Ducking behind a nearby parked car, she texted Joan: *"Chloe is leaving in her car. Harriet's with her. No time to wait for you. I'll follow them."*

Joan's answer came quickly. *"Damn. Keep me posted and let me know where to meet up."*

Chapter 4

As Chloe maneuvered her car out of the parking lot and onto the street, she remembered a photo of her mother's first car—a small hatchback. Her mother laughed whenever she described it, jokingly calling her car *a puddle jumper*. Chloe smiled—like mother, like daughter.

Still smiling, Chloe asked what direction to head in. Harriet glanced over her shoulder, pleased not to see her stalker, and she smiled too.

"I want to see the Werewolf of Walworth County!" Harriet said. "Though some call it the Beast of Bray Road. But I like the werewolf title. It's so much more gothic."

"Really? I remember hearing about that on TV occasionally, but you don't seem the type to be into crazy stuff that like," Chloe said and at once regretted her choice of words. "I don't mean that you are crazy. I'm just surprised."

"No offense taken. Some people might call me crazy," Harriet laughed. "But I love stuff like that. I watch all of that crazy—to use your word—stuff on TV."

"I love shows about ghosts, monsters, and all of that kind of stuff too," Chloe said. "It's my guilty pleasure, I guess. My mom loved that stuff too. But oh boy, not my dad. He thought it was all ridiculous. But Mom and I would eat popcorn and watch those types of shows late into the night—but never on a school night! That was the rule."

Chloe sighed. She was pleased that a happy memory had sprung up and hoped that this road trip would provide at least a temporary escape from her gloominess.

"We must be soul mates then, eh?" Harriet said.

Chloe looked over at her happy companion, and a wide, uninhibited grin formed on Chloe's face.

"Okay, werewolf hunting it is!" Chloe laughed and drove off. Chloe hadn't laughed in quite a while, and although the sound of her own laughter seemed somewhat unfamiliar to her, it also felt wonderful.

In the 90-minute drive to the small community of Elkhorn, WI, which had the dubious honor of being at the hub of the local werewolf craze, Chloe listened politely to her companion's chatter and enjoyed the beauty of the tree-covered rolling hills.

Chloe had little trouble finding Elkhorn. However, she was uncertain about the location of Bray Road and decided to ask for directions at a local gas station. At the mention of Bray Road, the station attendant sniggered. However, the directions provided were spot on.

As Chloe turned off the highway onto Bray Road, the sun started to set after a long day of heat and humidity. To Chloe, Bray Road seemed like any other country road. In fact, there wasn't much on it at all: a few farmhouses, some cornfields, several wooded areas, and a rambler-style house or two. It wasn't the creepy backwoods road that she had expected after listening to Harriet's nonstop chatter about the many werewolf sightings over the years.

Harriet asked Chloe to pull over to the side of the road,

turn off the headlights, and park, explaining that the darkness might entice the elusive werewolves out of their hiding places and into the safety of the night. Chloe obeyed, amazed at how seriously Harriet was taking this little adventure of theirs. However, Chloe also found herself looking into the darkness, hoping to spot a werewolf.

As they sat in the darkness, Chloe rolled down her window. Cool night air rushed in, replacing the artificial cold that the car's air-conditioning had been providing.

"Hetty, how long do you want to wait? It's getting foggy, and I don't know how safe it is to sit at the side of a dark road in the fog."

Harriet's eyes were fixed on the empty field to the side of them. After a moment or two, she spoke, "Just a little longer, please. It has only been a half hour or so."

Harriet reached into her tote bag, feeling the cool metal of her knitting needles. It was a dark, remote road, and she smiled, fully understanding the inherent danger of its remoteness.

"More like an hour," Chloe mumbled, lightly tapping her fingers on the steering wheel.

Suddenly, Chloe spotted something with glowing eyes running toward the car. "Oh shit! What's that?"

"Not sure . . . could it be a . . ." Harriet's voice trailed off as her grip on her knitting needles tighten.

Within seconds, a man jogging with his large dog approached the car. A quick grin crossed Chloe's face, and Harriet released her grip on the knitting needles. The dog was only a German Shepherd—not a werewolf.

They both tensed again as the man came over to the car's opened window, bending down as he eyeballed Chloe and Harriet. "Are you two ladies having car trouble? Or are you waiting for the Beast of Bray Road to appear?" His voice was gruff, and his stare intense.

"I prefer the title of *werewolf*," Harriet pointedly said.

"Call it whatever you want, lady. But you better move along," the man ordered. "The police routinely patrol this road and chase away the crazies. We have had enough of the werewolf fanatics over the years—trespassing on people's properties and whatnot." With those words, he jogged away, with his dog following. Before long, both were out of sight.

Chloe and Harriet looked at each other, unsure of what to do. The stillness was quickly fractured, however, as a large black raven landed on the car's hood. In unison, each let out a small yelp—much like two frightened pups. The fog swirled around the raven, giving it an almost otherworldly appearance. As it flew off, the raven shrieked an ominous warning of the dangers ahead.

Chloe shivered, not fully understanding the warning. However, the deep, inborn instinct that every living thing possesses forced both women to glance slowly over their shoulders. The man and his dog were coming back, jogging at a rapid pace. As the man and dog pushed through the fog, their very bodies seemed to shift with each swirl of the fog.

Although fear had made it impossible for either to speak, Chloe and Harriet locked eyes, instantly seeing that they shared a question. Were the man and his dog transforming somehow into werewolves?

A menacing howl cut through the night, and they shared a second unspoken question. Did the howl come from the man or the dog—or both?

As the dog's red eyes got dangerously close to the car, they heard its rapid panting. And they shared a third unspoken question. Could they flee in time?

Chloe broke free of her fear and whispered, "We need to get out of here."

Harriet nodded her agreement.

The man and his dog came to a stop. Both stood still, watching Chloe's little car struggle to accelerate before speeding away into the foggy night. He grinned, looking down at his dog. "Fools. People need to stay off this road. Isn't that right?"

Still panting, the dog howled—a ferocious, savage howl that echoed through the cool night air. Then the man and his dog turned their glare toward a white van as it pulled out of the shadows and headed in the same direction as the car.

After nearly thirty minutes of speeding down the interstate, Chloe pulled into the parking lot of a fast-food joint and put her head down on the steering wheel.

Harriet saw Chloe shaking and asked, "Are you okay? Are you crying?"

"Oh my god, no," Chloe said as she looked over her. "I'm laughing. That was so much fun! Scary, but fun!"

Harriet snickered and said, "I didn't expect anything like that to happen. That wasn't really my plan."

"That howl scared the crap out of me, but it was only a man out jogging with his dog on a foggy night, right?"

"I don't honestly know," Harriet truthfully answered. "Back there, however, I was pretty sure that a couple of werewolves were running toward us, and you were too."

Chloe nodded in agreement.

Rubbing her temples, Harriet spoke again. "The truth is everyone has some sort of monster they need to escape from in life—something that scares them or controls them."

Chloe smiled at this strange comment. "Yes, that's probably true. But we ran like a couple of scared kids."

"It doesn't matter if you go to battle or run the other way. My sister once told me that sometimes you have to run away in order to survive," Harriet whispered, looking directly at Chloe, still rubbing her temples. "The trick is to be strong enough to do it."

Chloe wasn't sure what monster Harriet had fought in her life, but the statement resonated with her.

"I agree, Hetty. But right now, I need a cheeseburger and a pop to survive. Let's eat." Chloe laughed, pleased that she could laugh again.

After eating, they checked into a nearby motel for the night. Luckily, the motel had plenty of vacancies, and they were able to get separate rooms. Before turning in, Chloe phoned her father and told him about her sudden road trip.

"Hi, Dad. I'm sorry to be calling you so late."

"You know that you can call me whenever you want. Anyhow, I'm not in the mood to sleep. Is there a problem?" Frank asked.

"No. I just wanted to let you know that I decided to take a last-minute road trip. We left tonight, and right now, we are not far from Elkhorn."

"What do you mean *we*?"

"I'm with an older woman who lives in my apartment building." Chloe hoped that her father wouldn't ask too many questions. It was a spur-of-the-moment decision, and Chloe was unsure how to explain it to him.

"Okay, I see. Be very careful. There are a lot of dangerous people in the world." He inhaled deeply, trying to control his increasingly rapid breathing.

"Wow, that's very cynical. Is everything okay, Dad? That doesn't sound like you."

"Sorry, I'm just tired. I couldn't sleep last night."

"Why, Dad? You sound worried. Something wrong?"

"No, sweetie, nothing's wrong. Um, I'm involved in a very tough case right now at the office." It was a lie, and it bothered Frank. He didn't like lying to his daughter, but he knew that it was necessary this time. He couldn't discuss what was really worrying him.

Frank quickly added, "But if you need me, please just call. I'll drop everything and come running."

"I know that you would, Dad. I love you, but please promise that you will take some time off soon. I think that you need a break."

"Maybe later, after all of this . . . stuff . . . is done with. But anyway, what's your itinerary?" Frank kept his voice level, trying not to alarm his daughter again.

"We don't really have an itinerary. I guess that we'll just wing it."

"On a practical note, do you have enough money for this trip?"

"Yes, of course," Chloe laughed. "I wouldn't hit the road without any money. I'm not crazy! I just gotten paid, and I have a little in my savings account. You know how frugal I am. I have plenty."

"Okay, good. Would you please call me every day so that I don't worry myself to death?"

"Sure, but please don't worry, Dad. I *am* an adult now, you know. I can take care of myself."

"I know, but even adults need to be careful when traveling. Good night, sweetheart."

Frank ended the call before he said too much. He didn't want Chloe to learn about the events of twelve years ago. With at least this much, Frank agreed with his two earlier visitors.

After the call with her father ended, Chloe flipped through the photos on her cell phone until she found the one that she wanted, a photo of her parents and her. It was really a snapshot of an old family photograph—one in which everyone was smiling. She had snapped it because she wanted to keep the memory close by. Chloe wondered if she would ever be that happy again.

As she climbed into bed and turned off the lamp, Chloe felt a little more alive and a little tougher. After all, Chloe grinned;

she had successfully faced fear twice that day—quitting her internship and escaping werewolves.

Amused with herself and her werewolf adventure, she drifted off to sleep.

∼

Frank paced back and forth in his living room for several minutes before finally texting Joan: *"Got a call from Chloe. She's on a road trip with the OLD BAT!"*

Joan shot an instant text back to him: *"We know. Edith followed them. They are at a motel. Edith's watching. Chloe's safe."*

"Not happy about this whole thing—none of it!"

"Me either, Frank."

"I'm taking a few days off and following Chloe myself!"

"Please don't."

"WHY???"

"Chloe would spot you right away. Edith and I can blend into the scenery better."

"She might recognize you."

"Not likely. I'm dead as far as she knows."

No response came from Frank. After a few seconds, Joan decided to text again. *"Does Chloe know who she's with?"*

"No."

"Good."

"I'm worried. I should tell her to come home."

"Please don't. Let Edith and me handle this as we agreed."

"OKAY."

Frank threw his phone across the room, put his head into his hands, and hoped that he was making the right decision.

∼

Harriet couldn't sleep. Looking at the clock in her motel room, she moaned. It was barely past midnight, and thoughts of Chloe kept her awake. Werewolves or not, it had been a surprisingly fun evening, and that troubled her.

Her head throbbed as she crawled out of bed and stumbled into the bathroom. She switched on the lights, slouched over the sink, and looked into the mirror. "You look like crap," Harriet told herself.

Suddenly, the lights dimmed, shrouding the room in semi-darkness. A shifting, shadowy figure appeared in the mirror; its molten eyes burning through the darkness.

"Abigail," Harriet whispered, quickly standing straight and tall, looking like a soldier awaiting orders.

"Surprised?" Abigail hissed.

"Um, yes. Are you . . . mad . . . at me?"

"You *failed* tonight."

"I'm sorry, but . . ."

"But?"

"I've been locked up for a long time, and tonight was fun. I don't really want the road trip to end so soon, and . . ."

"And?"

"I'm not sure about the plan anymore."

"Stick to the plan!"

"But the plan is to kill Chloe, and she's sweet."

"You know why Chloe must die."

"But . . ."

"Don't I always know what is best?"

"Yes."

"Do you want to have some fun first?"

"Yes."

"Enjoy the trip. Toy with her for a while. *Then kill her.*"

A piercing, shrill laugh came from the mirror. Harriet nodded in agreement.

When the laughter stopped, the shadowy Abigail growled, "Make it look like an accident."

"Why?"

"We won't be able to have more fun if you get locked up."

As the shadowy figure faded away, Harriet stared into the mirror, her thoughts drifting back to when Abigail first came to her. She was very young—not yet school-age. Alone and scared in her bedroom, a shadowy figure softly called from the darkness: "Don't be afraid, Hetty. Can I be your friend?"

Her bedroom was dark and bleak, lacking any of the bright, fanciful things generally found in a little girl's room. But the voice sounded cheerful and kind, and Harriet wasn't frightened by it.

"I don't have any friends," Harriet told the voice.

"I will be your friend."

"I would really, really like a friend. I'm Hetty. What's your name?"

"What name do you like?"

"My dolly was called Abigail, but Mommy took her away."

"Then my name will be Abigail."

Harriet never felt alone again. Each night, Abigail came to her in the darkness, slowly seeping into her soul, taking root, and transforming into her inner voice.

Chapter 5

Although the sun had just started to light the day, Chloe was already dressed and headed toward Harriet's room.

She lightly tapped on the door and was pleased that Harriet was also up. While Harriet finished packing her belongings into a tote bag, the two chatted politely, agreeing that the motel had seen better times but also agreeing that they had slept like the dead.

As they were about to leave, Chloe caught sight of a heart-shaped tin on a table in Harriet's room. "Oh, don't forget that. It's very pretty. Did a sweetheart give it to you?"

Harriet quickly put it into her tote bag and mumbled, "It used to have truffles in it. And yes, a sweetheart gave it to me a long time ago, but he broke my heart. Anyhow, I have something else in it now, something for my family."

For a moment, the pain of her long-ago broken heart surfaced, catching Harriet by surprise. Chloe noticed Harriet's moist, sad eyes and regretted drawing attention to the tin. However, something other than sadness suddenly flickered in Harriet's eyes, and Chloe flinched.

Breaking the mood, Chloe asked, "Where should we head next? Maybe a drive along the Lake Michigan shoreline up to the Door County peninsula? It's beautiful up there, I hear."

Gaining Harriet's approval, the two started off on the second day of the road trip. To catch the northbound interstate to Door County, Chloe first needed to head east to Milwaukee. However, as they approached Milwaukee, they opted for a more scenic route than the interstate.

Skirting along the coastline of Lake Michigan, Chloe stuck to the two-lane roads as much as possible. Although a much slower route than the interstate, they enjoyed catching views of the lake as they leisurely made their way.

Around noon, they stopped for lunch in downtown Manitowoc, a city located on the shore of Lake Michigan. After eating, they decided to enjoy the lake breeze and found a bench at the water's edge. Both soon became enthralled by the slow maneuvering of the S.S. Badger, a large passenger and car ferry, which was starting its voyage across Lake Michigan.

"I wonder if anyone has ever fallen off the ferry and drown?" Harriet asked.

"I'm not sure," Chloe said, slightly stunned by the morbid question.

"Why don't we wait for the ferry to return and book passage on it?" Harriet's eyes turned to Chloe and then back to the ferry.

Surprised by the question, it took Chloe a few seconds to respond. "I don't think it's a good idea to wait. The trip across Lake Michigan is roughly four hours, and then it turns around and returns to Manitowoc. Too long to wait."

Harriet reluctantly agreed to continue their trip to Door County. Chloe wasn't sure why, but she felt relieved to get back on the road. As they started to drive northward again, Chloe put her uneasiness out of mind, focusing once again on the scenery.

When they finally reached the Door County Peninsula, they

were tired but happy. It had been a long day, but one filled with sightseeing, the breeze off Lake Michigan, and lighthearted conversation. It had been a good day, both agreed.

Neither had spotted the white van which had followed them to Door County.

Since the night was closing in and the sky was filling with storm clouds, they decided to find a hotel for the night. However, at the height of the tourism season in one of Wisconsin's premier vacation spots, this proved difficult without a reservation.

After being turned away from several hotels, Chloe stepped into a local visitor center to ask for lodging suggestions. Unfortunately, the visitor center was overflowing with other vacationers, all clamoring for assistance.

Barely able to push her way into the visitor center, Chloe felt very fortunate when a young attendant walked over to her. She noticed that his name tag read *Christopher*. He quickly provided directions to a newly opened inn that was, as he described it, off the beaten track but likely to have a vacancy. Unfortunately, he disappeared back into the crowd before Chloe could ask for the inn's phone number to verify if, indeed, there was a vacancy.

Following the directions provided, Chloe easily found the inn, which was located on a rural, inland road. As they pulled up in front of it, she pointed to a vacancy sign in the window and was grateful for Christopher's suggestion.

Delighted that the inn was an old Victorian house, Chloe said, "It looks charming. I am guessing that the location explains the vacancy."

As they checked in, they met the innkeepers, Logan and Ellie, a couple in their late twenties, who explained that they had just purchased the old house a year ago and were busy renovating it. Eager to talk and share their story, the couple explained they wanted a different life than their parents. Neither of them wanted to be trapped in a large, sprawling city and be too busy to actually enjoy life. They had grown tired of having to take a three-hour drive to *visit* nature. After deciding to take a leap of faith, they took out a loan, purchased a run-down Victorian house, and turned it into an inn.

Chloe and Harriet listened intently, looking at each other from time to time. After the innkeepers finished their somewhat long story, Chloe was the first to speak, "I'm so impressed at how brave you both were. Do you have regrets?"

Logan and Ellie spoke in unison, "None."

Ellie continued, "We can't say that this has been easy. But we're doing something that we love. We are never going to be rich, but that's okay. This is the life for us; we feel more at peace here. And the scenery is just so beautiful here."

Chloe nodded her approval.

Harriet picked up their room key and said, "Both of you are lucky to be able to live your life on your own terms. However, most of us have *someone* that we need to answer too, unfortunately."

"So true," Ellie cheerfully agreed. "Oh, and the room directly under yours is totally empty. We haven't renovated it yet. Everything should be nice and quiet for you! Oh, just one quick question. How did you find out about this inn? Most people haven't heard about us yet."

"I stopped at the visitor center, and a young guy named Christopher told me about it," Chloe answered.

"I don't know a Christopher at the visitor center. He must be new," Ellie said. "But I'll make a point to call the visitor center tomorrow and thank him for the recommendation."

The storm clouds suddenly burst, releasing torrential rain. The ensuing thunder and lightning rattled the windows, and the innkeepers raced off to check if any were open, ending the conversation.

Unfortunately, there was only one room available. So Chloe

and Harriet agreed to share. Both were somewhat uncomfortable with the closeness that this entailed but neither spoke of this out loud.

Due to the thunderstorm that raged outside, Chloe and Harriet decided to eat a light meal provided by the innkeepers and turn in early. The two beds in the room were comfortable, and Chloe quickly fell to sleep.

However, Harriet was unable to fall asleep. She had an excruciating headache and rubbed her temples in an attempt to ease the pain. She had enjoyed the day with Chloe, and this unsettled her.

Each flash of lighting brought back ugly memories to Harriet—memories of her early life. She closed her eyes, but the memories refused to go. She saw her earlier life, first as an impish child and then as a resentful teenager. In the flashes of light, she saw her angry parents and her frightened sister. With each burst of thunder, Harriet also heard the long-ago words that her parents taunted her with: *Peculiar, odd, wicked.* Her parents' words were permanently etched in her memory, forever smoldering.

Harriet forced the images and words from her mind and softly said to herself, "I need to forget." With this statement still fresh on her lips, Harriet finally slept.

Well before dawn, Chloe awoke. Softly crying, she slid down to the floor, hugging herself. As the sounds of her soft, desperate cries found their way through Harriet's blanket of sleep, she woke finally free of her throbbing headache.

Seeing Chloe in such a state, Harriet slid out of bed and sat next to the younger woman. She pulled Chloe closer to her, wrapping her arms around her much like a mother comforting her child. Harriet was surprised by her own sudden act of kindness.

They sat like this, intertwined as it were, not speaking—but each sensing the pain of the other.

Eventually, Chloe whispered, "I was having such a horrible dream. I don't know why. This inn is charming. "

"What was the dream?" Harriet asked.

"I have this same dream from time to time. I'm running and running. I'm frantic in the dream that I will get caught by whoever is chasing me. I know that a shrink would say that the dream means that I have a problem in life that I'm avoiding. I suppose that's true," Chloe said.

Looking into the sad eyes of Harriet, she continued, "But this dream was different. This time, I ran toward my family's fishing cabin. I heard my mother repeatedly say, 'Be careful.' It was so real. It wasn't like most dreams. It was crystal clear. I saw my mother's face so clearly. It was like my mother was really in my dream. I know that this sounds really strange. My mother and my grandmother both died when I was only ten years old."

Chloe stopped talking and looked into Harriet's eyes as she waited for a response.

After a few moments, Harriet spoke, "I don't think that anyone should dismiss a dream as just a dream. Or, at the very least, you should never dismiss a dream that was powerful enough to touch your emotions. Maybe your mother really did come to you in the dream with a message. Maybe it was only your subconscious trying to reach you. What I learned in therapy many years ago is this: If you can decipher the meaning of your dreams, you might be able to understand what is really bothering you."

Chloe nodded, once again surprised at the wisdom that Harriet seemed to possess.

Harriet whispered, "Do you dream of your grandmother?"

Chloe took a few moments before answering. "Yes, sometimes. But for some reason, I'm always uneasy when I wake afterwards."

"Really?"

"Yes, but I don't know why. My mother died in a terrible car accident, and my grandmother took it very hard. She went to live with her sister in Albuquerque. Unfortunately, she had a heart attack at some point and died. Dad told me that the death of my mother broke her heart and spirit."

He was right, Harriet thought.

Chloe continued almost absentmindedly, "Whenever my grandmother was due to drop by, Mom fussed about everything—she wanted no dust and no clutter. The house needed to be in perfect order. I don't know why that was, but I know that my grandmother wasn't the hugs and kisses type. I don't really remember much else about her, except that she knitted. A typical grandma thing, I guess."

Harriet smirked and said, "That's an outdated image of a grandma. Maybe your grandma had more layers than you realized as a kid."

"Very possible, I guess," Chloe admitted.

Yes, very possible, Harriet thought.

Chloe continued to ramble, almost unaware of the older woman next to her. "I don't remember much about the day that Mom died. My therapist suggested that I'm blocking the memories because of my grief. But over the last week or so, bits and pieces of that day are starting to pop into my mind. I only wish that I remembered more."

"What bits and pieces? What do you remember?" Harriet's face grew pale.

Chloe sunk deeper into thought, her eyes staring at the floor. She was unaware of Harriet's concern.

"I adored Mom, and when she died, I was so sad—despondent is a better word for how I felt," Chloe said, and then added, "I just don't understand this dream."

"Maybe your mother had a reason to enter your dreams—

maybe she was warning you about some danger," Harriet unexpectedly suggested.

"I guess, or maybe it was just a dream."

Tears slowly pooled in Chloe's eyes. "My father's an attorney—just a small-town attorney, as he calls it. Most folks have a really negative image of attorneys, but my dad is a good guy. He has always been there for me. After Mom died, he had a rule that we ate supper together each night so we could talk. Even as a kid, I could see how much he loved me. Unfortunately, he was out of town at a conference on the night that Mom died, and he has no idea what happened back then."

"What do you *actually* remember from the day that your mother died?"

"I remember going to the nurse's office at school that day. I felt sick. Mom picked me up and took me straight to our family doctor. I remember the doctor giving me some sort of shot, which made me a little sleepy. As we were driving away, Mom got a phone call, and she was clearly upset afterwards. Mom then drove to the fishing cabin, not even stopping to take me home first. She just raced down the road to the cabin."

Harriet looked closely at Chloe and then quietly asked, "Do you know who called your mother, or why your mother needed to get to the cabin so fast?"

"No, I don't."

Chloe continued again, "About all that I remember clearly is that it was late spring, and it had just started sleeting. The road was very slippery, and I was relieved when we got to the fishing cabin safely. But I don't remember much of anything else."

"I'm so sorry for your loss. I understand what it is like to lose someone," Harriet gently whispered. She squeezed Chloe's hand, unnerved by the compassion that she felt for Chloe. It was not part of her plan.

"Somehow, my father and I managed to get through it." Chloe's voice was so soft that Harriet could barely hear it.

Chloe wiped the tears from her eyes and continued in a slightly louder voice. "Every weekend during the summer after the accident, we went on fishing trips together. The strange thing is that we never again went to the fishing cabin—not that summer, not ever. Dad never explained why, but he always looked uncomfortable whenever the topic of the cabin came up. Eventually, I stopped asking about it."

"If not at the cabin, where did you go fishing back then?" Harriet asked, only barely interested in the answer.

"Dad would just pick a lake at random. This is Wisconsin, you know, and there are a lot of lakes. We never really said much on those trips. We would just sit, sometimes not even casting a line out. But being out in nature helped us."

Harriet squeezed Chloe's hand again, and Chloe continued. "Dad and I just got on with life. There's really no other option when something terrible happens. But I don't think that I fully recovered from losing my mom. I still feel sad, or maybe the right word is empty. I feel more like a shell of a person than a whole person. And I'm still afraid of something—something that happened back then."

"Afraid of what?" Harriet asked, wondering what Chloe really saw all those years ago.

"I don't know."

Harriet let go of Chloe's hand and inched away.

"I haven't discussed any of this with my father. I don't want him to know how unhappy I am nor that I am still afraid of *something* from back then. He already worries too much about me, and I want to spare him. Frankly, the last twelve years have been hard on him, too."

"I'm sure that he knows," Harriet flatly stated. "Parents can see through whatever mask you wear, see who you really are, see what you are hiding."

Chloe nodded in agreement, very aware of the recent concern that she heard in her father's voice. "Hopefully, I'll start to remember more. I think that it's really important for me to understand why I've felt so uneasy all of these years."

Chloe rambled on, more to herself than Harriet, "When Mom and I got to the fishing cabin that night, she told me to stay in the car. She then went into the cabin, and I heard yelling. I couldn't make out the actual words. The next thing that I remember is Mom dropping me off at home. I don't remember anything in-between. Except Mom had blood on her."

Harriet focused her eyes closely on Chloe, and in a seemingly concerned voice, she asked, "Was your mother hurt?"

"To be honest, I don't really know if my mother was hurt," Chloe mumbled. "Unfortunately, I don't remember anything except bits and pieces. And I really don't understand how Mom's car ended up plunging into the Mississippi River. The Mississippi River is at least an hour from our cabin and in the opposite direction of our house. What was Mom doing in that area on a stormy night?"

That's a good question, Harriet thought.

"What do you think my dream was trying to tell me?" Chloe's voice was barely audible.

"You are the only one that can answer that." Harriet rubbed her forehead, trying to ease the start of another headache.

"But I don't honestly know."

"You know, Chloe. Deep inside your soul, you know the answer. They say that in the quiet of the night, as we dream, our souls whisper to us, guiding us to the answers we need. At least, that's what I read in a self-help book many years ago."

"Wow, Hetty. That's a nice thought. Do your dreams give you guidance?"

"No, not my dreams, but something else does," Harriet answered, holding her pounding head as she got up and climbed back into bed.

Harriet's answer puzzled Chloe. But like Harriet, she no longer wanted to talk. With a stretch of her arms and a muffled yawn, Chloe returned to her bed as well, falling back to sleep.

At dawn, Chloe woke to the sound of loud voices and banging in the room below. Smelling smoke, she jumped out of bed and quickly noticed that Harriet's bed was empty. Grabbing her phone, Chloe put on her robe and rushed toward the commotion, wondering where Harriet was.

"The fire's out," Elle, the innkeeper, said to the small group of guests who were gathering outside of the empty room. "Logan stamped it out, and I followed up with a fire extinguisher to make sure. Nothing to worry about now."

"What happened?" one of the guests asked.

"It's an empty room. So, we aren't sure how a fire got started in a wastebasket. But luckily, a passerby alerted us to the smoke," Elle explained. "We're very lucky that she saw the smoke."

As the other guests returned to their rooms, Chloe glanced around and saw Harriet at the other end of the hall, looking up at the smoke detector.

"Yes, we noticed that too," Elle said as she walked over to Harriet. "The battery's missing from the smoke detector. It's really strange because I'm sure that it had one."

"Yes, strange," Harriet said, smirking as she walked away. "Please let my friend know that I'm going back to our room."

Chloe walked over to a nearby window and was soon joined by Elle. Looking down at a white van parked below, Elle said, "That's our good Samaritan. Thank goodness for her! Oh, and your friend went back to your room."

Chloe nodded in response and stared at the woman standing next to the van, feeling certain that she had seen her before.

The good Samaritan looked up at their window, and Elle waved to her before walking back to her husband. Suddenly Chloe remembered—it was the woman who had saved her from getting hit by the bus.

The van quickly drove off. But Chloe lingered, looking out the window. It was strange, she thought, that the good Samaritan just happened to show up here as well. Remembering the stern warning her father gave her about safety, she wondered if she should be worried. But a gentle, familiar presence briefly wrapped around her, and Chloe somehow sensed that the good Samaritan wished her no harm. She also sensed one other thing—*don't tell Harriet about the good Samaritan.*

Chloe's phone rang, jarring her out of her thoughts. "I was about to call you, Dad," Chloe said as she answered the phone.

"Wow, not even a hello or good morning," Frank said, forcing a chuckle.

"I'm sorry. You aren't checking up on me, are you?"

"Maybe a little. Can't a dad worry about his kid?"

"I'm *twenty-two* years old, Dad. I'll be fine."

"What's your itinerary today?

"We're going to drive around Door County and sightsee."

"Sounds fun. But please be careful."

Rolling her eyes, Chloe said, "Bye, Dad. Love you."

≈

"Dammit, Chloe saw me," Edith said as she drove away from the inn.

"Then it's good that I got here last night," Joan said, glancing over at Edith. "I'll follow them today, and you can rest up."

"Okay, sounds like a good plan. And that'll also give me time to swap out this white van for some other color. There must be a branch of the car rental agency around here."

"Try for a color that won't stand out, like black maybe."

"I agree. I don't want to be spotted again. Where did you park your truck?"

"At the end of this road, behind an old, abandon shed."

"Joan, did your phone just beep?"

"Yes, it's a text from Frank. They're exploring Door County today. Chloe will need to drive past me on their way to the main road. I should be able to follow them easily."

"Good. I'll meet you at the end of the day and take it from there. By the way, where were you when I called last night?"

"Please don't laugh, Edith. I had planned on spending the night at an RV camp just outside of Madison. But when I got there, I couldn't sleep. I just kept worrying about Chloe. I decided meditating might help relax me. But while I meditated, I got a really strong feeling that I needed to go to the cabin and hide the letters there."

"I would never laugh at you. And as you might guess, I'm a firm believer in all things mystical. If you got a feeling to go to the cabin, then it was right to go there."

Edith stopped the van near Joan's truck. Before getting out, Joan asked, "Do you think that we are doing the right thing by following Chloe and not alerting her to the danger? Frank is really worried and me too. I feel like we are using Chloe as bait."

"Yes, that's exactly what we are doing. You have to set a trap to catch a rat, and a trap doesn't work without bait. I know that it sounds harsh, but that's the truth."

"I know. But she's my daughter, and I'm worried."

"The other option is telling her the truth."

"No, the truth is too horrible. We can never tell Chloe. I just didn't expect Chloe to go on a road trip."

"I didn't expect that either. To be truthful, I wasn't really sure what to do when they checked into the motel outside of Elkhorn. After a while, I finally called the motel and asked for

Harriet's room. But there was no one checked in under her name. I had no choice but to just sit in the parking lot and watch."

"Wow, she must have checked in under an alias. But how is that possible? They ask for ID these days."

"It wouldn't surprise me that she has a fake ID or two. That's just the type of thing that she would do."

"I'm worried, Edith. Do you think Chloe is safe inside a hotel where we can't see them?"

"I don't think anything will happen at a hotel. It would be a dumb move, and Harriet's a lot of things but not dumb."

Joan raised her eyebrows, silently questioning her aunt's reasoning.

"If she killed . . . um, I mean hurt Chloe inside a hotel, it's almost certain the hotel clerk would tell the police about Harriet—the traveling companion of the victim. I know Harriet well enough to be sure of one thing. She'll want to avoid the police. When she makes a move, it will be an accident that can't be tied to her or be somewhere isolated."

"That's not very comforting."

"I'm sorry, Joan. I know that Chloe is your daughter, and you're concerned for her. I'm concerned too. We need to keep tabs on them. That's the only way we will be able to keep Chloe safe during this *ill-conceived* road trip and grab Harriet. And nothing has changed. Telling Chloe the truth doesn't solve the problem. Only removing Harriet solves the problem."

"I guess you're right. I don't want my daughter to spend her life looking over her shoulder. That's too dangerous of a way to live."

"Unfortunately, we can't kick down a hotel room door and drag Harriet out to the van."

"I agree, Edith, but I wish we could do just that. By the way, what were you going to say if the motel put you through to Harriet's room?"

"I'm not sure. But it was a mistake to call. In all likelihood, Harriet would've hung up on me or worse. Maybe call the cops and say that I was stalking her or something. It would have been hard to explain to the cops why I was sitting in a dark parking lot watching her."

"Better to confront her in person?" Joan asked, staring at Edith.

"Yes, we can better control the situation that way. We just need to keep vigilant and watch for an opportunity to confront her when Chloe is not around." Edith's voice was firm and calm, and she hoped that Joan didn't know that she was faking confidence.

Joan and the dog got out and watched Edith drove off.

~

After a hearty Midwest breakfast of eggs, pancakes, bacon, and coffee, Chloe and Harriet stopped by the inn's front desk to check out. As Chloe handed over the room key, Elle said, "I just got off the phone with the visitor center. They never heard of Christopher. But we are grateful that you found our inn regardless of who pointed you in our direction!"

"Wow," Chloe laughed. "Maybe he was St. Christopher, the patron saint of travelers."

"A little divine help never hurts!" Elle laughed.

Harriet walked outside, rolling her eyes.

Chloe joined her a few minutes later, and they continued their road trip, neither speaking of the night before nor the early morning fire. Their itinerary was simple, drive up one side of the peninsula and then back down the other side.

As they drove, Chloe and Harriet admired the beauty all around them, occasionally stopping to get a closer look at some of the rocky bluffs and beaches. Chloe admired the tenacity of the trees that had taken root on the rocky bluffs, standing guard over Lake Michigan, and defying the odds as they stubbornly survived. A bit like herself, Chloe thought.

Around midday, Chloe and Harriet came across a small sign pointing the way to a lighthouse. Both found the idea of seeing a lighthouse intriguing. After a short drive, they discovered a parking lot and the path, or rather a causeway, to the lighthouse, which sat on a nearby island. Both laughed as they hurried over the causeway, avoiding as much of the shallow water as possible.

As they reached the lighthouse, Harriet tried coaxing Chloe to climb the stairs to the top of the 90ish-foot lighthouse, insisting that the views would be stunning. But Chloe declined, admitting to a fear of heights. Harriet's smile camouflaged her annoyance as they walked back to the car and drove off.

Eventually, they stopped for a late lunch. Catching a view of the lake as she parked, Chloe suggested that they get takeout and eat outside.

Once they had their takeout food in hand, they strolled over to the nearby beach. The beach teemed with other tourists, and the laughter and squeals of summer fun filled the air. They walked a little further and located a picnic table just far enough from the beach to muffle the touristy sounds but still close enough to enjoy the lake view.

"This is a nice spot, isn't it, Hetty?" Chloe asked, glancing at the beachgoers as she ate.

"Not really. I can still hear the noise. Eating inside might have been a better option after all," Harriet grumbled.

"Really? The lake's so pretty, and I like watching the families on the beach. It reminds me of happier times—of family vacations with my parents. What about you? When you were a child, did your family go on any *fun-packed* vacations?" Chloe laughed.

"Oh god no! There was absolutely no fun when I was a kid," Harriet sneered.

Startled by both Harriet's answer and her tone, Chloe said, "There must've been some fun times, I hope."

Harriet looked squarely at Chloe. "You shared a lot about yourself last night. Maybe I should do the same."

Chloe felt self-conscious, realizing that she had blurted out her life story to a virtual stranger amid the storm last night. Chloe seldom spoke of her family's tragedy even to her friends.

"My parents died when I was a teenager," Harriet said, her voice flat, almost lifeless. "I was not my parent's favorite, to be sure. To be honest, I was a bit difficult and odd. I have a sister, which my parents seemed to like better. My sister is younger than me—about two or three years, if I remember right. I always envied her pretty green eyes. Anyhow, I lost touch with her for many, many years. And when I finally reached out to her, it didn't go well. Unfortunately, we'll probably never mend our differences."

"I'm sorry that you aren't close with your sister."

"It is what it is. I was never close to her anyhow—nor to my parents for that matter. There was no love in my family, at least not for me. My parents often punished me for one little thing or another. They were very cruel. But I suppose that they had no idea how to really deal with me. As a child, I referred to them as the Evil Queen and her hatchet man."

Stunned, Chloe was barely able to whisper, "I'm so sorry."

Harriet nodded, silently cursing Chloe for her resemblance to the Evil Queen. She then calmly continued her story. "After my parents died, I lashed out at everyone—especially those trying to help me. I was a real pain in the ass to my social worker and my foster parents. As a result, a judge committed me to a youth behavior center. However, they couldn't hold me after I turned eighteen, and I was released. Luckily, a trust fund had been established for me from my parents' estate, and I used that to start my life over. I went to college and got an accounting degree. After that, I tried to live a perfect life. At least, it was perfect for a while."

Harriet never took her eyes off the lake as she continued to speak. "I've been afraid to really expose the true me to anyone. The pain of not being loved as a kid stays with you. I really felt rejected by my parents in a sense. And I have tried to avoid feeling that pain again. But when I was much, much younger, I met a young man and became pregnant. But, unfortunately, he didn't love me as much as I loved him. To be truthful, I don't believe that he loved me at all. And ultimately, he rejected me as well."

Harriet grew silent, and for a moment, it appeared that she might cry. Chloe stared at the older woman, unsure of what to say.

However, Harriet quickly regained her composure and continued. "I kept the child and tried to be a perfect mother. But in the end, she rejected me also. The only thing in life that I could always count on was my inner voice. And there are times when I am not fond of that either."

Harriet sat quietly for a few seconds and then added one final thought. "As a young woman, I moved far away from where I grew up. I was trying to run away from my problems—and from my inner demon, I guess. But the sad truth is this: Unless you solve the problems that keep you awake at night, they just move with you. You cannot outrun them."

At the end of her raw disclosure, Harriet walked to the car. Chloe watched her closely, noticing that she seemed so very tired. She was deeply impressed by Harriet's honesty and felt a strong connection with her. Although both of them carried a profound sadness within, Chloe felt the connection was more than that. She seemed oddly familiar to Chloe.

Chloe thought about her dream from the night before, wondering if it was trying to tell her something? Confused, Chloe returned to the car also, and the two continued their trip.

By the end of the day, they found themselves driving out of

Door County and heading toward the Northwoods. Or rather, Chloe thought, they were heading *Up North* as her father would say. She smiled briefly at that thought.

However, both Chloe and Harriet had been too distracted by the scenery and by their deeply personal conversation to notice that a pickup truck had been shadowing them throughout the day. They also paid no attention to the black van that was now following them.

Chapter 6

As Chloe steered the car north, the views of the woodlands and the breeze through the car windows acted like a tonic. And the mood became lighter. The two easily agreed that Up North was, indeed, a paradise.

Eventually, they found themselves in the city of Rhinelander, one of northern Wisconsin's popular tourism spots. Since it was getting dark, they decided to spend the night there. Exhausted and hungry, they grabbed a couple of cheeseburgers and checked into a local hotel, pleased to find two available rooms at the height of the tourism season.

As soon as Chloe entered her hotel room, she looked under her bed just as she had every night since she was ten years old. Finding nothing except dust, Chloe wished that she hadn't felt compelled to look. The reason behind her fears remained fuzzy to her. Although her mother's death had been traumatizing to her, Chloe felt it went deeper than that. And she hoped that the answer would surface along with more memories.

Chloe phoned her father, filling him in on the day's events

and her current location. But just before ending the call, she suddenly decided to ask a question. "Did Grandma have a twin—not your mom—but Mom's mom?"

Chloe didn't know why she blurted out the question, nor why she said twin rather than sister. She also didn't understand why she sensed a sort of vague duality about Harriet.

"Neither of your grandma's were twins. Why?"

"I know that it sounds goofy, but the older woman that I am traveling with reminds me so much of Grandma Harriet. She even sort of sounds like her."

"They say that we all have doppelgängers out there."

"They don't look alike, but there's something about her."

"Sorry, I have another call coming in. Sleep well, sweetheart, and stay safe. No foolish risks," Frank said before abruptly ending the phone call.

∽

Frank answered the incoming call with one word, "Status?"

"They're in Rhinelander," Edith answered. "I'm parked right outside of their hotel."

"Chloe just called me. Her traveling *buddy* reminds her of Grandma Harriet!"

"Oh shit. I really hope that Chloe doesn't start to ask her questions."

"Why? Never mind, I know. Chloe can't find out what happened twelve years ago."

"Exactly." Edith, however, also worried what Harriet would do if questioned unexpectedly by Chloe, hoping that she wasn't as easily angered now as when they were children.

"Can't you just find the old bat's room and talk to her?"

"I don't think that's a good idea. I know Harriet, and she's likely to cause a ruckus if we try that. We can't risk drawing

Chloe's attention. It's better to wait until Chloe is nowhere around."

"When I agreed to go along with this, both you and Joan promised that Chloe would be safe. Is she safe?"

"Yes, we're watching very closely and will not make a move until Chloe's safely out of the way."

Frank ended the phone call without any further discussion.

Edith saw Joan pull into the parking lot and waved her over to the van. Joan hurried over to the van's open window, and Edith quickly updated her on Chloe's activities and her call with Frank. Both looked toward the hotel and knew that they shared a question. *Could they keep Chloe safe?*

"Joan—do you think they saw either of us tailing them today?"

"It didn't seem so, at least not when I was following them. What about you?"

"Not that I could tell." Edith yawned and stretched her arms.

"I'll watch the hotel tonight, Edith. I'm a night owl by nature."

"Thanks."

"Edith, how are we going to handle tailing them tomorrow? There are a lot of scenic, narrow backroads around here. Depending on what route they take, it'll be tough not to get spotted by them, especially if two vehicles are tailing them."

"Good point. We'll need to take turns like we did today. Since you're taking the night shift, so to speak, I'll follow them tomorrow. And you can find a place to catch some sleep during the day. I'll call you late afternoon and let you know where we are so that you can take over."

"Agreed."

≈

Chloe and Harriet slept, undisturbed by nightmares. Not

waking until the early morning, they both felt refreshed and hungry as they met up in the hotel lobby.

After devouring another hearty, homestyle breakfast at a nearby restaurant, Chloe asked if they could skip making any firm plans for the day, suggesting that they hit the backroads and go wherever the roads might lead. Chloe flashed a small, tentative smile, explaining that she wanted to be adventurous—to really see and feel the Northwoods.

Harriet quickly agreed. "It'll be nice to be away from the crowds."

"Yes, I agree. Nature was a huge part of my childhood. I went on nature hikes with my mother and on fishing trips with my father. I really miss those things."

Before leaving Rhinelander and heading deeper into the Northwoods, they sought out what Chloe drolly referred to as the *famous* statue of the Hodag monster—a mischievous creature of local folklore. They drove around for a few minutes until they spotted the statute in front of the local visitor center. Chloe quickly parked nearby.

"It's a dinosaur," Harriet said, looking over at the statute.

However, to Chloe, it resembled something closer to a lovable cartoon creature, and she laughingly said, "He's so cute!"

"If only all monsters were that cute," Harriet quietly mumbled.

"We need to take a picture!" Chloe laughed again and hopped out of the car, followed by Harriet.

Chloe handed her cellphone over to a fellow tourist, who happily consented to take their photo. As he snapped the photo, Chloe pulled Harriet close, giving her a sideways hug. Harriet smiled, slightly blushing. She hadn't expected a hug, and she felt her defenses crumbling, feeling a bond form with Chloe. The photo captured a shared moment of love.

Harriet's inner voice hissed, *pull back from Chloe,* and she obeyed. Although startled slightly by the abrupt end to the moment, Chloe gave a warm smile to Harriet.

Thanking their fellow tourist, the two got back into the car and drove out of Rhinelander. Steering the car down the main highway, Chloe soon saw a sign, indicating that they were driving through a section of the Chequamegon–Nicolet National Forest. After a few more miles, she turned off onto a small, gravel road. A cloud of dust followed them as they meandered through the dense forest.

As she drove, Chloe was especially captivated by the trees, noticing that some seemed to touch the clouds, while smaller ones lived in the shadows. She felt the trees—pines, maples, oaks, and birch—were woven together like a family, and this made Chloe miss the family that she once had.

As the car bumped along the road, they got deeper and deeper into the forest. They soon started to spot some of the forest's wildlife—a fox, a raccoon, and even a wild turkey, to name but a few. Chloe also caught sight of several cardinals perched tightly together on a tree branch, and she pointed them out to Harriet.

Chloe laughed and said, "Don't they say cardinals are messengers from Heaven? Maybe someone is trying to tell us something."

Harriet raised her eyebrows but said nothing. A coldness suddenly surrounded Harriet, and she felt a shiver pass through her. She understood the message: *Don't hurt Chloe.* But her inner voice told her to ignore it, and so she did.

Before long, they came upon a crossroad, and Chloe stopped the car, wondering which way to go. She could see that their road dead-ended just ahead. So, turning either left or right onto the somewhat smaller gravel road seemed the only option. Shrugging, Chloe turned left.

"We're in the middle of nowhere. I've not seen another person for quite a while." Harriet remarked, smiling broadly.

Grateful for the cloud of dust that marked their new direction, Edith turned left as well, careful to keep a safe, discreet distance behind them.

As Chloe's car crawled along, they caught sight of wildflowers along the side of the road. Both were particularly taken by the tiny wild violets nestled in fallen pine needles. Chloe inhaled deeply, smelling the fresh air, laced with the scents of the wildflowers and the pines.

Both seemed to be under a spell cast by the forest and by the creatures who called it home. For now, at least, Chloe felt free of the emptiness and fear that plagued her. Eventually, they came to a wooden bridge, which beckoned them even deeper into the wilderness.

"It looks really old. Should we cross it, Hetty?" Chloe asked.

"You wanted an adventure, didn't you? The worst that might happen is that we fall into the river." Harriet turned her head away from Chloe to hide her smirk.

Chloe drove slowly over the old, creaking boards of the bridge and was relieved when they got safely across. Harriet glanced over at Chloe, silently admitting to herself that she was enjoying Chloe's company. However, Harriet knew that she needed to stick to her plan—her inner voice demanded it.

After a short while, Harriet asked Chloe to stop the car, pointing to several paths that led even deeper into the forest.

"I think wild raspberries are growing over there," Harriet said. "My grandmother used to take my sister and me raspberry picking. She lived in Maine. Whenever my sister and I visited her, Granny would drive us out to this one particular little dirt road, and we would pick tons of raspberries."

"What a wonderful memory," Chloe said. Then, unexpectedly, a memory of her own grandmother telling a similar story came to her.

"Do we have time to pick some today?"

"We have time, Hetty. But those paths seem to lead into some really dense forest. Do you think it is wise? I mean, no one is around, and we could get lost."

Chloe once again felt the gentle presence nearby, and as goosebumps formed on her skin, she sensed that she should stay in the car. "Hetty, I think that we should just keep driving."

"We can't pass up getting out and walking into the forest . . . just a little . . . to pick some raspberries. It's like the forest is calling us." Harriet quickly exited the car and started walking down the nearest path.

Chloe jumped out of the car and hurried to catch up with her. Harriet quickly found a patch of berries and began popping them into her mouth. She looked at Chloe, smiling. Actually, grinning was a better word for it. Chloe marveled at how innocent and childlike Harriet seemed at this moment. Chloe smiled, dismissing her hesitation to leave the car.

Standing in the lushness of the forest, Chloe felt a sense of reverence as she looked up at the looming trees around her. As the wind swirled through the trees, Chloe watched the branches danced to a heavenly song that only they could hear.

At that moment, Chloe knew that she was standing in a very spiritual place—a place of beauty capable of touching one's soul. As she breathed in the fresh, pure air, a truth grew within her heart and soul. She was the creator of her own roadblocks to life, a nurturer of her grief-fueled sadness, emptiness, and fears.

Chloe also knew that she needed to free herself of these soon. If not, she feared she would only exist in the shadows like a small sapling, failing to fully live.

Harriet walked over to Chloe and said, "I'm not sure, Chloe, which path we should take into the forest."

"Me either."

"I guess we should just pick one and try it," Harriet said. After a few seconds, she added, "Someone told me once that the only way to find the right path in life is to admit that you've been walking down the wrong path."

Chloe was stunned by her odd statement and simply nodded, accepting the strangeness of Harriet's wisdom.

"If only it was that easy," Chloe said quietly.

"Life is never easy," Harriet replied, starting down one of the paths. Chloe followed behind.

The wind weaved its way through the trees, gently caressing them, and Chloe felt a deep sense of peace as the two continued down the path. They walked deeper and deeper into the forest, occasionally stopping to enjoy the wildflowers or look up at the numerous birds as they fluttered by, chirping songs for the forest and its visitors to enjoy.

As they walked, Chloe accepted that nature was filling her emptiness in much the same way that one fills an empty beer mug. Oh crap, Chloe smiled—silently asking herself, *Is that really the only way I can explain it?* Chloe rolled her eyes, quietly accepting it as a *Wisconsin thing.*

A question started to slowly take root in Chloe's mind. And she started to wonder: was it *too* much of a coincidence that my grandmother told a story about berry picking too?

"Hetty, I have a question," Chloe finally said. "My grandmother told a similar story about her granny and raspberry picking. Are you related to my grandmother, by any chance?"

"Oh goodness no, sweetie. I don't even know who your grandma is." Harriet flinched as her inner voice growled: *She suspects who you are. End things now.*

Although her inner voice demanded action, Harriet found it difficult to keep the plan in the front of her mind. She was enjoying Chloe's company too much.

Never Tell Chloe

Finally, they found themselves standing at the shore of a small lake. The crystal clarity of the lake water was so stunning that they couldn't find a word worthy of it. The lake seemed to absorb the beauty surrounding it, reflecting it back in a masterful painting on its surface.

Chloe and Harriet walked to the very edge of the lake, standing so close that their shoes soaked up a tiny portion of the lake itself. Both giggled like young girls about their wet feet. They peered through the crystal surface of the lake and studied its underwater world.

The two companions stared at the wonderment of what they saw. They watched the aquatic plants sway with the movement of the lake currents. They watched fish swim by, leaping up as if to introduce themselves to their visitors. Their eyes next moved back to the surface of the lake, and they watched the ducks glide gracefully by, and the toads and frogs leap about.

They noticed a fox, or perhaps it was a small timber wolf, on the other side of the lake, lapping up the fresh water before running back into the safety of the forest.

"Maybe it's a hodag," Chloe said, laughing. "They say that hodags are shy."

Chloe and Harriet stood silently, unable to speak any words that could describe what they saw and felt at this moment. Yet, both sensed the other's feelings of wonderment.

"I wish I could take a photo of this with my phone," Chloe said. "But I jumped out of the car so fast that I forgot it."

Suddenly, Chloe darted a few feet into the lake, pulling out an old beer can. Angry, she muttered, "I can't believe this. How dare someone show such disrespect."

"What do you mean? It's only one beer can," Harriet said.

With a sad, half-smile, Chloe explained, "When I was a kid, my parents took me to hear speeches by a local environmentalist. Her speeches were really more like sermons. She talked about how nature was almost divine in a sense and how being out in nature nurtures the human soul. Even as a kid, I was drawn to that truth." A thought suddenly came to Chloe: *The forest needs to be protected.*

"At one of her events, she handed out copies of a prayer, asking God to protect nature. I said it every night before bed as a kid. I was such a dork."

"Don't call yourself names!" Harriet barked, flinching as she remembered the hurtful names that her parents once hurled at her. Calming down, she asked, "Do you still say the prayer?"

"No, but I remember it clearly . . . I pray to God, to the Universe, to the angels, to all good things known and unknown in this world. I pray for the protection of the trees, of the lakes, of the animals, and of the air and wind itself. I pray for the protection of Mother Earth."

Pausing for a second to gather her thoughts, she continued. "Please, God, I beg you to protect nature from people. Please wrap a heavenly, divine shield around nature, around the world itself. We have forgotten what it is like to walk barefoot on Mother Earth, and I pray that Mother Earth can forgive us. Amen."

"Amen," Harriet echoed, amused.

"I don't know where that memory came from. It just popped into my mind."

"I didn't know that you were such a spiritual, outdoorsy type. You seem more an indoor gal."

Chloe was taken aback by this description of her; however, she knew it was accurate. Chloe seldom ventured out into nature anymore. As the fishing trips with her father dwindled, and he threw himself back into his work, Chloe chose to hide from the world—first in her childhood bedroom and now in her apartment.

"When I was younger, I was very outdoorsy. Both of my parents loved the outdoors.

"Here, take my hand and let me help you out of the lake. It's slippery," Harriet offered.

Harriet's inner voice growled; no words, just a growl. Harriet understood the command and jerked her hand back. Chloe fell backwards, going underwater. As Chloe struggled to surface, she could see Harriet glare down at her and then walk away. Chloe pulled her head just above the surface. However, her feet teetered on the edge of an underwater drop-off, and she plunged into deeper water.

As Harriet walked away from the edge of the lake, she stopped, shocked by the sight of Edith emerging from the nearby bushes.

"What the hell are you doing here!" Harriet shrieked. Edith ignored her as she frantically rushed toward the lake.

Harriet grabbed a fallen branch and struck Edith with it. In a rage, she hit Edith again and again—until she was lying still on the ground. With the strength of someone much younger, Harriet dragged Edith back to the bushes, hiding her from sight. Straightening her blouse, Harriet silently congratulated herself; that problem was solved and solved very quickly.

Turning toward the sudden splashing sounds she heard, Harriet was shocked as she watched Chloe crawl onto dry land.

"Are you all right?" Harriet asked, hurrying over to Chloe. "I was trying to find something to pull you out with." Grateful for the plentiful trees and bushes, she was certain that Chloe could not have seen Edith.

"Yes, I'm okay," Chloe gasped, trying to calm herself.

Chloe felt chilled from the cool lake water. She was also chilled by Harriet's earlier glare. Shaking her head as if to rid herself of that thought, Chloe forced a chuckle and said, "It's been a while since I took a swim in a lake."

Chloe didn't share the details of her near-drowning with Harriet. She closed her eyes for a moment, her heart still beating wildly. She had panicked in the water, thrashing about and sinking ever deeper. As she fought to hold her breath, an iridescent light pierced through the lake, and she heard a soft, female voice.

"Stay calm," the voice said, and Chloe grew calmer.

"Look up," the voice said, and Chloe did.

Above her, a log drifted along. With a sudden burst of energy, she pushed upward and grabbed ahold of the log. Pulling her head above the water, she inhaled, filling her lungs with air. Regaining some strength, she pushed off from the log and swam to the shore.

Chloe silently thanked whoever or whatever saved her.

After calming down, Chloe suggested they head back to their car as the sun was setting. Retracing their steps on the same path that brought them deep into the forest, they saw two young bear cubs hurry up a large pine. Hiding within the branches of the pine, the cubs wailed in fright, calling for their mother. The mother bear was nearby and quickly started toward her cubs.

Chloe and Harriet froze in their tracks, uncertain of what to do. The mother bear ran to the base of the tree that was cradling her cubs and stopped. Growling at the two humans, she stomped and pawed threateningly on the ground. Chloe and Harriet understood the warning. The mother bear was protecting her young cubs; no translation was needed.

They backed away, slowly moving backwards down the path. The mother bear continued her warning until they turned a bend and were out of sight. Chloe and Harriet started running, tripping often on the uneven path. The light was limited as the forest grew darker. Finally, too tired to run any longer, Chloe and Harriet stopped to rest.

Chloe was the first to speak, "I'm not sure if we are still going in the right direction. We haven't crossed that little stream we waded across earlier today. Do you think that we took a wrong turn somewhere?"

"I'm not sure," Harriet said. "Everything looks different in the dark."

The two continued down the path and stopped again. "What was that?" Chloe whispered.

Harriet had heard it also. Something was following them. As the moon pushed its way through the wispy, featherly clouds, they turned and saw their pursuer—a cougar. The cougar sat, staring at them, as if trying to decide if it was worth the trouble to attack two lost humans. They stood very still, barely breathing. After a few moments, the cougar leaped back into the forest, disappearing within seconds.

Chloe held her chest; her heart was pounding faster than she thought possible. Chloe stared silently into the night for a few seconds and then whispered, "I thought that we were going to be a nighttime snack for the cougar."

"I guess nature also has an evil, dangerous side to it." Harriet rubbed her temples. She had a headache; her inner voice was angry.

"No, not evil. Dangerous maybe. But there's danger everywhere. You can slip in your bathtub and die. Or get hit by a bus on the way home. But nature is not evil. A mother bear protects its young. A cougar stalks its next meal. A bear is a bear. A cougar is a cougar. They aren't evil. They're just doing what nature requires of them to survive. Evil is a serial killer, a mass shooter, a genocide, or someone who murders their own family. These are evil. Humans can be evil, not animals."

"Yes, that's true. Only humans can choose evil over good."

Chloe nodded in agreement. Harriet had spoken a truth. But a chill ran over her. Despite still being wet from her *swim*, Chloe was sure that the chill came from a source deeper within her. She sensed that something was terribly wrong.

Chloe and Harriet continued down the path, more loudly this time, announcing their presence to the wildlife, hoping to avoid any further encounters. Harriet began to lag behind Chloe. After a short while, Chloe felt increasingly uneasy and very slowly glanced over her shoulder, catching sight of the large branch that Harriet had raised high in the air.

Chloe jumped to the side of the path. "What the hell?"

"Oh goodness," Harriet mumbled. "I didn't mean to scare you. I thought that I heard something again."

Chloe looked into the dark forest, first to the left and then to the right. She didn't see nor hear anything—until she spotted two glowing eyes deep in the darkness. "Oh crap, what is that?"

Surprised at the sight of the eyes also, Harriet said nothing. Soon they heard the reassuring hoot of an owl as it announced itself to the night.

"Thank goodness, it's just an owl," Harriet said, dropping the branch. However, her eyes continued to scan the dense, dark forest, wondering if Edith was following.

"Let's keep moving," Chloe said, motioning for Harriet to take the lead. Chloe was unnerved but not by the owl.

Soon they spied fireflies, seemingly dancing in the cool night air—flowing in and out of the trees as their lights decorated the forest. "How amazing," both said at the same time.

Another small creature, however, fluttered at the side of the path. At first, they were puzzled by what it was.

"Perhaps a hummingbird or a very large butterfly?" Chloe whispered.

They stood, watching until Chloe spoke again, tentatively offering another guess, "Could it be an angel?"

"I don't know," Harriet said. As she stared at the strange creature, she felt unsettled, her heart pounding so loudly she could hear it.

Chloe sensed that it was a gentle presence—perhaps the same one who had just saved her from drowning. Chloe whispered, "My heart is saying that she is here to help us."

They watched as the fluttering creature illuminated the darkness that surrounded it. They could see that a soft, delicate aura encircled her small, feminine form—a form only a foot or so in height. Her aura slowly, silently pulsated, producing a dazzling blend of colors: gentle shades of rose, violet, and green, but mostly of blue. If the creature drifted too far off the path and into the forest, she seemed to disappear for a moment, absorbing the protective colors of the forest.

As the shimmering creature moved down the path ahead of them, the lost companions followed, thankful for its light. After a short while, the creature came to an intersecting path that veered in a different direction. Hovering at this spot, she pointed to the new path before disappearing into the protective camouflage of the forest.

Trusting this strange little creature, Chloe headed down the new path, and Harriet followed. The path was very narrow, and in darkness again, the two were barely able to push their way through the trees, ferns, and twisted vines that lined the path. However, after a few minutes on the new path, they saw the little stream.

Even in the darkness, the stream sparkled, reflecting the brilliance of the moon and the stars as it rolled over its rocky bottom and weaved gracefully around larger stones. After wading across it, the two caught sight of the road and quickly sprinted the rest of the way down the path and hurried into the safety of the car.

"I'm not sure if anyone would believe how we found our way out," Chloe said, staring into the darkness.

"It doesn't matter if anyone else believes. It only matters if you believe. People are too wrapped up in everyday living to have time to believe in things like angels and demons," Harriet said.

Chloe wasn't ready yet to openly acknowledge that she had

encountered an angel. However, Harriet could see the belief in Chloe's eyes, and it unexpectedly touched her.

Harriet's walls were crumbling, and this worried her. She counted on her walls to hide her true intentions. She couldn't afford to expose anything more to Chloe.

Chloe stared straight ahead and asked, "Hetty, did you push me into the lake?"

"Of course not. I slipped and lost my grip on your hand." Harriet started to cry. A few forced tears had always helped her sell a lie.

Although they spoke no other words, Chloe and Harriet's eyes met for a brief moment. Chloe wasn't sure if she believed Harriet as she started the car and drove into the darkness.

Although her inner voice wasn't happy that she failed again, Harriet was tired from the long day, and she decided that the plan could wait a little longer. In fact, at this moment, Harriet wanted her inner voice to go silent for a few hours, like it had been for twelve years while she was at the institution, only roaring back when Joan unexpectedly visited.

∼

As Edith emerged from the forest, she watched the taillights of Chloe's car fade from her sight.

Bruised, she stumbled, inch by inch, down the road to the black van that was hidden out of sight. No longer able to stand easily, she slid to the ground and leaned against the van. Angry that she didn't have the strength at that moment to follow them, Edith made a phone call instead.

"Joan—I lost them. Well, sort of. I know the direction that they went."

"Oh crap. I knew something was wrong. You were supposed to call hours ago."

"Sorry, I lost track of time. They went into the damn woods, and I had to follow on foot."

"Oh geez. Where are you?"

"Just outside of Rhinelander, and Harriet attacked me."

"Are you okay, Edith?"

"Yes. Sore but no broken bones."

"Someone needs to follow them. Are you up to that?"

"I have to be. We need to protect Chloe. I can catch up with them. I just need to rest for a second. Where are you, Joan? Today made it very clear that when we confront Harriet, it'll take at least two people to handle her."

"I drove as far as Wausau. It seemed like a logical, central spot to wait."

"Good idea. I wish that we knew where they were heading."

"I might know. Frank called me a little while ago, wondering where Chloe was. She hadn't called him yet tonight, and she also wasn't answering her phone. I told him that if there was a problem, you would have called me. Anyhow, she's been talking endlessly about taking a trip to the Apostle Islands this summer. What's interesting is that Chloe and I were planning a trip there also before . . . before I left."

"Very interesting. Do you truly feel in your gut that Chloe will head there next?"

"Yes."

"Then why don't you starting driving there now, and I'll keep following her from my end."

"Are you sure? Shouldn't I meet up with you so that we can follow Chloe together?"

"I don't actually know where I am, and by the time, I figure it out, you could be halfway to the Apostle Islands. And if you are wrong about the Apostle Islands, then we will adjust our plans tomorrow. I'm going to get back into the saddle now, as they say, and catch up with them."

Joan ended the call with one word, "Okay."

Sitting in the parking lot of a local drive-in, Joan understood how dangerous her mother was. She also understood that her mother had to be dealt with—one way or the other. When she left Wisconsin twelve years prior, she had only taken her fears, her emptiness, and of course, her dog.

Joan popped a deep-fried cheese curd into her mouth. Her dog barked and licked her lips. Laughing, Joan said, "Don't complain, Molly. I saved the last one for you. Aren't we just a couple of cheeseheads? You know what they say: Once a cheesehead, always a cheesehead."

As the dog scarfed down the last cheese curd, Joan remembered another bit of advice that the old man had given her back in Oregon: *If you encounter a roadblock in life, look for a way around it.*

Good advice, she thought, but this time, ramming through the roadblock might be the only option.

Chapter 7

After driving for about an hour, Chloe and Harriet found themselves in a small village nestled next to an equally small lake. A small village is perhaps stretching the truth somewhat, Chloe thought, knowing that her father would call it *just a wide spot in the road.*

A welcome sign that showed the population not by a numerical count but only as *Happy* beckoned travelers to enter. Harriet sneered quietly as they drove by the sign, but Chloe smiled.

It only took a few minutes to drive from the welcome sign to the far end of the village, where an old, white clapboard church sat. Chloe sensed a peaceful quietness in the air, feeling that the village and its old church reflected a charm only found on Christmas cards.

After pulling into the church parking lot, Chloe hopped out of the car and discovered that the church was locked. Darn, she thought, it would have been nice to take shelter for the night in the church. Exhausted from their adventure in the forest and nearly out of gas, Chloe and Harriet opted to sleep in the car rather than look any further for shelter.

As Chloe looked over at the tired old woman next to her, she silently chastised herself for thinking she was dangerous.

"I know this is gross," Chloe said. "But I have to pee. I am going to find a tree to hide behind, and well, you know what I mean. It's not like we haven't done that quite a few times today."

Harriet laughed, and they both got out of the car to *find a tree*.

After returning to the car, Chloe checked her phone and noticed several missed calls from her father. She hoped he wasn't too worried.

"Dad, I'm in a sweet little place about an hour north of Rhinelander. I'll call you tomorrow," Chloe whispered into her father's voicemail. She was grateful that he hadn't answered. She was too tired for a long conversation.

As they drifted off to sleep, the birds sang lullabies to them, and the nearby trees stood guard against the night. Chloe felt safe in the parking lot of the old church.

Neither had seen the black van as it pulled behind the church.

In the early morning light, Chloe was the first to wake, believing for just a second that her cat had been snuggling close to her. She rolled down the car window, inhaled the cool morning air, and listened to the morning songs of the birds. Her ears slowly attuned to the sounds of the trees, whose leaves rustled in the cool morning breeze.

These early morning sounds brought memories of her mother to Chloe. She remembered hiking with her mother in the woods near the family fishing cabin. As they hiked, they talked and laughed, and her mother would tell her to listen to the wind, hug the trees, roll in the grass, and skip down the paths—suggestions that brought giggles to Chloe as a child.

After hiking, they would return to the cabin so that her mother could paint. She was an artist, and Chloe sighed as she pictured her mother's messy art smock. Although her mother sold only an occasional painting at local art fairs, her mother's art was magical to Chloe.

Chloe also remembered that her mother often tried to explain the essence of art to her as she painted. Closing her eyes, Chloe could almost still hear her mother speak: *"An artist must put a little of their own soul into their work. There is a difference between a doodle and a drawing, a stale landscape painting and a work of art, a dime-store novel and a literary masterpiece, or a greeting card verse and poetry. Art must evoke a reaction, a connection. An artist needs to almost give birth to something intangible, something alive in and of itself."*

Chloe had loved watching her mother swirl her brush on the canvas, producing fairy tale images of nature and its animals—both real and imagined. Chloe remembered how her mother's eyes sparkled with life and imagination while she painted.

These were happy memories, and Chloe was grateful for them. However, these memories brought with them another sadder memory. Chloe painfully remembered that her mother was only happy during brief periods. Mostly, she seemed neither happy nor sad—but rather, almost detached. It wasn't that her mother didn't do all of the appropriate things that a mother should. It was simply that Chloe didn't always feel the emotions behind the actions. Chloe decided to discard this particular memory, choosing to remember the happier ones.

Chloe looked over at the strange old woman, amused that she was talking in her sleep, saying the name Abigail over and over again. Chloe wondered who Abigail was.

Chloe couldn't shake the feeling that they were connected in some way. It wasn't just the earlier raspberry story, she thought, but also her slight New England accent. She silently asked herself—One coincidence can be explained away but two?

Harriet woke a few minutes later, stretching and feeling refreshed. "I know that we slept in the car. But wow, I feel great—reinvigorated, in fact. It must be all of the fresh air that we got yesterday."

"Yup, I agree," Chloe said. "My mother would say that nature has a way of healing people. It is just something in our DNA. We need to feel, see, and inhale the outdoors once in a while. Most of us live so separate from nature these days. Mom always said that we were created to live with nature, not separate from it."

After taking a deep breath of the fresh air, Chloe added, "We have lost touch with Mother Earth, and it's killing our very souls. Anyhow that's what my mother would say."

"Based on how good I feel right now, I agree with your mother," Harriet said.

Chloe's eyes drifted over to the trees, and her thoughts followed. "Last semester, I read an essay on the environment, and part of it really stuck with me. I re-read it so many times that I've pretty much memorized it: *Once upon a time, we needed to fish in the lakes, hunt in the forests, and use the stars to navigate. Kids played barefoot, and young men picked wildflowers to give their sweethearts. Our hands and feet touched the earth daily. Our eyes saw the beauty of nature every day. Most of us don't do any of those things these days. We live and work in air-conditioned buildings, stare into computers all day long, or work in factories for hours and hours each day.*"

"Wow, you aren't the typical carefree twenty-something, are you?" Harriet snickered.

"Sorry, I know that I'm a nerd."

Harriet laughed. "Probably, but didn't I tell you not to call herself names? Anyhow, being smart isn't a bad thing. Nerd or not, you certainly aren't what I expected."

"How's that?"

"To be honest, I expected someone your age to be a self-absorbed, spoiled brat."

Chloe's mouth dropped open.

"However, that's not who you are. You're a sweet, smart young woman, and that's the truth." Harriet's face twitched slightly as she fought against her fondness for Chloe.

Chloe blushed, not expecting the compliment. She wondered, however, why Harriet asked to go on a trip with her—especially since she expected to be traveling with a *self-absorbed, spoiled brat*.

Suddenly an old man riding a lawn mower turned into the church's parking lot.

"Oh my god," Chloe said. "I wonder if he has a key for the church. I don't mean to be gross again, but I really need to pee."

Chloe hopped out of the car and dashed over to him before Harriet could respond. After listening to Chloe explain her *situation*, he laughed and unlocked the front door of the old church. Chloe waved to Harriet to come, but she yelled back that she would wait. Surprised at the response, Chloe hurried into the church and quickly found the restroom in the basement.

After a short while, Chloe returned to the main level and sat on one of the old oak pews. It had been a long time since Chloe had been in a church—twelve years to be exact. However, the quiet beauty of the church was surprisingly comforting to her this morning. Chloe glanced around the church, noticing how the morning sun poured through the stained-glass windows, painting the church in a blend of gentle colors. She especially admired the vintage oak altar, which seemed to be so lovingly polished that it glistened.

The old man sat next to Chloe and said, "This old church is beautiful, isn't it? It dates back to the 1850s. There aren't many people left in this little village, and the church even lacks a pastor these days. As you can guess, it's hard to get a pastor for these little out-of-the-way churches. But those who love this church still show up here every Sunday. They sing a few hymns, share a few stories, and enjoy a potluck lunch."

After a brief moment, the old man added, "If you're ever searching for a place to belong, to feel love, or to feel safe, please remember this church. It always has been the history of this church to welcome everyone. It's our belief that a church like Heaven itself should never be viewed as an exclusive private club. God loves all of His children regardless of their social status, skin color, troubled souls, religion, or lack of religion."

His words touched her, and Chloe felt an unexplainable bond with him, feeling like she had known him for years.

"It's nice to know that there are places like this in the world. It feels so peaceful here," Chloe said.

The old man took her hand and smiled. This simple gesture broke through Chloe's defenses, and she blurted out, "I'm always so sad . . . so afraid."

The old man took a few seconds before responding. "You need to remember that there has always been both good and evil in the world. However, even in the darkness of nights, the stars in the sky break through the darkness. And in the morning, the light of the sun overtakes the night. It's in this same way that good always wins over evil. Search for the light in the world—or be the light."

Chloe sat very still, absorbing the old man's words.

The old man bent closer to Chloe and whispered a warning, "I don't mean to be rude, but never turn your back on someone who won't enter a church."

He then put on an old fishing hat almost entirely covered by shimmering silver lures, stood up, and before turning to leave, he said, "I'm heading out to the creek to do some fishing. Nothing better for the soul—that's what I say, anyhow."

Chloe followed him to the door and watched as he rode

off on his blue lawn mower, slowly fading away in the distance. However, his warning hung in the air after he left. Chloe took another look around the church and walked outside into the light.

"Are you sure that you can wait?" Chloe asked as she approached the car. "There's a bathroom right there in the church."

"I'll wait for the gas station."

"Okay, that's your choice. I need to gas up the car anyhow."

Getting into the car, Chloe shivered briefly as she looked into Harriet's dark steel-blue eyes, and an unexpected rush of memories came to Chloe. In particular, she remembered hiding whenever her grandmother visited. And she remembered why. Her grandmother wasn't very grandmotherly—no chocolate cookies, no sleepovers, and no hugs.

However, the memory that really shook Chloe was of her grandmother sitting on the porch of her family's cabin, knitting as she angrily swatted mosquitos. She stole a quick look at the knitting needles sticking out of Harriet's tote bag in the backseat. Knitting—another coincidence, she wondered?

As she drove to the local gas station, Chloe decided to phone her father as soon as she was alone, hoping that he could fill in a few blanks for her.

Upon completing their respective tasks at the station, they decided to eat a quick breakfast in the car before departing the village. After finishing the coffee and two mildly warm breakfast sandwiches bought at the station, they both agreed that they were too hungry to judge the quality of the food. But they readily agreed that the coffee was hot and very strong. If they didn't already feel invigorated by the very force of nature itself, they felt the coffee alone would have done the trick.

Chloe had pulled the car to the side of the station so they could in eat a less busy, more private area. However, as she scanned the area, she decided that going back into the station was the only option for a private call with her father. But before she could do so, Harriet asked, "Where should we go next, Chloe?"

The question startled Chloe for a second. She hadn't been thinking about their next destination. "I don't know. Where do you want to go?"

"I've never ventured this far north before."

"Wow, that's too bad, Hetty. It's beautiful up here."

"Yes, I guess so."

"Um, I noticed your accent, Hetty. Where are you from originally? Have you lived very long in Madison?"

"I lived in that general part of the state for most of my life," Harriet answered, avoiding any further explanation.

Before Chloe could pry any further, Harriet turned the conversation back to the question of their next stop. "Why don't you pick where we head next? Is there anything in this part of the state that you might want to visit?"

"Actually, yes. The Apostle Islands."

"Then that's our next stop."

"They are *officially* known as the Apostle Islands National Lakeshore," Chloe said, her lopsided grin revealing her sudden enthusiasm for their next stop. "I've wanted to visit there for a long time."

Chloe chose not to share her mother's long-ago promise to plan their next family vacation there. Her mother's death stopped those plans, and the memory was much too melancholy to be shared over breakfast, she felt.

"I'm guessing that it will take about two hours to get there, which means that we'll have a full day to sightsee and have some fun," Chloe said.

Sounding like a well-informed tourist guide, Chloe continued, "The options are almost endless—sailing, kayaking, canoeing, camping, fishing, touring lighthouses, scuba diving, sightseeing cruises, or hiking in the woods."

"Hmm, I'm not sure about hiking in the woods again!" Harriet said, laughing.

"Maybe a nice, safe sightseeing cruise around the islands?" Chloe didn't want another hike with Harriet either.

Harriet nodded her agreement.

With the day's plans finalized, Chloe excused herself and headed back to the station's restroom to phone her father in privacy. When his phone rang, Frank was relieved to see his daughter's caller ID. He had resisted the urge to call her when he first woke, not wanting to appear overly concern.

"Good morning, Chloe."

"Hi, Dad. It's really pretty up here. I forgot how much I loved the outdoors."

"Where are you off to next?"

"The Apostle Islands. We're planning to take a sightseeing cruise. But I have some quick questions first."

"Sure, what's up?"

"I know you said that Grandma Harriet didn't have a twin. But if I remember right, she had a sister. What's her name? And do you remember the color of Grandma Harriet's eyes or her sister's?"

"Chloe, are you okay? Why all of the questions? Is something up? If you sense any sort of problem or danger, you need to end the trip right now and come home."

Frank instantly regretted his outburst. But he was worried. Chloe was too far away for him to protect her. A heaviness suddenly set into his chest, and for a second, he felt that he might be having a heart attack. Frank took several deep breaths and calmed himself down.

"Dad, is there something wrong? You sound really, really stressed out."

"Sorry. I'm being over-protective. You've never taken a vacation without me."

"Dad, I'm fine. Don't worry, okay?"

"Okay, sweetie. The only sister that your Grandma Harriet had is Edith. She was a couple of years younger than your Grandma Harriet, but I don't remember the eye color for either."

"I vaguely remember meeting Edith once."

"Yes, you met her once. Edith was visiting Grandma Harriet around the time of your mother's car accident. She took your grandmother back to Albuquerque with her right after that."

"Oh, so that's how Grandma Harriet ended up in Albuquerque. It sounds like they were very close sisters. Does Aunt Edith still live in Albuquerque?"

"Yes, Edith still lives there."

"Do you have an address or phone number for Edith?"

"No, sorry." It was a lie, and Frank felt guilty about having lied once again to his daughter.

"Oh, that's too bad. I thought that I might reach out to her. I don't know much about Mom's side of the family. Anyhow, what did Grandma Harriet do for a living? And what does Edith do for a living?"

"Your grandmother was an accountant. Edith is an artist. Again, why the questions?"

"I was just thinking about family, I guess." Chloe knew that it was a vague answer, but she didn't want to tell her worrisome father that she was sensing some sort of family connection with Harriet.

"I see."

"Oh, just one more question—have you ever heard of someone called Abigail?"

"No." A one-word response was all that Frank could manage as he slouched slightly forward, barely able to catch his breath.

"Okay, thanks. I'll give you a call later today. Bye, Dad."

After the call ended, Frank quickly texted Joan: *Apostle Islands. Sightseeing cruise.*

Joan texted back: *Thank you. Already in the area.*

Frank took a deep breath and then another one. Then he texted Joan again: *Chloe asked who Abigail was. I didn't tell her. Please, please keep our daughter safe.*

Joan stared at the words for several seconds before texting back: *I'll protect Chloe. I promise.*

※

As they headed down the two-lane highway toward their next stop, it was apparent to Harriet that Chloe was distracted by something. However, Harriet decided against questioning her, preferring to avoid any further revealing conversations.

Chloe wondered about the strange coincidences that surrounded the older woman sitting next to her, and she decided to do some internet sleuthing to find her Aunt Edith, or rather her Great-Aunt Edith. And if possible, phone her. Chloe wanted to find out who Harriet really was and hoped Edith could help.

The drive ended as they arrived in the historic city of Bayfield, a small city of roughly five hundred souls perched on the shores of Lake Superior. At first glance, it seemed to have more trees than residents and tourists combined.

Chloe drove through part of Bayfield's historic district in search of the Apostle Islands Visitor Center, soaking in the flavor of what they saw. They were especially awed by the beautiful Queen Anne houses and the flowering gardens that graced their lawns. In the downtown area, they were equally delighted by the variety of cafes, gift stores, artisan shops, and galleries. Chloe felt a touch of melancholy, realizing that her mother would have loved the artsy vibe.

Their unplanned tour of the city ended at the visitor center located in the old Bayfield County Courthouse, an elegant and imposing brownstone building. They hurried inside and inquired about cruises. They were delighted to learn that there was a daily, narrated 55-mile cruise.

Since the cruise was set to depart soon, they quickly hurried to the dock, paid their fares, and settled into seats on the upper open-air deck of the boat.

Once the cruise was underway, the captain began narrating, sharing tidbits about the history and scenery of the area as the boat pushed its way through the choppy waters of Lake Superior. Harriet suggested they stand by the boat's railing to catch better views. The two held tightly onto the boat's railing to steady themselves.

After a short while, Harriet pointed to a scenic bluff with one hand, and while Chloe was distracted, she placed her other hand on Chloe's back. She hesitated briefly and then gave a gentle nudge. Caught off guard, Chloe slipped, nearly falling overboard. Luckily, a woman raced over, quickly pulling her to safety.

Several of the passengers gathered around Chloe, asking if she was alright. Chloe assured all that she was. However, since her rescuer had instantly blended back into the crowd of passengers on deck, Chloe didn't know who had actually saved her. Unhappy that she couldn't thank her, Chloe was keenly aware, however, that she needed to be rescued—once again.

As the incident unfolded, Harriet had stepped away, distancing herself from the commotion. After the crowd thinned, she walked back over to Chloe and asked, "Are you okay, Chloe?"

"Yes, of course, I just slipped," Chloe said in a shaky voice. In truth, Chloe felt more uneasy than okay.

"Take a few deep breaths. It'll help you calm down."

Chloe followed the advice, but it only slightly calmed her. She silently asked herself: *Are two accidents in two days merely another coincidence? Or was I shoved?*

"Hetty, um, where were you when I slipped?"

"I stepped away right before your accident. It was getting

really crowded by the railing, and people were jostling for better spots. I'm happy that you are safe." Harriet gave Chloe a quick hug to bolster the lie.

"Thanks for the hug. I really needed that," Chloe said, feeling foolish for wondering if Hetty had shoved her. It was *just* an accident, she decided.

"Let's just forget about it and enjoy the rest of the cruise," Chloe said, pushing any unsettling thoughts out of her mind.

"Wonderful idea," Harriet smiled, pleased that Chloe had believed her.

As the cruise continued, the lake's cool fresh water splashed the passengers on the open-aired decks. Although not necessarily shared by all, Chloe and Harriet were delighted to feel and taste the waters of the mighty Lake Superior. Both were, however, also happy that they had followed the advice of the friendly park employee and had worn jackets. Despite it being a warm and sunny day on land, the experience onboard was much cooler—in fact, somewhat chilly. The two agreed that the formidable winds of Lake Superior delivered more of an arctic experience than a tropical one.

Eventually, Chloe noticed that Harriet kept glancing over her shoulder.

"Is everything okay?" Chloe asked.

"Oh yes," Harriet said, smiling to conceal the lie. "But I might have spotted someone that I know, a woman wearing large hoop earrings. Did you happen to see anyone like that?"

"No, sorry. If you want, we can walk around the boat and try to find this woman."

"No thanks. It was probably only my imagination." Harriet had gotten only a quick glimpse of the woman who saved Chloe—a woman wearing large hoop earrings.

As the boat continued on its planned route, they became fully engrossed in the sights again. They especially enjoyed the views of historic lighthouses and of the nesting eagles on the sandstone cliffs.

Both were also profoundly struck by the sea caves and arches. As the wind twisted around and through these mystical formations, the two imagined the reverence that the early indigenous people must have felt. A reverence they also now shared. They further gained a greater respect for the early schooner captains, who sailed through these picturesque islands, praying to survive the often defiant but beautiful Lake Superior.

Toward the end of the cruise, the two women spotted kayakers paddling near the caves. Harriet casually commented on the dangers of kayaking in rough waters.

The offhand comment brought back another long-ago memory to Chloe, a day that she spent kayaking with her mother just a week or so before her mother's death. The kayak overturned, and they were washed down the river by the currents. Fortunately, both Chloe and her mother were excellent swimmers and made it to shore safely.

After the ill-fated adventure, Chloe remembered her mother repeatedly saying, "Always be careful, Chloe." How appropriate that advice still seemed, she thought.

When the cruise ended, the two exited the boat, having enjoyed the cruise despite Chloe's *accident*. Chloe suddenly and happily proclaimed that visiting the Apostle Islands was almost a spiritual experience—like being granted a glimpse of heaven itself. Harriet didn't respond as she glanced around, trying to spot anyone who might be following. Seeing no one, Harriet was relieved as they walked away from the dock.

Since it was now early afternoon, Chloe and Harriet found a quaint diner and ate their orders of fish and chips like two hungry seafarers. They spent the rest of the day roaming the streets of Bayfield, visiting various shops and galleries. They came across a restaurant near the docks by early evening and decided to splurge, choosing to dine rather than just grab a bite to eat.

After dining and exhausted from their touristy activities, they found two hotel rooms available at a nearby inn. Although once again surprised that they could acquire two rooms so easily at the height of the tourist season, Chloe decided to accept it as random luck—mixed with a bit of mysterious magic. After checking into the hotel, the two agreed to meet up in a couple of hours on the porch that encircled the inn.

Delighted to have some time alone, Chloe sat down by the desk in her room and pulled her notebook computer out of her tote bag. She was determined to find some answers. Chloe was surprised at how quickly she located her Great-Aunt Edith. According to the internet, Edith was a locally well-known artist in Albuquerque, who also owned an art gallery.

Searching further, Chloe located a photo of Edith and was shocked—Edith was the good Samaritan. Chloe then noticed a partially obstructed image of another woman in the background of the photo. The woman was wearing large hoop earrings. Unable to tell from the photo, she wondered who this woman was. Chloe's stomach knotted up; something odd was going on.

Chloe quickly located the phone number for Edith's art gallery. Although uncertain of what she wanted to ask, Chloe called and left a message on the voicemail, hoping that Edith would call back.

Chloe got up and paced around her room. She wasn't sure what to make of this new information. She definitely sensed that something strange was going on—something tied to Aunt Edith and her grandmother. She also wondered about her nightmares and mumbled, "What am I not remembering? What is the reason behind the fear that I still have from that night?"

She sat back down at her computer, determined to find out what she could about the accident that killed her mother. After a lengthy internet search, Chloe found a small news article on the car accident. Despite its brevity, the article summed it up pretty well, Chloe thought.

Chloe re-read the short article several times: *Car plunged into the Mississippi River just north of La Crosse, WI. Adult woman presumed drowned along with family dog. It is believed that the inclement weather and icy road conditions contributed to the accident. Due to heavy spring rains and melting snow, the river is at flood stage. The search for missing woman has been called off due to dangerous conditions.*

Chloe, of course, had known that her mother had died in a car accident. However, she wasn't told that her mother had drowned. Since her mother was an excellent swimmer, that bit of information was unsettling to her.

The short article also brought a terrifying memory to Chloe. Closing her eyes, Chloe seemed transported back to the awful day of her mother's death.

~

Chloe felt sick, sleepy, and cold in the backseat of her mother's car. The car was parked outside of the cabin, and the freezing rain pounded on the windows of the car. Chloe's head popped up just enough to watch Aunt Edith drive off. Despite the pounding rain, Chloe could hear yelling coming from the fishing cabin, but she couldn't make out the words. Chloe fought to keep her eyes open. Suddenly she was jolted fully awake at the sound of a gunshot. Frighten and alone in the car, Chloe sneaked a peek out of the car window and watched her mother stagger over to the car.

As her mother got into the car, Chloe was shocked at the sight of her mother's swollen eyes and her bloody blouse. Next the puppy leapt into the car, barking, then growling, and then barking again. Chloe followed the puppy's glare, putting her hand over her mouth, trying but failing to stop a scream. The puppy was barking at Grandma Harriet, who loomed in the doorway of the cabin, pointing a gun in their direction and laughing. Terrified, Chloe was unable to speak—unable to even ask her mother what was happening.

Chloe then saw a bullet burst forth in a fiery cloud from Grandma Harriet's gun. Luckily, however, her mother quickly hit the gas pedal, and the car raced ahead. The bullet missed hitting the car. Soon Chloe and her mother were speeding down the highway. Her mother was driving too fast for the weather conditions, and Chloe held onto the puppy as the car repeatedly fishtailed. When her mother finally pulled into the driveway at their house, Chloe sat frozen in the backseat of the car, glad to be home, but too frightened to move.

Chloe's mother sat still for a moment in the car, tearless and enraged. Forcing herself to appear calm, her mother got out of the car and then tried to coax the puppy out. The puppy stubbornly refused to do so. Chloe's mother then opened the car door nearest to Chloe. She helped Chloe out of the car, took her hand, and led her into the house. Next, Chloe's mother helped her into bed, gently tucking her in, explaining that it was just a bad dream, and telling Chloe to forget everything. Looking into her mother's eyes, Chloe remained speechless. Chloe didn't understand what she saw in her mother's eyes, but it scared her.

Next, her mother gently kissed Chloe on her forehead and quietly walked out of her bedroom. It was the last time that Chloe saw her.

∽

As she opened her eyes, tears flowed down her face. She had blocked the ugliness for so long that the memory was both startling and therapeutic. She was starting to remember and understand the reasons for her fear. However, Chloe knew that there was more to the story, and she wanted to know *all* of the story.

Chloe suddenly noticed the clock, and she was surprised that it was almost time to meet Harriet. Forcing herself to calm down, Chloe quickly freshened up and exited her hotel room.

By chance, Chloe and Harriet met at the top of the grand staircase in the inn. Chloe suggested taking the elevator; however, Harriet smiled, saying that she was not too old for the stairs. As they descended the stairs, Chloe took the lead, with Harriet close behind. As they started to descend, Chloe felt a soft nudge from behind and stumbled, missing a couple of steps before catching herself again.

Chloe's jaw clenched, as did her fists, and she fought to control her anger. This time, doubt didn't cloud her mind; Harriet shoved her. What she didn't know was why. Chloe stood still, steadying herself and quickly weighing her options—scream at the old woman, slap the old woman, or both . . . or neither.

From behind, she heard Harriet quietly asked, "Are you okay?"

A favorite saying of her father's suddenly popped into Chloe's mind—*you catch more bees with honey than vinegar.* Chloe made her decision. She would pretend that once again she accidentally slipped. She had too many unanswered questions, and Harriet was the key to the answers. Alienating her was too risky.

"I'm okay. It must have been the wine at dinner. I'm not used to drinking," Chloe said, trying to keep her voice light. "I'm going to go slower the rest of the way down. Why don't you go ahead of me?"

Chloe winced as she saw a slight smile on Harriet's face as she passed by.

When they reached the porch, they sat quietly and watched as the setting sun brushed the sky with gentle streaks of yellow and burgundy.

"Wow, the sky is beautiful," Chloe whispered.

Harriet gave a quick, noncommittal nod. She wasn't interested in the sky.

"It's odd that I'm having so many accidents lately," Chloe said, giving a sideways glance at Harriet. Chloe hoped her *casual* statement would lead to a deeper conversation.

However, Harriet didn't respond. Instead, she sat, staring vacantly into the early night sky, lost in her thoughts. She wasn't sure if she wanted to obey her inner voice. Her growing fondness for Chloe was at odds with the plan. After a short while, she excused herself, explaining that her headache was returning and that she was retiring to her room for the night.

Remaining behind, Chloe sat in silence for a time. At first, she thought about Harriet and the odd coincidences surrounding her. But her mind quickly drifted to the strange, otherworldly experiences of the last few days. She knew that most would be uncomfortable or even frightened by such things. However, even as a child, Chloe often sensed unseen but gentle spirits around her. Such things didn't scare her.

Although unwilling to risk the ridicule of nonbelievers and openly admit it, Chloe intuitively knew the truth, however. She softly whispered to herself, "I'm not crazy. These things are real. I feel it in my bones."

Chloe decided to take a walk. She didn't have any particular destination in mind; she just wanted to walk. The coolness and quiet of the night were calming to her.

As she walked, Chloe asked the night a simple question, hoping for some sort of magical response, "How can I find the answers that I seek?" Receiving no immediate response, Chloe continued to walk in the darkness.

As Chloe turned the corner, she got her answer but not in words. A dead streetlight flickered on, and her cat appeared, sitting where it seemed the two realms of life and death momentarily co-existed.

Taking a few more steps toward the light, a discarded news clipping blew into Chloe's path. Picking it up, she saw the road trip's next stop. She looked up in time to watch her cat slowly fade away, and the streetlight flicker off. Chloe was thankful for the guidance.

As she turned back toward the inn, Chloe removed her shoes, delighted to feel the cool earth as she walked. With each step, Chloe grew more hopeful that she would soon find the answers that she sought. Just before reaching the hotel, Chloe remembered to text her father about her plans for the next day.

Chloe was unaware of the two women who were walking in the darkness behind her.

Chapter 8

After Chloe entered the hotel, Edith and Joan sat on the porch of the inn.

"Chloe left a voice mail for me," Edith whispered.

"Oh crap," Joan whispered back as she fidgeted with her hoop earrings.

"Should I phone her?" Edith closed her eyes, still feeling tired and sore from the previous night, and waited for Joan's answer.

"No, we agreed to never tell Chloe anything. How in the world could we ever explain all of this anyhow? She'll think that we're crazy . . . or worse, that we're the monsters and not that evil, old woman."

"Agreed. Somehow we need to grab Harriet and get her back to Albuquerque. Then we can figure out what to do next."

"I followed Mother after she left the porch, and she went directly into her room. Unfortunately, there were too many people around to grab her."

To watch the inn from a more discreet distance, the two returned to the van. The dog, which had patiently waited in the van, greeted them with a soft bark and a tail wag. As Joan took the dog for a short walk, Edith stared into the night, praying for protection from the darkness in her sister.

After Joan returned with the dog, all three settled in for a long night of surveillance. Shortly, however, the dog suddenly snarled, and the two women jumped at the sight of Harriet approaching the van.

"Holy shit!" Edith yelled. "I think that she's pointing a gun."

Edith quickly started the van and sped away, leaving Harriet standing alone in the parking lot. Harriet calmly put her cell-phone back into her pocket. As she walked back into the inn and to her room, she flaunted a triumphant sneer to those she passed.

Edith parked the van down the street and sighed deeply. "My heart's still pounding. I know that this spot is further away from the inn. But thankfully, we can still easily watch both the inn and Chloe's car from here."

"Maybe we should just kill the wicked old bitch," Joan said, glaring into the night.

"Joan!" Edith snapped, unsure if Joan was serious. "Don't say that. She's my sister and your mother."

"But how else can we finally end this nightmare? You somehow convinced the old bitch to go into a nuthouse in Albuquerque for the last twelve years. But she's out now, and the nightmare is starting all over again."

"Don't say nuthouse. It was a mental institution—a hospital."

"We need to fight fire with fire."

"The sad truth is sometimes when you fight fire with fire, you only get a much bigger fire."

"I should *not* have gone to visit her at the institution," Joan whispered, fighting the tears that wanted to fall. "After all my years of trying to heal, it seemed necessary to face her again and tell her that I forgave her. You know, so I could move on as they say. Start my next chapter in life. But she just stared at me. No words. Nada. She just stared. She clearly wanted nothing to do with me."

"Don't blame yourself, Joan. You had no way to know how things would turn out. I thought that it was a good idea, too. Forgiveness is a powerful way to heal old wounds."

"Do you think that Mother actually murdered anyone?"

"I have no way to know for sure but maybe. May God forgive her if she has."

"Do you think that Mother would really harm Chloe?"

"I don't know that either for sure. If she really wanted to do so, she certainly is capable of it. It's more like she is toying Chloe. I think that she enjoys making people squirm. She used to do that with our parents—well, they were your grandparents."

"Were your parents really as horrible as you claimed?"

"More so."

Edith and Joan fixed their eyes on the inn again, hoping for *nothing* to happen. The dog growled as a woman approached the van.

Rolling the window down, Edith greeted the woman standing in the dark. "Hello, Gladys. I'm very pleased that you could come. Did you have any problem finding the inn?"

Gladys got into the backseat of the van as she answered, "None, but please fill me in on what is happening. You didn't explain much in the call."

Edith briefed her on the events from the last few days.

"Oh, geez. I'm glad that you called me. I honestly sense a darkness over your family." Gladys nervously looked toward the inn.

"Are you sensing anything in particular?" Edith asked.

"No, nothing like that. I'm not psychic. It's just a gut feeling that I get when I encounter these situations," Gladys answered.

"We called you only a few hours ago. Where do you live that you could get here so fast?" Joan asked, noticing that Gladys's long, single braid had gotten grayer and longer over the last twelve years. But Joan approved, feeling that it made Gladys look like a wise old sage.

"I don't really have an address. Sadly, in my profession, I travel a great deal. I'm currently staying at a wonderful spiritual retreat about three hours from here. I need to recharge my body and soul from time to time."

"In your profession, I'm guessing that's very necessary. There's a lot of evil in the world," Edith quietly said.

"Unfortunately, yes," Gladys agreed. "Tell me exactly how I can help."

"Joan and I have discussed this, and we both agree. What was started twelve years ago needs to be finished. I told you what is going on, but I haven't told you yet about my actual plan. If I can't convince Harriet to voluntarily return to Albuquerque with me, I'm going to kidnap her. But either way, we want to finish what was started."

Edith looked at Gladys, trying to gauge her willingness. Without flinching, Gladys said, "I'll do whatever is necessary. I failed you back then, and I strongly feel that Harriet needs to be dealt with. If not, she'll only become increasingly more evil."

Edith's eyes teared up, and she mouthed, "Thank you."

"Well, um, I had an ulterior motive when I agreed to Edith's plan to call you in," Joan said, looking at Gladys. "Harriet roughed up Edith last night, and this made one thing *very* clear. It'll take at least two people to handle her."

Edith looked at Joan, raising her eyebrows in a silent question: *What are you up to?*

"Since Gladys is here now, I'm going to leave. I need to take care of something," Joan announced, surprising the other two women.

"For how long?" Edith asked.

"I'm not sure. But since there're two of you, I can be spared for a while." Joan and the dog got out of the van.

"I'm confused," Edith said. "Don't you want to help protect Chloe?"

"I'm very serious about protecting Chloe," Joan answered in a low, firm voice. "That's why I need to go. Frank just texted, and we now know where they're heading tomorrow. Chloe's in her room and is safe for now. It's unlikely that anything is going to happen anymore tonight."

"Are you coming back tonight?" Edith asked.

"No. But I'll meet up with you as soon as I can."

∽

Still feeling triumphant from the fright that she put into her sister and daughter, Harriet stood in front of the wall mirror in her room, watching a shadowy figure form.

"Abigail, did you see how scared Edith and Joan were?" Harriet asked, laughing loudly.

"Yes! You were magnificent."

"I feel so powerful."

"Are you ready yet to take care of Chloe?"

"I think so. My mother was mean to me."

"Yes, your mother was very, very mean to you."

"And Chloe looks too damn much like my mother."

"Yes, Harriet. Chloe looks just like your mother."

"Abigail, can I tell you a secret?"

"Of course."

"It's really tough to look at Chloe."

"I understand, Harriet."

"But Chloe isn't mean like my mother. Are you sure that my mother is hiding inside of her?"

"Harriet, I would never lie to you."

"I know, Abigail."

"So tell me again, Harriet, why Chloe must die?"

"My mother's hiding in her."

"And?"

"Payback. I hate Edith and that ungrateful daughter of mine!"

"Very good, Harriet. Don't hesitate again."

"I won't."

The shadowy figure emerged from the mirror, embraced Harriet, and slowly faded away.

Harriet walked to the window and watched Joan drive off. In the darkness of her room, she laughed and then whispered to herself, "It's too late to run again, dear. Twelve years of my life were wasted because of you. And holy hell, I felt such guilt about your death. But you weren't dead, were you? Soon you and your dear Aunt Edith will regret those twelve wasted years as much as I do. But sweet, innocent Chloe will pay the price, not you. Then you'll understand pain like I do."

∼

After several hours of driving, Joan pulled into the parking lot at Frank's condo. The sun hadn't yet risen, but despite the early hour, Joan texted him: *Can we talk?*

Frank texted back: *Yes. Where are you?*

Joan replied: *In the parking lot outside.*

An out of breath Frank was sitting in his wife's pickup truck in less than two minutes. The dog sat between the two, looking from one to the other. Then with a yawn, the dog curled up and went to sleep.

"Has something happened to Chloe?" Frank quickly asked.

"No, Chloe's fine. Aunt Edith and Gladys are keeping watch."

"Gladys? Oh, good grief, that didn't work out well last time. Is that Edith's plan again?" Frank shook his head in disbelief.

"It's part of it. Aunt Edith still hopes that Mother will just miraculously agree to go back to Albuquerque with her. But she has a Plan B. However, I honestly doubt if either of Aunt Edith's plans will work."

"Dammit, this is a nightmare."

"Don't worry, Frank. I have my own Plan B. I promise that Mother will never harm, threaten, or in any way hurt Chloe. You have my word on it." Joan pointed to a paper bag on the floor near his feet.

Frank was shocked by what he saw in the bag. "Whatever you're thinking, please don't do it."

Joan ignored his plea and stared straight ahead. "Frank, I'm so sorry for everything but especially for disappearing for the last twelve years."

Frank didn't respond.

"But these last twelve years have toughened me up. I've learned how to survive on my own. I've learned how to be my own person. Before I left, I didn't feel anything at all—not happiness and not sadness—just emptiness. I don't know how to explain it except that I functioned like an actress playing a part."

After taking a deep breath, Joan said, "However, I've really worked on healing myself over the years. But I needed to leave to do that. I needed to leave to actually feel alive."

"You had a child!" Frank yelled. "I can understand how you might want to leave me if you weren't happy. But you left your child also."

"I know. But I wasn't a real mother to Chloe. I was just faking my feelings most of the time. As she got older, Chloe would've figured that out and grew to resent me in much the same way I resented my own mother. I didn't understand it back then, but I also spared her my family's legacy of evil."

"Oh please, you're now just trying to justify what you did.

Chloe loved you. Your supposed death left a huge hole in Chloe's heart as well as in my heart."

"I'm so sorry. I really am. But I scared myself twelve years ago. The rage that I felt on that night twelve years ago was beyond anything that I can explain. It was well beyond anything that could be called normal. I felt it in my bones—like it was actually part of me."

Frank remained silent, unsure of what to say. What happened all of those years ago was truly beyond anything that he could call normal.

"I believe, Frank, that evil is contagious. I've read that some scientists believe memories of pain and trauma can be passed from one generation to the next in our DNA. In my family line, I believe this includes evil itself."

Joan stopped speaking for a short time to let Frank absorb her words, and then she continued to explain, "I believe that is what happened to me back then. On that awful night twelve years ago, I felt such rage, such evil. I felt it deep in my bones. I wanted to kill Mother that night. I had never felt anything close to that before. I had always resented my mother, but I never felt the urge to kill her. My rage, the evil inside of me, was triggered that night."

Joan went silent, but more for herself than Frank. Joan knew that once again she was feeling the rage, and it scared her. Over the last twelve years, Joan had prayed, meditated, and willed the evil out of herself. And she eventually felt free of it, until now.

Finally, Joan continued, "For the last twelve years, I prayed that Chloe would be spared my family's legacy. I prayed that there wasn't any evil stored deep inside of her DNA. I don't want Chloe to know about any of the horrible things that have happened in my family. I don't want those terrifying images planted in her mind. I'm putting an end to this one way or another."

"Joan, I don't know about your family. But there's nothing evil about our daughter."

"I want you to know something, Frank. I made sure Chloe was safe before I disappeared. You see, I had planned to kill my mother before I left Wisconsin. I drove to her house. But instead of finding her there, I found a for sale sign in front of the house. I called the real estate company, and the agent blurted out that the *poor woman* who lived there had just lost her daughter and moved to Albuquerque. So since my mother was gone, I felt that Chloe was safe."

"Edith handled things very fast after your death . . . I mean, disappearance. Harriet was in Albuquerque within a week."

"A few days later, I decided to drive to Albuquerque. When I got there, I discreetly followed Edith and discovered that Mother was in a psychiatric hospital. That confirmed to me that Chloe would be safe."

"I don't know what to say, to be honest. Thank you, I guess."

"Over the years, I monitored you and Chloe, as well as Aunt Edith, via the internet. I never saw anything odd popping up on anyone's social media accounts or anywhere else. As far as I could tell, Chloe remained safe."

As the dog continued to sleep, Frank looked closely at Joan. Rather than evil, he felt that Joan acted more like a wounded animal back then, protecting her cub before running off to die alone. Or he supposed, to heal alone. In doing so, Frank now knew she gave up a daughter that she clearly still loved. Any anger that he felt toward her was gone.

Frank pulled a large envelope from his pocket and handed it to Joan. Without opening it, Joan was certain of its contents. Frank said nothing as he got of the truck and watched his wife drive away. Although he would never openly admit it, he hoped that Joan could end things with her mother—in whatever way proved necessary.

As she drove down the street, Joan wasn't sure if she should meet up with Edith and Gladys right away or take care of a few more things. Within minutes, however, Joan spotted a sign at a gas station advertising fishing bait, and she remembered her conversation with the old man in Oregon. Joan managed a half-smile and decided to follow his advice to tied up loose ends. She had two more tasks to do before it got much later in the day.

First things first, Joan thought as she drove toward her old neighborhood. As she passed her former home, Joan saw a swing set in the backyard. Joan was pleased that Frank had sold their house to a young family, and she hoped they were happy there.

However, that wasn't the house that she was seeking. Rather, Joan was heading to her childhood home only two blocks further down the same street. Joan begrudgingly gave her mother credit for her skillful manipulation of Frank. With a sweet smile and an offer to help with the down payment, Harriet had charmed him into purchasing their house. Less than two months after their marriage, Joan found herself living down the street from her mother.

Joan always knew living so close to her mother was a mistake—a mistake that fueled her ever-growing resentment of her. However, she was too meek to stand up to her mother back then. As she parked in front of her childhood home, Joan no longer felt meek.

Joan was determined to find out what, if anything, was buried under the lilac bushes in the backyard of her childhood home. It might seem like a strange thing to want, Joan silently thought. But since childhood, she had been haunted by a recurring nightmare, always waking afterwards to the scent of lilacs. Joan had never been able to let go of a nagging, lifelong question: What were the lilacs bushes hiding?

Although their yard was always perfectly manicured, her mother had never shown any interest in flowering plants of any sort, preferring the low maintenance of rock gardens. So even as a child, Joan had been surprised by her mother's sudden desire to plant the lilac bushes—and not just one bush, but three lilac bushes planted tightly together in a row, forming a strange, out of place flowery plot at the back of the yard.

Joan waited in her truck until finally the garage door opened. She watched a woman back out her car and drive away. Seeing no other vehicle in the garage, Joan hoped that no one else was in the house. Joan petted her dog, telling it to *stay*. The dog sat very still, seeming to understand that something important was happening.

Joan put on a cap, pulling the visor down to partially hide her face. She got out of her truck, carrying a garden spade. Joan had decided on a spade, feeling that a shovel would draw too much attention. She glanced around her, noting that the neighborhood at this early hour looked quiet. She then quickly ran into the backyard of her childhood home.

Hurriedly, she dug below the lilac bushes, repeatedly shoving the spade deep into the ground and tossing the dirt behind her. After a few feet, the spade hit something solid.

"Oh my god," Joan said out loud. "What is that?"

"What are you doing?" a nosy next-door neighbor yelled.

Startled, Joan jumped up, yelling, "Call the police. Someone is buried below these bushes."

Before the nosy neighbor could respond, Joan raced back to her truck and drove off. Joan felt lucky the neighbor didn't follow her. Without a description of her truck or plates, the neighbor could only provide the police with a vague description of a crazy woman in a cap.

Chapter 9

Well before the sun rose, Chloe knocked on Harriet's hotel room door, waking her.

"There's a place that I really want to go to next," Chloe said, not explaining anything more. Chloe sensed it was important not to share the name of their next destination.

Harriet agreed to dress and meet Chloe by the car. However, she didn't ask about nor was she interested in their destination. It was time to finally finish the plan. She decided to let the day and her inner voice control how and when that would happen.

Chloe drove south toward a small village roughly thirty miles west of Wisconsin Dells, a touristy community in south-central Wisconsin. Opting for a scenic route rather than a busy highway, Chloe guessed that the drive would be nearly six hours long.

Initially, neither spoke—in part due to the early hours and the hypnotic early morning fog. But Chloe was also distracted, wondering why her Great-Aunt Edith hadn't returned her call.

Early on in their route, however, they passed through one of the national forests in Wisconsin. They were surprised to encounter a flagman, who stopped the traffic coming from their direction. Chloe poked her head out of the window and yelled, "Has there been a car accident?"

The flagman walked over to the car. "No. It's a clean-up day. We do these a few times throughout the year. We're pulling out items that were illegally dumped in the ditches."

"Really?" Chloe asked.

"You would be surprised what we find: old sofas, used appliances, tires, rusted cars, and lots of trash," the flagman explained. "We've seen just about everything."

Backing away, the flagman looked down the road and waved them through. Then, as their car slowly moved past the road crew, they saw what caused the delay. An old, rusted car had been pulled from the ditch.

As the car's speed picked up, Harriet said, "I don't know why anyone would get rid of a vintage Cadillac Eldorado like that. I owned one once, and it was so much fun to drive. You could pick up anyone in a car like that. It was really a magnet of sorts."

A vision of her grandmother driving a red Cadillac Eldorado flashed into Chloe's mind. Chloe gave a sideways glance at her traveling companion, curious who this old woman really was. However, Chloe's outrage over the dumping of trash in the forest overrode her curiosity, and she didn't spend much time wondering about this latest strange coincidence.

Chloe glared into the morning fog, not speaking. Eventually, she broke her silence. "I was an intern at a law firm until very recently, and one of their clients was a man whose company was guilty of illegal dumping. It was a very successful asbestos removal company. They would go in and remove asbestos from homes and businesses, which is a good thing, of course. However, the problem came with the disposal of the asbestos."

Chloe clenched the steering wheel tighter, trying to control her outrage. "Instead of taking it to the proper landfill that handles hazardous waste, the owner burned the asbestos materials in large piles on some so-called worthless rural land that he owned. No one really saw or cared what he was burning out there. But this was horrible because it released asbestos into the air."

Harriet nodded her understanding but did not speak. The story didn't interest her.

"And then he disposed of the ashes near a creek—which was near a farm, and so on," Chloe explained. "Just to save money, he polluted the environment and exposed countless people to a dangerous health risk."

Harriet nodded again, trying to look interested in the story as Chloe continued to talk.

"A whistleblower in his company turned him in. And he was charged with violations of the Federal Clean Air Act. I'm not sure why he wasn't charged with violating any other environmental laws, but he wasn't. The law firm was able to negotiate a deal with the federal prosecutors. He avoided jail time and only got a fine. Every time that client entered the office, I felt sick to my stomach. His eyes looked so hard and evil."

Not fully listening, Harriet yawned. After a few seconds, she absentmindedly responded, "Evil can be difficult to recognize. Often, it's hidden deep within a person, unseen until it's too late."

Harriet knew that she was sharing a truth about herself, but she felt confident that Chloe was unaware of it. Feeling pleased with her ability to shield her true self, Harriet smiled—a sly, devious smile.

Hopeful that today's destination would provide answers, Chloe glanced over at Harriet, wondering why this peculiar old woman made her feel so uneasy—so often. Of course, she knew the *nudges* explained some of the unease, but the story behind them was what Chloe really wanted to know.

Harriet returned the glance, and as their eyes briefly met, Harriet saw a difference in the younger woman. Chloe's eyes reflected an almost intangible change—a transformation from a frightened girl to a woman. Harriet was uncomfortably happy for her, but she decided not to let that change her plan.

Indeed, Chloe was becoming more and more aware of the changes in herself as well. Certainly, Chloe felt more alive and less empty. However, she also felt that her calling was coming into focus—a love of nature. Or rather, she felt called to protect nature.

However, the fear that forced her to look under her bed every night—to hide from life—still lingered. Chloe sensed the reasons behind this fear were buried in her nightmares, in her emerging memories, and perhaps with her traveling companion. Determined to find answers, she decided not to let her uneasiness about Harriet change her plan.

For the next few hours, Chloe and Harriet chatted about the scenery, the weather, and not much else. Finally, within an hour of their destination, they decided to stop to fill up the gas tank and get something to eat. They quickly found a gas station a few miles later in a small community along their route.

Since it wasn't yet noon, the fast-food restaurant that they located nearby was virtually empty. After ordering their customary cheeseburger, fries, and pop, Chloe and Harriet sat in a back booth. As they ate, Chloe finally let Harriet know their destination.

"Why the village of Howling Hills?" Harriet asked.

Chloe took a deep breath and then plunged forward with a short explanation—in fact, a very short explanation. "Last night, I took a walk after you went up to your room, and this old newspaper clipping blew onto the sidewalk in front of me. When I picked it, I recognized the story in the clipping. It was about the Howling Hills Spiritualist Camp."

"I've never heard of this camp." Harriet's eyes locked on Chloe, wondering when to make her move. Her inner voice urged quick action, but Harriet knew that the restaurant was much too public. She needed to wait a little longer.

"I actually had read this same article several years ago when it first appeared in the Madison newspaper. This spiritualist camp has existed for more than 140 years."

"Have you ever gone there before?"

"No. My father doesn't believe in psychics and such things. He says those who believe in these types of things are a little goofy. When I mentioned the article to him, he rolled his eyes. So I never went. But I really feel that it's important for me to go there now."

Chloe looked closely at her traveling companion, noticing the dark rings under her eyes. Chloe wondered if the long road trip was taking a toll on her. "Are you okay? You look tired."

"I'm fine. I didn't sleep last night; too many memories keeping me awake. But maybe we should avoid this camp. Why waste time visiting psychics? Why not head over to the bluffs on the Mississippi River? It's only another 90 minutes or so from here. I hear that the views are wonderful from them."

"Sorry, but I really feel that I need to go to this spiritualist camp. I've never felt more alive, and I have the forest, the lakes, and the fresh air to thank for that. But I'm searching for answers to some questions that I have, and who knows, maybe a psychic can help." Chloe was not willing yet to openly declare her belief in the mystical.

Despite Harriet's reluctance, they returned to the car and headed in the direction of the camp. They drove through the picturesque countryside, dominated by steep hills, towering bluffs, and lush green panoramas of farms fields, valleys, and trees—whose colors blended together like those on an artist's canvas.

Although neither said it aloud, Chloe and Harriet were again soothed by the scenery as the car glided up and down the hills.

In less than an hour, they arrived at their destination—Howling Hills, a village of less than one thousand living souls. Mindful of Harriet's reluctance to visit the camp, Chloe sought the assistance of her phone's GPS for directions, avoiding a possible time-consuming, street-by-street search.

Chloe quickly found the steep street that led up to the camp, which sat atop an imposing hill. Chloe backed up her little economy car to secure a running start and told Harriet to hold on. Chloe pushed the gas pedal down, and the car flew up the hill, leaving the little village behind. Landing on the crest of the hill, the car seemed to guide itself through the rustic old gate—a gate which appeared to have welcomed visitors to the historic camp for many, many years. Chloe parked the car in the gravel parking lot among the smattering of other cars.

The camp consisted of numerous tiny white cabins that radiated a rustic coziness and were nestled among towering pine trees. The cabins appeared to be relics from an earlier, less commercialized era—when resorts only needed to offer the allure of nature and not free Wi-Fi and indoor waterparks. Some of the cabins were freshly painted and welcoming; however, some were still awaiting their turn at a facelift.

The tiny cabins encircled a large, park-like area, which appeared to Chloe to serve as the spiritual center of the camp. Its many trees provided a shield of sorts, helping protect the camp from Wisconsin's hot, humid summers. The center of the camp also featured a large firepit, a gazebo, and several buildings. However, one building, in particular, stood out from the others. It was a large white building, which bore the word *Chapel*.

As Chloe and Harriet walked from the parking lot into the camp, Chloe felt as if she had somehow slipped into an earlier era. She could envision the hordes of long-ago believers, dressed in the cumbersome clothing of the late 19th century, arriving by train, and then ascending the steep hill to the camp. She could almost feel their sorrows and their hopes of finding comfort in their era of deadly wars and equally deadly pandemics. Yet, as Chloe stood still for a moment, she sensed that those who travel to this camp in modern times share much with those of long ago.

However, the spell that held Chloe was interrupted as a golf cart sped by. Chloe didn't get a good look at the driver. But she smiled at the sight of a small, white dog bouncing about on the passenger seat, guessing that the dog would have preferred to walk.

Chloe steered Harriet toward a somewhat larger white cabin near the entry of the camp. "I think that must be the camp's office."

"Yes, and apparently, it's a gift shop also," Harriet grumbled, pointing to the sign in front of the cabin.

It was clear to Chloe that Harriet wasn't happy to be at this camp. However, Chloe felt strongly that this stop on their road trip was important, and she ignored Harriet's hesitation.

Chloe eyed the larger cabin, finding it as charming as the smaller cabins. However, everything was charming here, she thought—except the box-like building next to the camp's office. It looked to be a small motel, with identical doors lining the length of the building. She had read that the camp offered lodging in the charming little cabins, but she wasn't aware of the motel. Hmm, Chloe thought, this motel was probably a *must* for those not willing to step back into time—and not willing to give up modern plumbing.

As Harriet took a few steps away from her, Chloe glanced around again, feeling something intangible in this little historical camp, an aura of sorts. Chloe inhaled deeply, breathing in the thick texture of the camp's air. The air seemed almost mystical to her. With each breath, Chloe felt a deep sense of peace and instinctively knew this to be a very spiritual place.

A breeze whooshed past Chloe, leaving behind a message: *You must remember.*

Chloe walked over to Harriet and asked, "Hetty, do you want to get a reading from one of the psychics?"

"No, never. I don't want these people messing with my thoughts."

"I don't think that is how it works. I've read that an ethical psychic won't read you without your permission. I can't force you, of course."

Chloe then said—with a quiet firmness in her voice, "I believe that it's important that I get a reading."

Entering the camp office, Harriet ignored the young woman, who was behind the counter, and wandered around the small space, glancing at the crystals and other spiritual items for sale. However, Chloe stopped immediately at the counter and asked about the availability of a reading. The young woman explained the cost and pointed to a list of the day's available psychic mediums. Chloe selected one of the mediums, booked a time, and paid.

With Harriet in tow, Chloe left the office and started down the circular dirt path toward the cabin that the medium was located in, reaching it in just minutes. However, once there, Harriet abruptly hurried away, mumbling, "I'll wander around while you have your reading."

Somewhat amused at the speed of Harriet's departure, Chloe sat in a lawn chair a few discreet feet from the cabin. She still had ten minutes before her appointment. As she studied the cabin, Chloe decided that its purple door and the delicate flowers planted in front easily made it one of the most charming in the camp.

Harriet hurried down the path and entered a large white

building, unaware of the word *Chapel* on the other side. Once inside, she discovered that the Chapel occupied one end of the building. The other end consisted of an old-fashioned camp dining hall. Walking through the dining hall toward the chapel, she heard echoes from its storied history. Stepping into the chapel, Harriet felt an icy chill and knew that she was not welcome there.

Chloe watched Harriet bolt out of the large building and start to scurry about—feeling that she looked like a rodent trying to find a way out of a maze. She took note that others at the camp were watching Harriet very closely as well.

At that point, the psychic medium opened the cabin's door and motioned for Chloe to enter.

Once inside, the psychic medium introduced herself as Annie and asked Chloe to sit across from her at a small table. Next, Annie explained that she would say a prayer before beginning the reading, asking the Universe, Mother-Father God, and the arch angels to protect them from dark energy. She further explained that she prays to only receive messages of the highest good. Chloe nodded her understanding.

After the prayer, Annie held Chloe's hands and began speaking, "There is a spirit here. She is coming across as a grandmother spirit. Her name starts with F—maybe Flora or Flo; something like that."

"My grandmother on my father's side was Florence. She died before I was born. I never knew her."

"Although she passed before you came into this world, she's still very much aware of you. She tells me that she prefers to be called Flo. And your Grandma Flo is worried about you. You need to be careful of the dark. Do you understand this?"

"No, what does she mean?"

"I'll ask her."

Annie went silent for a moment. "What she's showing me is a car accident. I also see water and blood. Do you understand?"

"Yes, my mother died in a car crash and drowned. My grandmother on my mother's side, Grandma Harriet, died from a heart attack about a month later."

"Your Grandma Flo says no. Neither your mother nor your other grandmother is on her side of the veil."

"I'm not sure what you mean. What veil?"

"Your Grandma Flo is talking about the veil between our realms, between the living and the dead."

"Oh, I see, but I don't understand why they aren't on her side of the veil. That doesn't make any sense to me. We had a dog named Molly, who also died in the accident. Do you see Molly?"

"Your Grandma Flo says no; the dog didn't die in the accident."

"I don't understand. I was told that my mother and dog both died in the car accident."

"I can only tell you what I'm being told."

"Okay, I understand."

"Your Grandma Flo is warning you that a darkness is coming, and I'm now seeing the car accident. The car plunged into water, maybe a river." The psychic held Chloe's hands tighter.

"Yes, that's right. The car plunged into the Mississippi River, but it happened about twelve years ago. I don't remember much about that time frame."

"Grandma Flo says that you need to remember."

"I wish I could remember more."

"Your Grandmother Flo is warning you again about the darkness. I'm not clear what she means exactly. Let me ask her for more."

Annie went silent, closing her eyes—seemingly trying to pull more information forward from the other side. Annie squeezed Chloe's hands even tighter, and Chloe sensed fear in Annie's grip. Annie then started speaking again.

"She is saying that you need to remember what happened. You are in great danger."

"Oh my god."

"She keeps saying that you need to find the letters."

"Letters?"

"I'm seeing an old shack near a lake. Does this make sense?"

"Yes, my family has a fishing cabin."

"Maybe look there. There must be a connection, or I wouldn't get that image."

"Okay, I will."

"I'm also getting a vision of a pitchfork. I know it sounds hokey, but that's my symbol for a dark entity, like a demon, maybe. I'm not sure exactly what to make of this. Your Grandma Flo is no longer here. But she kept saying the same thing over and over: *remember*."

Annie released Chloe's hands and said quietly, "I think that there's a darkness trying to harm you. A very real negative presence—maybe a demonic entity. This isn't something that I normally encounter in a reading. I generally focus on messages of love and light. But your Grandma Flo is very concerned about you; she's worried about your safety. However, she said that you have both a grandfather spirit and a guardian angel who have been protecting you. Your Grandma Flo also said that you should remember to call on the angels for protection. You'll need their protection. Again, she kept repeating that you need to remember."

"Thank you," Chloe mumbled. With puffy, wet eyes and a tissue in hand, Chloe left the cabin in search of Harriet. She wandered a few minutes but didn't spot her. Too distraught to look any further, she went to her car and discovered a note on the windshield. It read: *I'll be waiting for you at the diner in the village below. Love, Hetty.*

Chloe crumbled the note, tossed it into her car, and walked

back into the camp. "Love—yeah, right. Hetty will have to wait," Chloe mumbled to herself. "I'm not ready to leave yet."

Chloe aimlessly wandered about, noticing a fox peeking around the corner of a cabin and a hawk squawking as it flew over. Next, she stopped to admire a building with the words *Spirit Lodge* painted about its blue door. Images of animals covered its outside walls. Chloe inhaled deeply, sensing that the animals were telling her to use her instincts, to defend herself, and to be resilient—to survive the darkness.

Chloe felt compelled to crossover the lawn to one particular tree—one of the many soaring pines that dotted the camp. A small sign identified it as the Healing Tree.

Chloe sat in one of the weathered, plastic lawn chairs that were clustered around this tree. She quietly looked up at the tree and then down at the ground. A frog hopped by, and a butterfly floated past. Chloe wondered if these were also trying to tell her something. Then in a voice barely above a whisper, Chloe asked the Healing Tree for help. As she sat under the pine, Chloe started to remember the days leading up to the car accident.

Like snippets from an old movie, some of her repressed memories played in her mind. First, quick flashes of arguments between her mother and Grandma Harriet came into focus. Chloe remembered her disbelief; this had never happened before. In fact, her mother had never raised her voice to anyone. She also saw images of her younger self hiding as the arguments raged, trying but unable to catch little more than a word or two.

Next, fragments of arguments between her mother and father flashed into her mind. Her father yelling, "All of this is nonsense." Her mother sobbing, "No, it's real. Mother is dangerous."

Chloe felt the worry and confusion of her younger self as her childhood home became a battleground.

Another memory pushed its way to the surface, the arrival of Aunt Edith. Chloe remembered that everything changed after that. The house grew quieter. Grandma Harriet stopped coming over, and hushed talks took place between her parents and Edith. It was obvious even to young Chloe that her mother was worried about what she called *the situation.*

Chloe flinched at the memory of her father leaving on a business trip in the middle of *the situation.* Even as a child, she sensed that her mother grew more anxious after he left, and it was then that Chloe started to ask questions about what was going on. Her mother explained that Grandma Harriet was ill. However, her mother would not say anything further, leaving young Chloe confused and frightened. Chloe shook her head at the memory. Nothing was explained to her, not then and not now.

One last snippet popped into her mind—an image of her mother sitting alone, staring at a photo of Grandma Harriet. There was a look of fear in her mother's eyes. Chloe wondered what really happened at the family fishing cabin twelve years ago.

Chloe continued to sit under the Healing Tree. Closing her eyes, she tried to pull more memories out of the shadows of her mind. After a few unsuccessful minutes, Chloe opened her eyes to find Annie sitting next to her. Surprised, Chloe lifted her eyebrows as if to ask why Annie was there.

"I don't want to frighten you," Annie said. "However, the other mediums and I wanted to let you know that we all sensed a very dark energy from the older woman that you were with."

Chloe stared at her, not sure what to make of the information except that she also sensed something strange about Harriet.

"Be careful. Never invite darkness into you. It has no power over you unless you give it," Annie warned. "Most of us here don't deal with this type of extremely dark, negative energy, but there are those that do. Please take this card and call her for help."

Never Tell Chloe

Chloe took the business card and watched Annie hurry back to her peers. When she read the card, Chloe was only mildly surprised by what she read. After putting the card into her purse, Chloe got up and headed to her car. She had a few questions for Harriet.

When Chloe got into her car, she found a necklace with a silver crucifix on the passenger seat. Although not sure who placed it in her car, Chloe put it on. It brought a feeling of comfort to her.

As they discreetly watched from the van, Edith and Gladys were delighted that Chloe had put the crucifix on. They had placed it in her unlocked car only a few minutes before. Believing in its power, the crucifix also brought a sense of comfort to Edith and Gladys.

However, they were confused about why Chloe was alone. They had drifted too far behind and had only just arrived. Until now, Chloe and Harriet had been inseparable, and they wondered if something had happened between the two.

Chloe stiffened her jaw, steeling herself for whatever was to come next. She drove down the steep hill into the village below. As promised, Harriet was at the local diner, smiling and talking to the other patrons.

When Harriet got into the car, she noticed a difference in Chloe—a coldness had replaced the previous sweetness. Forcing a smile, she asked Chloe if she had enjoyed her reading. Ignoring the question, Chloe wasted no time in driving out of the village. The black van followed unnoticed.

As the car flew down the highway toward Madison, Harriet started to laugh. The laughter was menacing, a sound as cold and hard as ice. Chloe shivered but not just from the sound of the laughter but also from a memory. Chloe heard this same laughter one other time—twelve years ago at the fishing cabin.

Harriet sensed that Chloe knew the truth or at least part of it. She could see the disdain in Chloe's eyes. "What did those witches at that camp say about me?"

Chloe did not respond. Instead, she stared straight ahead and accelerated.

"Answer me!"

"They are not witches!" Chloe snapped but said nothing more in response.

Harriet's anger grew, and she tried grabbing the wheel. But Chloe's own anger was stronger, and she shoved her away. Harriet tried again and then once again, causing the car to veer in and out of the lane each time. Finding Chloe stronger than expected, Harriet gave up, sitting in silence until they finally reached Madison.

Flying down a highway off-ramp, Chloe slowed the car down and pulled into an empty parking lot.

"Who are you? Are you my grandmother?" Chloe asked, her anger more apparent with each word.

The only answer Harriet gave was another cold, shrill laugh.

"Get out of the car! Get out!" Chloe screamed.

Harriet glared at Chloe but did not move. Chloe got out of the car, walked around to the passenger side, and dragged her out. She reached back into the car, grabbed Harriet's tote bag, and tossed it onto the ground. As Harriet steadied herself and picked up her bag, Chloe drove away.

However, as Chloe pulled out of the parking lot, the black van pulled into it. But instead of following Chloe, they focused their attention on Harriet, who stood alone in the middle of the parking lot.

"Now is our chance. No one's around," Edith told Gladys as the van came to a stop. Gladys nodded in agreement.

Edith quietly opened her door and approached Harriet, gently asking, "Harriet, would you please come with me?"

Startled, Harriet took several steps backwards. "Don't come near me," she hissed.

"Harriet, we only want to help you," Edith said quietly.

"Harriet's not here. I *am* Abigail."

Gladys quietly emerged from the van and inched closer to Harriet, trying to avoid spooking her.

"Let us help you," Gladys quietly offered.

"I'm not going anywhere with the two of you!" Harriet's voice was loud and hard.

They quickly charged Harriet, hoping to forcibly maneuver her into the van. However, she jumped out of their reach and sprinted down the street, quickly disappearing out of sight. Her speed would have surprised most people but not them. They knew that Harriet wasn't an ordinary old woman.

Edith placed a phone call as they stood in the empty parking, unsure of what to do. "Joan, we tried to grab Harriet, but she got away."

"Damn. Where's Chloe?"

"We don't know. We followed them back to Madison. Chloe pulled into a parking lot, left Harriet there, and then drove off. Sorry, but we don't know where either of them are."

"Shit. Well, at least, Chloe isn't with her anymore."

"Harriet will try to track down Chloe."

"I know. I'll call Frank and check if he has heard from Chloe."

"Where are you, Joan? We haven't seen you since last night."

"I'm in Madison also. I'll call you back as soon as I can." Joan exited the divorce attorney's office and rushed to her truck.

Edith and Gladys returned to the van and waited to hear from Joan.

Chapter 10

Chloe returned home to find several police cars and a small crowd in front of her apartment building. Unsure of what had happened, Chloe parked farther down the street and walked back to her building. She didn't want to answer any questions from the police—not yet, at least.

"What's going on?" Chloe asked a young woman in the crowd.

"It's really awful. They found a woman tied up in her apartment."

"Dead?" Chloe quietly asked, fearing the worst.

"No, the ambulance just left with her. It was one of the tenants. A grad student, I think. From what I overheard the police say, the victim was badly beaten. They also said that an old woman had been hiding out in the apartment for a week or so. Scary, eh? No one suspected anything."

"Oh my god."

Chloe hurried back to her car and phoned her father.

"Dad," Chloe sobbed. "Something awful has happened."

"Tell me what is going on."

Chloe quickly filled him in on the situation at her apartment building and also told him she parted ways with her traveling companion.

"Are *you* okay, Chloe? Are *you* safe?"

Chloe heard fear in her father's voice. It matched the fear in her own voice.

"Dad, I'm starting to remember some things from twelve years ago," Chloe sobbed and then began to speak rapidly. "I remember the night that Mom died. Mom drove us out to the fishing cabin. She told me to stay in the car. There was a lot of yelling in the cabin. I don't know about what. I saw Aunt Edith rush out and drive off. Then more yelling. Next Mom screamed. Very loud like she was in pain. Then she ran out of the cabin. Mom was battered up. Grandma Harriet stood at the door. She pointed a gun at the car and shot but missed."

Trying to control her sobs, Chloe continued, "Mom stepped on the gas pedal. And our tires spun in the mud. I could hear Grandma Harriet laughing like some sort of crazy person. Mom then drove us home."

Then in a rush of words, Chloe finished her story, "But after we got home, Mom didn't sound like herself. She sounded strange—eerily calm. She helped me into my bed. I was so afraid that I was trembling. I was afraid of what I just saw, and I was afraid of Mom. But Mom told me that I was just having a bad dream and to forget everything. She then kissed me on the forehead and said goodbye. That was the last time that I ever saw her. Dad, what really happened back then?"

"Oh Chloe," Frank whispered, his voice barely audible.

Chloe took a deep breath, forcing herself to calm down, and asked, "Dad, do you know what really happened back then?"

"Yes."

"Is Grandma Harriet alive? Is she a killer?"

"Yes, she's alive. Killer, maybe."

"Oh my god, Dad."

"There's a lot more to the story, but there isn't time to tell you now. You need to go somewhere else. You aren't safe by your apartment. I'll tell you everything that I know as soon as I can."

"Thank you," Chloe said, grateful that she would soon know the truth. Chloe then quickly filled him in on her psychic reading and the mysterious letters.

When Chloe concluded, her father was silent for a moment before responding. "Letters? I don't understand that, but we can look for them later. I need to get you somewhere safe first. You certainly won't be safe at your apartment and probably not at my condo. Your grandmother undoubtingly knows where I live. A hotel might be best."

"Dad, I'm going to the cabin. I'm sorry, but I feel that it's really important for me to find those letters."

"You sound very determined."

"I am."

"The cabin is pretty isolated. Is there any way that I can change your mind?

"No, Dad. I'm going there. I want to find those letters, and Grandma won't know that I'm there. That makes it's a safe place, right?

"I guess, but I'm going with you. Meet me at my office, and we can drive there together."

"That's really out of the way, Dad. Can you meet me there instead?"

"Okay, I'll meet you at the cabin but be careful. We should both get there around 10 o'clock tonight."

Careful not to draw any attention, Chloe slowly pulled away from the curb, focusing on the three things she needed to do: fill up her gas tank, drive to the cabin, and find the letters.

The fishing cabin sat on a large tract of unblemished woodland about an hour from the Mississippi River in an area dominated by soaring bluffs and narrow two-lane roads. Chloe's parents had purchased the cabin because of its remote location, feeling that it offered a private refuge from the outside world.

Her grandmother often joked that no one would be able to hear a scream coming from the cabin. In retrospect, Chloe found her joke chilling, and she was upset that such evil had touched a place connected to so many of her cherished memories.

As Chloe drove, a few of those memories filled her thoughts. Chloe fondly remembered her mother's easel on the cabin's porch and her father's canoe in the nearby river. She remembered the shared laughter, the hikes, and her puppy.

Chloe eventually turned off the road onto the mile-long driveway which led to the cabin. As her car bounced along the dirt driveway, pushing its way through the overgrown grasses and low-hanging branches, Chloe took a deep breath and wondered what she would learn in the coming hours.

When she reached the cabin, Chloe was disappointed that her father hadn't yet arrived. She was also shocked at the poor condition of the cabin. In her memory, the small cabin oozed charm—as if it had been snatched out of a fairytale. She remembered her father had always joked that it looked more like an English cottage than a fishing shack.

Getting out of the car, Chloe grabbed her purse and a small shopping bag as distant lightning signaled that the humid day was giving way to a stormy night. Using the light on her cell phone, Chloe surveyed the cabin. The white paint on the outside of the cabin was peeling, and the roof was sagging slightly. Inside, despite the layers of dirt and cobwebs, things were still relatively intact. Although the overstuffed couch and chairs looked soiled and unusable, Chloe was pleased that the wooden table and its chairs seemed sturdy. In fact, it appeared that someone had cleaned the table and chairs recently. Chloe wondered who had done so.

Reaching into the shopping bag, Chloe removed a small, battery-powered lantern and set it on the table. She had decided to buy the lantern at the gas station before heading to the cabin and was very happy now that she did. Despite its small size, the lantern fully lit the cabin.

Chloe quickly moved around the cabin, desperately searching. She opened cabinet drawers, flipped over the mildewy couch cushions, and stomped on the floor, hoping but failing to find a hiding place under the floorboards. Chloe stopped, took a deep breath, and slowly scanned the cabin.

She spotted a painting of an angel hanging on the wall and walked over to it. She looked closely at it and was surprised by its unspoiled condition. Chloe suddenly recalled the day that her mother had hung the painting. She wasn't much more than a toddler at the time, and like most, memories from such early years were fuzzy to her at best. But this long-forgotten memory seemed very vivid to her at the moment.

~

"This is a painting of your very own angel, Chloe."
"Really, Mommy? She's my angel?"
"Yes, she's your guardian angel. She came to me in a dream and asked to be painted."
"She's so pretty. So many colors! Can I take her home?"
"No, sweetie, the angel said to hang the painting here."

~

Chloe smiled. She recognized the angel in the old painting. The angel had been painted in the colors of rose, violet, and green—but mostly, in heavenly blue. It was the same angel that had led Chloe and Harriet out of the forest two nights ago.

After taking the painting off the wall, Chloe discovered a small book taped on its back. Chloe removed the book, careful to avoid damaging it. She rehung the painting and sat at the table to read the book.

Chloe realized, however, that it was actually a small pocket folio rather than a book. As she opened it, Chloe found several old letters that had been written twelve years ago. For the next hour or so, Chloe read the letters, discovering some of the truths that had been hidden from her.

March 8

My dear niece Joan:

We have never met, but I am your Aunt Edith. I'm the sister of your mother, Harriet.

I fear that you will be deeply upset by this letter, and for this, I am sorry.

However, I write to you for one simple reason: I believe that your daughter, Chloe, is in danger.

I write also because I feel an obligation to warn you. I cannot just look the other way. Aren't those who do nothing to stop evil also responsible in some way for the evil?

I will get to the bottom line, as they say. Your mother, Harriet, is determined to harm your young daughter, Chloe. This is something that Harriet has told me personally.

I know this sounds crazy, but I believe that Harriet is possessed by a demon. You may think that I am mad, but I firmly believe this.

To fully understand the danger that your daughter is in, you need to know the awful history of our family. I doubt that your mother has shared any of it with you.

From my earliest memories, my sister, Harriet, and I suffered relentless verbal and physical abuse. Our childhood home was not a happy place, to say the least. Although I don't like to drag these memories out into the light, I think that you need to know.

First of all, my parents were ruthless in their verbal abuse of Harriet, relentlessly calling her horrible things, such as odd, disgusting, and evil. Sadly, they also physically abused Harriet.

I'm two years younger than your mother, and I am ashamed to say that I often hid as my parents abused your mother. Actually, torture might be a more accurate word. At times, my parents would tie Harriet to a chair and then do dreadful things: sometimes hitting her, sometimes burning her with cigarettes, or sometimes worse. At other times, they would lock Harriet in her bedroom without food for days.

I remember one particularly dreadful incident very well. My mother, without any provocation, burnt Harriet with a hot iron. Harriet never screamed; never said a word. I think that Harriet's lack of a response is what made it so much more frightening to witness.

You are probably wondering why no one reported such horrible abuse to the authorities, and the answer is really simple. No one knew. We were homeschooled and had little contact with anyone outside of the house.

I was also abused, however, not as harshly as Harriet. Somehow, Harriet brought the worst out in my parents. For you see, my parents believed that Harriet was possessed by a demon. They thought that she was born a bad seed, as they often called her.

Indeed, the evil in our house was very real. I saw it every day. I saw it in my parents, and I saw it in my sister. I lived in fear of the rage in their eyes and in their actions.

However, I also admired how Harriet defied the abuse.

For example, Harriet frequently laughed at or spit in my parents' faces as they abused her. Harriet had some special tricks that she would do just to rile up our parents, such as reciting the Lord's Prayer backwards. It infuriated our parents, and of course, this always resulted in another beating of Harriet.

I remember other strange things about Harriet as well. Her voice would suddenly sound like someone else entirely; sometimes a man, sometimes a woman, and sometimes a beast. Harriet also cut herself, cussed profusely, had fits and convulsions, and refused to look at a cross.

At times, Harriet would turn on me, hitting or cussing at me. I knew then, as I do now, it wasn't Harriet who was hurting me. It was her rage, and when it boiled over, I was an easy target. However, after these incidents, Harriet would always beg my forgiveness.

At other times, Harriet would come to me, warning me of a future incident, telling me to hide, to be quiet, and to stay safe. In her own way, I felt that Harriet tried to protect me back then.

Please don't get me wrong. I feared Harriet, but I also loved her, then and now. I know that this is difficult to understand—to fear and love the same person. Perhaps this strange combination is due to the horrific childhood that we shared.

You may be wondering if the abuse ever ended. Yes, but not until Harriet murdered our parents.

When Harriet was fifteen years old, she overheard our parents' plan to send her to a mental institution. This enraged Harriet. I'm not sure why. Any place would have been better than our home. But this angered Harriet so much so that she took the iron skillet and beat our parents to death.

God, please forgive me. I did nothing to prevent the murders. I just stood still and watched, getting splashed by their blood. I was too afraid to move or to scream. I was barely able to breathe.

The scene is forever burned into my memory.

However, the deafening screams of our parents resulted in calls to the police by the neighbors. Although the police rushed to our house within a few minutes of the neighbors' calls, our parents were already dead by then.

In my nightmares, I still see Harriet holding the bloody skillet and hear her hysterical laughter as the police approached her. I remember how difficult it was for the police officers to subdue Harriet. The officers testified in Court that Harriet acted more like a wild beast than a teenage girl.

Because of the horrific child abuse that Harriet suffered, she was convicted of manslaughter rather than murder. Due to her age and her diminished capacity caused by the years of sadistic abuse, the judge sentenced her to a mere three years. She served the time in a locked ward in a mental institution. She was released when she turned eighteen.

Luckily, I was placed in a foster home and cared for by a very loving family. I also received psychological counseling. I consider myself very lucky for both of those things as they were the first steps on the long path to my eventual healing.

Through the years, I always hoped that Harriet had received the counseling that she needed as well. However, Harriet never contacted me after she was released, and I never tried to find her either. In fact, I didn't see Harriet until about two years ago.

It was then that Harriet showed up at my art gallery in Albuquerque unannounced. Harriet said that she had stumbled across a story about my gallery on the internet. She said that she had always wondered how my life had turned out.

I was honestly pleased to see her. I often wondered how

her life had turned out as well, and I was delighted to hear that she had a wonderful daughter and granddaughter.

I know that this letter is getting really long, but you must know our dreadful family history. It is the only way that you will understand the danger that Chloe is in.

Although I didn't understand as a child, I now see Harriet's behavior back then as signs of demonic possession.

Please know that I do not condone my parents' horrible abuse. I think that they also suffered some sort of demonic influence. I firmly believe that a contagious sickness had affected our whole family.

And this is where the story gets muddled. Was Harriet born with the darkness already in her, as my parents alleged? Or did the darkness enter my sister's soul as the result of the abuse?

I don't honestly have a definite answer for you. If not demonic in nature, however, I still believe her to be dangerous.

Most mental health professionals would say that Harriet was psychologically damaged by the abuse, and that her actions are the result of madness, not demonic possession. Of course, this is a very valid, mainstream conclusion. I just don't accept it because of what I'm about to explain next.

After her first visit, Harriet began to routinely visit, staying for a few days or so at a time. Everything seemed fine at first until Harriet started to disappear for long stretches of time during her visits.

When I asked her about this, Harriet laughed and said she was only having a little fun. However, I had already started to sense in her the same darkness that I feared as a child. To say that I was concerned is an understatement.

I followed her one day and watched her lure a young, teenage prostitute into an abandoned building. Harriet tied her up and beat her.

I'm ashamed to say that I reverted back to the frightened kid sister and did nothing. I just went home.

However, when Harriet returned later, I asked her why she had beaten that girl.

Harriet said that she was beating her because Abigail told her to do so. Harriet calmly explained that Abigail was the demon who befriended her as a child. Harriet actually used the word demon!

Harriet further stated that Abigail speaks to her—that Abigail is her inner voice. I don't really understand what Harriet meant by that.

I was too stunned to speak for a minute or so. But after a deep breath or two, I asked if the girl was still alive. Thankfully, Harriet said yes.

However, Harriet laughed and said that not every girl survived the beatings. She claimed that the desert holds a lot of her secrets.

I asked what in the world did she mean by that. Harriet laughed again but never actually answered the question. Her laughter was chilling—just as it was on the day that she murdered our parents.

Harriet then confessed that she was trying to build up her courage to kill her granddaughter, Chloe.

I was so shocked that I could only manage to say one word—why?

Harriet's response was this: Chloe looks too much like our mother!

I screamed at her to get out and not come back, and thank God, she left.

This was two days ago, and I have been worried about Chloe's safety ever since.

Hopefully, Harriet wasn't telling the truth. Maybe Harriet was toying with me in the same way that she toyed with our parents.

Would a family resemblance be enough for Harriet to kill her ten-year-old granddaughter? I don't honestly know. I hope and pray that it is not.

I suppose that I should have tried to phone you, but how would I have explained all of this in a phone call?

Please be careful.

Sincerely,
Aunt Edith

March 14

Aunt Edith:

To say that I was shocked by your very long and very disturbing letter is an understatement. I almost fainted, to be honest.

I have shown your letter to my husband, Frank, who was also shocked by it. He's an attorney and was able to confirm at least a small part of your claims. Your parents were indeed murdered. However, since it involved minors and child abuse, the court records are sealed.

Both Frank and I have shown the letter to my mother, and understandably, she was upset by it.

We aren't sure how to respond to your claims about a demon named Abigail and the beating of teenage girls. Those claims are bizarre.

However, my mother suggested that you were possessed as a child, not her. Or rather, this is what she believed as a child.

According to Mother, you were a tattletale, maliciously

reporting back to your parents anything (true or not) that might ignite their wrath toward my mother. Mother said that you took much pleasure in watching their violent abuse of her.

As a point of clarification, neither my husband nor myself believe in demonic possession.

Mother confessed that yes, she was involved in the deaths of her parents. However, she said that it was self-defense. Mother explained that on that awful day, she was being violently beaten—worse than most times. She felt that she might be killed. As a result, Mother grabbed the skillet and fought back. The judge took all of this into account, and the charges against her were dismissed. However, the judge ordered Mother confined to a mental institution—from which she was released after a few years.

Mother said that her past was too painful for her to share with me—or with anyone. She tried to put her awful childhood behind her and start over.

Mother confirmed that she had visited you several times. However, Mother was deeply saddened to find out that you had not fully escaped the family's dark past. Mother mentioned your heavy alcohol use.

It was very painful for me to watch Mother cry as she told us her story. I don't believe that I have ever seen her cry before.

I have gone to church and prayed over this. I have also asked my pastor's guidance on how to respond to your letter.

With the concurrence of my husband and my pastor, I am writing to let you know that I believe Mother. She would never harm my daughter, Chloe.

Both Mother and I forgive you for the lies you wrote, and I will pray for you.

However, we ask that you never contact us again.

Sincerely,

Joan

Never Tell Chloe

~

March 21

Dear Joan:

    I suppose that it is no surprise that you would believe your mother over me. She is your mother, of course. However, I want to clear up a few points from your letter.

    I have indeed dealt with alcoholism in my life. However, I have spent many hours and dollars on counseling as well. And I had put all of that behind me until your mother showed up.

    She has a knack for convincing people to do whatever she wishes. In my case, it was to have just one drink to celebrate our reunion and then one drink over a shared meal. Before I realized what was happening, I was drinking too much again. Please be aware that I have thrown myself back into counseling, and I'm starting to conquer my drinking problem once again.

    With regard to the assertion that I was possessed as a child, I can only say that I lived amid evil and did what was needed to survive. So yes, as a means of survival, I became the tattletale that your mother described me to be.

    However, what concerns me is this: Did your mother tell you that she has started to have nightmares about our childhood again and that the darkness in her is very much alive again?

    Did she mention that from time to time throughout her life, Abigail has, in fact, returned and coerced her into doing awful things?

    Did your mother say that she is worried that she might not be able to resist hurting Chloe?

    Did your mother tell you that she sought me out because I am the only other person in the world who would understand the horror of our childhood and understand why she would be so bothered by Chloe's resemblance to our mother?

I am, indeed, the only one who would understand. We were captives in the same hell as children.

I can fully understand why Harriet embraced a demon as a child. Back then, Abigail was her defense against our parents.

I didn't lie when I wrote that your mother is possessed. I remember the rage in Harriet's eyes when we were children, and I see that same rage in her eyes now.

I fear my sister, Harriet. Or, to be more precise, I fear the demon she calls Abigail.

I can understand why our parents tried to beat the demon out of Harriet.

Don't get me wrong. Our parents were vile, and their actions unspeakably immoral.

However, it's clear that Abigail is back once again. Maybe she never really left. I don't know, but I do know that Abigail has Chloe in her sights.

As a child, I was too afraid to stand up to our parents and to Abigail.

My defense was to hide, to lie, and to close my eyes. In some ways, I was a collaborator, and I am so very sorry for that.

I don't feel that I can look the other way any longer. Harriet is my sister. I didn't help my sister back then. I must help her now.

I have decided to come to Wisconsin. I don't have an exact date picked yet, but it will be sometime soon.

Please be aware, I have been put in touch with a woman in Wisconsin who handles exorcisms. With her help, maybe we can free Harriet from her demonic influence.

Please, please help me free your mother from this demon.

Edith

Never Tell Chloe

∼

MARCH 25

EDITH:

YOU MUST BE MAD! YOU WANT TO DO AN EXORCISM! HOW VERY MEDIEVAL OF YOU!

PLEASE KNOW THAT I WOULD NEVER HURT CHLOE! I CAN KEEP CHLOE SAFE FROM ABIGAIL!

DESPITE THE FAMILY RESEMBLANCE, CHLOE IS EVERYTHING THAT OUR MOTHER WAS NOT!

CHLOE IS A DELIGHT – LOVING, WARM, AND INNOCENT! SHE IS PART OF THE PERFECT FAMILY THAT I CREATED!

STAY AWAY!

HARRIET

∼

March 31

Aunt Edith:

Please come to Wisconsin at your earliest convenience.

Mother and I have constantly been fighting about your letters, and I'm concerned about Mother's overall mental health. Mother is saying some very strange things—mostly about Chloe's resemblance to her mother. She has also started to claim that Chloe is destroying our perfect family.

If that isn't awful enough, I'm also becoming increasingly worried about an old memory that has been haunting me for years.

When I was around ten years old, I started to get a little sassy with Mother as all children do. However, Mother was a *stickler for perfection. I had to behave perfectly at all times. I had to always dress perfectly and so on. She so desperately needed to have everything appear perfect. I realize that I'm repeating perfect over and over, but it was the word that she constantly used.*

I want to be clear, however. Mother never physically nor verbally abused me. But oh my god, when I acted up, the looks that Mother gave me could make a hot summer day turn frigid.

One night, I was sent off to bed early for being sassy. At some point later, I heard Mother leave the house. I looked out my window and saw Mother drive off in her Cadillac Eldorado. It was a real eye-catcher. Mother adored it, but she rarely drove it. She generally drove the sedan.

After an hour or so, Mother returned, and I went to the top of the stairs to tell her that I was sorry.

However, Mother wasn't alone. She had returned with a teenage girl. I vividly remember that the girl looked so sad. She was also very dirty and appeared to be drunk or maybe on drugs. I was surprised that Mother brought her into our home. Mother was such a clean freak. The house was always spotless.

I was certainly bewildered but also curious. I decided to keep quiet and watch. However, what I saw was horrifying.

As I watched from the top of the stairs, Mother put duct tape over the girl's mouth, tied her up, and beat her. I'll skip the sordid details, but the girl quickly collapsed on the floor. The girl was bloody, and I'm not sure if she was still alive after the beating.

Mother then looked up at me and smiled. I have always believed Mother knew that I had been watching the entire time.

Mother came up to me, and in her sweetest voice, she told me to hurry back to bed. Mother followed me into my room, tucked me in, and told me that I had a bad dream.

She then told me that only bad girls needed to be beaten, and she calmly advised me to always be a good girl. Mother then kissed me on my forehead and left.

The next morning, there was nothing out of place in our house. The house was as spotless as always. It was as if nothing had happened. I convinced myself that just as Mother had said, it was a bad dream.

However, I never stepped out of line again. I was too afraid to be anything but perfect.

There is one other thing. Mother planted some lilac bushes in our backyard the following day or so. This has always bothered me. She hated flowers.

I no longer believe that this was just a dream.

I'm worried and not sure how to handle Mother and this situation.

Unfortunately, my husband isn't convinced that there is anything to worry about. He feels that my childhood memory was, indeed, only a bad dream. He also doesn't believe that Mother is capable of what you suggest.

Please hurry.

Joan

Chloe sat straight up in the chair as she finished reading the last of the letters; her world had changed forever two weeks after the last letter had been written.

Chapter 11

Chloe's hands shook as she put the letters back into the pocket folio. Although they filled in many of the missing pieces for her, the letters left Chloe stunned and frightened. She expected to learn a few family secrets but certainly not what she read. But she finally understood why her mother had seemed depressed and detached so often.

However, Chloe didn't understand why nor how the letters came to be hidden in the cabin, and questions raced through her mind. She mumbled, "Is my grandmother mad? Or do I sense actual evil in her? Is a demon controlling my grandmother? Could someone really be possessed? Or, for that matter, do demons really exist? And if not, are my grandmother and great-aunt both somehow gripped by madness—a sort of shared psychosis?"

Reaching into her purse, Chloe pulled out the business card that she was given at the spiritualist camp earlier in the day. The card simply read: *Gladys* S*hepherd, Demonologist.*

Chloe dialed the phone number, not sure of what questions to ask. When Gladys answered, she was surprised to hear that Gladys had been expecting her call.

Never Tell Chloe

"I'm not sure what to ask," Chloe said. "I think that my grandmother may be possessed—and maybe a murderer. And I think that she wants to kill me."

"Chloe, your grandmother isn't the murderer. She *is* possessed by a demon," Gladys said, her tone firm and authoritative. "The demon is the murderer. The signs of mental illness and possession are very much the same. However, there *are* differences—supernatural strength, noxious smells, an aversion to holy water, a refusal to enter a church, and so on. These were all present in your grandmother's case."

"What do you mean—in my grandmother's case?"

"Twelve years ago, your Great-Aunt Edith contacted me, and I met with her and your mother. I also met with your grandmother. Before agreeing to perform an exorcism, I insist on an initial meeting with the subject to determine if an exorcism is appropriate."

"I don't understand. My grandmother wanted an exorcism?"

"No, she didn't. She refused to meet me, but your mother tricked her into going out to your family's cabin. We thought that it would provide a private location for my meeting with her. However, things didn't go well."

"Did you try to do an exorcism?"

"No. After talking with your grandmother, I left to mull over the situation before committing to anything. However, it took me less than an hour to call Edith with my decision—an exorcism was warranted. Unfortunately, I wasn't able to actually conduct the exorcism. Like I said, things didn't go well that day."

"Please explain what an exorcism is exactly." Chloe's voice quivered, exposing her growing fear.

"I don't know if I can cover everything in a phone call. But I'll give you some of the basics. A demon cannot be killed. So the solution is never to just kill a possessed person. The person would die but not the demon."

"I don't want to kill my grandmother!"

"Of course not. We don't either. So there's only really one option. The demon must be forced back to hell through exorcism. If not, the demon will just attach itself to another victim, and the evil will continue."

"I'm getting scared."

"That's understandable. This is scary stuff. But you must understand one thing. Liberating someone or someplace of a demonic possession must be done carefully, forcefully, and by someone who knows how to do it. In an exorcism, we must always call upon the power of Almighty God for help. Only God has the power to send the demonic entity back to hell; humans can't do it alone."

"Oh my god."

Glady added one last point. "You must never show any fear in front of a demon or any dark force. Good is always more powerful than evil. You must believe this to be true. I always ask God's angels to surround me in their white light for protection. And it's always best to do an exorcism in a holy place, such as a church."

"Can you help me? I'm at our family fishing cabin. It's located just off . . ."

"We know where the cabin is, and we're already on our way. When we get there, we'll figure out how to handle the situation. Your grandmother will likely show up there as well—she has you in her sights. Please be careful and *please* don't attempt an exorcism until we arrive."

"We?" Chloe said into a silent phone. Gladys had ended the call.

Chloe held the phone to her chest, scared and alone. Her father hadn't yet arrived.

Joan had called Edith almost an hour prior with an update; Frank was meeting Chloe at the fishing cabin. Edith's two-word response was *oh shit,* and Gladys's was *bad omen.* The three women decided to quickly head to the cabin.

Joan passed her aunt's van on the highway and arrived at the cabin's driveway well ahead of her aunt and Gladys. However, rather than turning into the driveway, she decided to park her truck out of sight about a mile or so from the cabin on a nearby dirt road. She wanted the element of surprise on her side. She had a plan.

Just as her truck came to a stop, rain burst from the dark, menacing clouds above. Joan and the dog quickly jumped out of the truck, landing in mud. Undeterred, they immediately raced toward the cabin, pushing their way through a shadowy, overgrown path. It proved a difficult and time-consuming effort, however.

As she pushed her way along, Joan suddenly stopped at a nondescript spot and dropped to her knees, unable to catch her breath. Although unrecognizable to her eyes, Joan's soul remembered this particular spot; it remembered the pain.

The dog suddenly raced ahead toward the cabin, leaving Joan alone in her pain. Watching the dog as it jumped over, wiggled under, and raced around the trees, twigs, and fallen logs, Joan tried to marshal her strength and head to the cabin as well. She needed to protect Chloe. Joan willed herself to rise only to fall again, rolling down a slight slope and landing under a large pine tree.

Joan sat under the pine, protected from the rain but not from the memory. Rocking back and forth, she now remembered this spot and the taste of its dirt. Joan had no broken bones, no sprains, no bruises. However, the memory had pulled her to the ground and refused to let her go.

Joan closed her eyes, not wanting to see where she was. The dog soon returned, nuzzling close. Joan heard the dog's breathing, felt the dog's warmth, and sensed its concern. Yet, she remained unable to rise.

"Molly, you remember this spot too, don't you?" Joan mumbled.

∼

Just as Chloe started to phone her father, the cabin door squeaked opened. *Abigail* had arrived.

Abigail smirked. "I hope that you weren't calling your daddy because he can't make it."

"Where's my father?" Chloe's voice was surprisingly calm. She refused to show fear.

Abigail grinned, baring her teeth. "After you dropped me off earlier today, I needed to acquire a car. As luck would have it, a silly person left their car idling in their driveway. Wow, how trusting is that? I got in the car and drove straight to your Daddy's office."

"Where's my father!"

"I left him lying in his own blood," Abigail laughed. "He wouldn't tell me where to find you, but then I remembered this fishing cabin. Lots of memories here!"

Chloe said nothing in response, but her glare screamed loudly. She was angry.

"Didn't your Mommy and you come by here to visit me—you know, on the day that your Mommy died," Abigail taunted, laughing louder and louder.

Her fanatical laughter drove the years of Chloe's hidden grief and fear to the surface. The grief flowed as tears, but the fear turned into rage. And the rage fueled Chloe's strength.

Armed with her rage, Chloe lunged at the evil, old woman, kicking and punching her.

Abigail stopped laughing and slammed Chloe against the floor. Chloe quickly rose back up. At first, Chloe's rage matched Abigail's strength as the two fought—good against evil. Or, more precisely, it was rage against evil. However, with each of Chloe's rage-driven blows, Abigail's strength increased, and Chloe's diminished.

In time, Chloe collapsed to the floor, sobbing. Abigail hovered above her fallen prey. Chloe could feel Abigail's hot breath, hear her panting, and smell her sweaty stench.

"Giving up already?" Abigail hissed. "Your rage was so sweet to taste."

Chloe felt too weak to fight back any longer. She silently conceded—Abigail wins. The demon is too strong. As she curled up in pain, fearing Abigail's final deadly blow, the wind started to howl outside, and the rain began to pound against the walls of the fragile cabin. Chloe heard the thunder getting closer and saw the fury of the lighting through the cabin's window.

And then Chloe heard another sound, a closer sound. It was a growl, not the growl of a beast but that of a mere dog. Chloe turned her face in the direction of the growl, fighting to see out of her swollen, bloody eyes.

Abigail backed away, hissing, "I hate dogs." And with those three words still hanging in the air, Abigail ran outside into the storm.

Wiping away her tears, Chloe looked into the eyes of the dog who had saved her. As it nuzzled her, Chloe sensed its sweetness. A thought flashed in her mind—the dog was Molly. But she wondered how that could be. Molly had been gone for twelve years. Was the dog real, she wondered? As the dog swiftly disappeared back into the night, Chloe inhaled deeply, trying to calm herself. Real or not, the dog had toughened Chloe's will to survive.

Chloe knew that she needed to fight back. If not, she feared that she wouldn't survive the night. She also sensed that Abigail would not stay outside in the storm for long. She knew that the demon needed to be forced back to hell—even if she had to do it alone.

Chloe tried to stand but failed. As she slid back to the floor, she knocked down the painting of her guardian angel, and it rested on the floor next to her.

Hugging the painting, Chloe remembered something that Gladys said: *An exorcism should be done in a holy place.* As far as Chloe was concerned, nature was the holiest of places. Forcing herself back on her feet, she removed the silver crucifix from her necklace. Holding the crucifix in both hands, she headed into the storm.

"Old woman," Chloe yelled over the storm. "Where are you?"

"Right behind you," Abigail hissed.

Turning around, Chloe faced her. The rain poured from the dark sky, and the force of the wind made it difficult for Chloe to stand. However, Abigail remained upright, unaffected by the formidable force of the wind and the rain. Abigail started to laugh; the sound of which was menacing.

"Your laughing pisses me off, old woman," Chloe yelled.

Chloe held the cross out in front of her and started the exorcism. "In the name of the Father, the Son, and the Holy Spirit, I demand that the demon named Abigail return to Hell!"

"Oh, my goodness," Abigail laughed. "You are trying to do an exorcism! And what's that? A tiny, little cross? How cute!"

Chloe yelled over the rain, making up the words and hoping that help arrived soon. "I call upon all things good in Heaven and on Earth for help in sending this demon back to hell."

Abigail stepped toward Chloe, and Chloe quickly moved backwards, her fear evident.

Despite the storm, both Chloe and Abigail heard the van approach. The van quickly slid to a stop in the mud, and Edith and Gladys jumped out, bracing themselves against the van as they fought to remain standing in defiance of the angry storm.

Turning toward the van, Abigail leaped through the storm and grabbed ahold of a long gray braid, twisting its owner forcibly around to face her.

"Gladys! How wonderful to see you again," Abigail laughed, wrapping her hands around Gladys's neck. As the grip tightened, Gladys started to collapse.

"Stop!" Both Edith and Chloe screamed. Abigail let go, and Gladys fell into the mud.

Abigail turned to face Chloe. She raised her hand, and with one fierce blow, Chloe crashed to the ground. She then spun around and glared at Edith. The fury in her eyes burned through the darkness, paralyzing Edith.

Gladys rose from the mud. She then quickly pulled a large crucifix from her pocket and held it high. Abigail froze in place.

"Chloe, get up and run to the cabin!" Gladys yelled, lowering the crucifix briefly as she pointed to the cabin.

As Chloe struggled to stand, Gladys screamed as Abigail hurled her against the cabin. Chloe fought against her fear as she watched Gladys's limp body bounce off the cabin and crash back into the mud. If not dead, she knew that Gladys was at least knocked out.

Edith ran over to Gladys, shielding her from the approaching Abigail. "Please don't kill her! We only want to help you!"

Abigail laughed, easily grabbing Edith and tossing her several feet in the air before she too landed motionless in the mud.

Chloe was now alone in the fight against the demon. She ran toward the safety of the woods, begging all things good in Heaven and on Earth to help. Yelling through the roaring storm, she begged the angels to protect her. She called out a prayer to God, asking him to send the demon back to Hell.

Slipping in the mud, Chloe fell over a fallen tree. As she tried to get up, she screamed out in pain. Unsure if she had broken a bone or if her ankle was only badly sprained, Chloe knew that she could not flee any further.

Dazed and afraid, Chloe looked up and watched the stars push their way through the dark storm clouds. Although the wind had diminished, the thunder and rain persisted. However, the sight of the stars comforted Chloe, and she softly asked the stars and the angels to surround her in their light and protect her from evil.

Abigail walked over to Chloe, each step slow but deliberate. She then bent down and picked up a rock.

Chloe was too weak to fight anymore, and she looked up, hoping to find a flicker of humanity in the eyes of her grandmother. Instead, only the cruel, angry eyes of the demon looked back at her.

"Are you afraid, Chloe?" Abigail growled.

"I don't fear you." A calmness overcame Chloe; she felt pulsating energy surrounding her.

"No fear? I don't believe you."

"The angels will protect me."

Abigail laughed loudly but soon grew quiet. She lowered her rock and said one word, "Joan."

Chloe followed Abigail's stare toward the nearby woods and was shocked by who she saw standing at its edge. Both had grown older, but Chloe recognized them.

As the early morning light filtered through the trees, Joan had found the strength to rise. Finally free of her long, crippling panic attack, Joan and the dog had rushed toward the cabin.

"Molly, sit," Joan whispered to the dog.

Joan stepped out of the woods and stared at her mother, calmly saying, "This needs to end."

"I killed you twelve years ago. How are you still alive?" The voice was no longer the shrill voice of Abigail. It seemed that the demon had retreated, leaving Harriet in control—at least for now, Chloe thought.

Covered in mud, Edith fought to regain her senses. As her blurred vision cleared, Edith was startled to see Harriet and Joan standing face to face. Edith forced herself up and prayed out loud, "Oh please, God, don't let any harm come to Joan or Chloe."

Edith then saw a decorative heart-shaped tin in the mud. She recognized the tin instantly. It was Harriet's prized possession and where she had kept a photo of Joan. Edith picked it up, opened it, and discovered a handgun inside. The handgun looked to be roughly six inches long, the kind of small handgun that one can easily conceal. It was the only thing in the heart-shaped tin.

Unfortunately, Edith wasn't surprised by the discovery. She removed the handgun, dropped the tin back into the mud, and stumbled closer to her sister. Harriet turned and faced her sister. Wet and shivering, Edith stood still, pointing the handgun at her.

Unsure of what to do, Joan took a few steps back into the edge of the woods, joining her dog and silently standing guard over Chloe.

"Are you Harriet or Abigail?" Edith asked, holding the handgun in her shaky hands.

"I'm both. We are forged together," Harriet answered, walking toward Edith. Her pace was slow, more like a tired old woman than a fierce demon. Harriet slowed to a stop and then collapsed to her knees in front of Edith.

"This needs to end," Edith said, unknowingly repeating Joan's words.

"I know," Harriet said. "Give me the handgun. I'll end this now."

Collapsing to her knees also, Edith looked into her sister's eyes and whispered, "I'm sorry. I should have helped you when we were kids."

Harriet took the handgun from Edith. She then pointed the gun first at her own head and then at Edith's head, asking, "Should I kill you or me?"

Trembling, Edith responded with one word, "Neither."

Ignoring her sister's response, Harriet turned her eyes toward a new threat. Between the claps of thunder, police sirens could be heard in the distance.

Edith used this distraction to snatch the handgun back, and Harriet lunged at her. The two sisters fought for control of the gun, pulling each other down into the mud. Shocked, Chloe remained motionless, helpless to intervene in the battle she was witnessing.

Chloe jumped at the sound of the first shot from the handgun and then again at the sound of the second shot. Chloe saw the mud splash as the second shot plunged into it, but she didn't see where the first shot had gone.

Afraid of what would happen next, Chloe stared at the two women—each now holding tightly onto each other. As they embraced, the small handgun rested in the mud, ignored by both. Edith started to pray, with her head turned up toward the heavens. Chloe strained to hear her. Despite the thunder and rain, Chloe heard most of what was said. Edith was asking God to free her sister from the demon.

Harriet broke free of her sister's embrace and stood. As she did so, it was clear that Harriet wasn't wounded. But as Edith struggled back to her feet, blood ran down her arm. At the sight of the blood, Chloe felt lightheaded for a moment. The last person that Chloe had seen covered in blood was her mother.

However, fear quickly replaced her lightheadedness as Chloe watched her grandmother walk toward her. Chloe scooted up into a sitting position, grabbing a nearby stick to use for protection. Over her shoulder, Chloe heard her mother's voice.

"Don't worry, Chloe," Joan said. "I will *not* let your grandmother hurt you."

Harriet stepped over Chloe and walked into the woods, soon standing face to face with her daughter.

Pointing a loaded handgun at her mother, Joan ordered, "Walk ahead of me."

Harriet obeyed, and the two women, followed by the dog, marched single file down the newly formed path. After a short time, they exited the woods near where Joan had parked her truck. Joan stole a quick glance behind her and was pleased that the rain had washed away their tracks.

Joan opened the truck's door and motioned for the dog to jump in.

"Get in the pickup truck, old woman," Joan said, glaring at her mother. Harriet obeyed, eyeing the snarling dog as she did so. The dog inched over slightly, barely allowing her enough room to sit.

They drove off, unseen by the arriving police.

~

Edith turned toward the deafening sound of the siren and watched the squad car stop in front of the cabin. Despite being weakened by her wound, Edith walked over to Gladys and helped her up. Both women were grateful to have survived the night.

The siren went silent as Frank and a police officer emerged from the squad car. Knowing that there would be questions to answer, both women walked over to the squad car.

Immediately noticing the blood on Edith's arm, the officer asked, "Have you been shot?"

"Yes, but . . ."

"Is the shooter still here?"

"No, she's gone," Edith said, scanning the area for Chloe and thankful to spot her in the distance. Frank also spotted Chloe and immediately started in her direction.

"Shit! Frank, wait until I secure the area," the officer yelled. Frank ignored him.

The officer drew his gun and did a quick sweep of the immediate area, concluding that the shooter had indeed fled.

Holding onto a nearby tree, Chloe forced herself to stand as she watched her bruised and bandaged father rushing to her. Relieved but in considerable pain, Chloe concluded that she hadn't broken a bone but instead had merely sprained her ankle.

Chloe drew the fresh, morning air deep into her lungs and silently thanked the angels for the armor that they had wrapped around her in the darkness. Chloe then looked up at the sun, thankful for the gift of a new day.

The morning sun had climbed higher in the sky, and the clouds were finally departing. To Chloe, it seemed that the storm had cleansed the woods. As if the events of the night before had never occurred, the birds started to chirp out their morning songs, and the wildflowers danced in the breeze.

"Chloe, are you okay?" Frank asked his daughter as they hugged.

Chloe nodded yes, and Frank hurriedly explained, "Your Grandma Harriet came after me in the parking lot at my office. She kept hitting and kicking me. It was like she was in some sort of violent frenzy. Right before I blacked out, my secretary screamed at her that the police were en route. When I woke up in the ER this morning, I was told that she had also stolen my car. I pleaded with the police to head out here. I was so afraid that we would be too late. I'm so sorry. I love you so much."

"I love you too, Dad."

Helped by her father, Chloe made her way to the squad car.

"I'll radio for an ambulance," the officer said as he looked at Edith. "You're bleeding."

"No, please don't," Edith said. "I don't want to go to the hospital."

"Okay, that's your choice, but I think that you should reconsider. Does anyone else need an ambulance?" he asked. All declined. Chloe denied she was in pain; Gladys explained that she was only bruised, and Edith laughed that the bullet had only scratched her arm.

He gave a quick nod and said, "I was filled in on some of the details on the way here. Is anyone else around here? Where is Harriet? I think that's the name that I was given."

"No one else is here, and my grandmother, Harriet, walked into the woods over there," Chloe answered, pointing toward the woods.

"Was she the shooter?" the officer asked.

"Yes. Her gun is in the mud over there," Edith answered and pointed in its direction.

The officer retrieved the gun before hurrying into the woods. He soon emerged from the woods and explained, "I don't see her nor any footprints, but the woods are really dense in there. We might need a canine unit to help search the area."

The officer radioed in, requesting assistance. Surprised that the officer hadn't immediately done so upon arriving at an obvious crime scene, Frank assumed that the officer was inexperienced.

"Chloe, I understand that you spent several days on a road trip with the suspect, unaware that she was your grandmother. How could you not recognize your own grandmother?" the officer pointedly asked.

Chloe glared at the officer. She didn't feel like answering questions. Her father squeezed her hand, silently suggesting that she cooperate.

"I had been told that my grandmother died twelve years ago. It never occurred to me that she was my Grandma Harriet. She called herself Hetty, and she certainly didn't look like the grandmother that I remembered from my childhood."

The officer eyed Chloe closely. "You didn't know that Hetty is a nickname for Harriet?"

"No, I didn't."

"Then you had no idea at all who she really was?"

"No," Chloe firmly insisted. "*My* Grandma Harriet always had her hair perfectly styled, and her makeup flawlessly applied. *My* Grandma Harriet's clothing was always stylish. *My* Grandma Harriet looked like she stepped out of a 1950s TV show, wearing pink lipstick and a pearl necklace. *This* old woman didn't look anything like that. *She* looked frumpy, wore no makeup, and practically had a buzz cut. And frankly, she was scrawny. *My* Grandma Harriet was definitely not skinny. She actually was a little chubby."

"Harriet would have said voluptuous," Edith quietly interjected.

"Okay," the officer said, softening his tone. "I understand. However, I want to talk with each of you separately to find out what happened here."

The three women essentially gave him the same story: *They arranged to meet at the cabin to discuss options. All described Harriet as a deranged and dangerous woman, who violently attacked each of them. No other details were shared.*

After speaking with each, he explained that a thorough search of the cabin and the surrounding area would happen as soon as additional officers arrived.

In a surprisingly short time, more squad cars started to arrive, and Frank asked, "Do we need to stay here during the search? I would like to take everyone back to my condo. It's been a rough night, to say the least. If you have any other questions, you have my phone number and address."

"That should be fine," the officer said. "The vehicles, however, will need to stay here for the forensics team. I'll ask one of the other officers to drive you to your condo."

Although thankful that they could leave, it surprised Frank that they could go before a detective had arrived.

"Can I get my purse before we go? It's in the cabin," Chloe asked, walking toward the cabin.

"Wait, I'll retrieve it for you," the officer said. "I'll have to check it for anything suspicious, like a gun or whatever." He hurried into the cabin, quickly returning with the purse.

"Nothing suspicious inside," the officer announced as he handed the purse to Chloe. She stole a quick look inside, relieved that the small pocket folio was still there. Surprised again, Frank was dumbfounded that the officer allowed the purse to be removed from the crime scene. He was definitely inexperienced, Frank thought.

Soon Frank and the three women were en route to his condo. During the drive, all sat quietly, too numb to talk. Each was also aware that they shouldn't speak in front of the officer who was driving.

Chapter 12

Once inside of Frank's condo, the four weary and battered souls dropped their defenses and relaxed. Frank graciously offered the three women an opportunity to wash up, providing bandages as well as towels and washcloths. Next, Frank raided his closet, returning with clean t-shirts and sweatpants for the women to change into.

After they had washed and changed, Frank and the three women sat at his kitchen table, holding tightly onto the bottles of beer that he had also supplied.

"Kind of early to drink, Dad," Chloe said, smiling at her father.

"Sweetheart," Frank laughed. "I think that all of us deserve a beer after last night. Oh geez, Edith, I forgot about your drinking ... um, problem. Do you want something nonalcohol?"

"No, actually, I really need a beer right now, but my limit is one drink per day."

Each sat wordless, staring at one another until Chloe quietly said, "I wish that I had been told about all of this from the start. If not twelve years ago, then at least a few days ago when Grandma Harriet first reappeared."

All nodded in agreement.

"However," Chloe continued. "I can understand why you would want to protect me from finding out about Grandma Harriet. She is no ordinary grandmother, to be sure. And I honestly appreciate that each of you risked your lives to protect me."

"Chloe, I'm sorry," Frank said. "I should have told you everything as soon as I knew. But we wanted to protect you from the very, very ugly truth. But that was wrong. You're an adult now, not a child."

"Dad, I understand, and I love you. I also have a confession of sorts. When Grandma Harriet headed into the woods, she was following Mom. I don't know why, but I didn't tell the police that I saw Mom. Edith, did you know that Mom was alive?"

Edith glanced at Gladys and then at Frank and said, "Yes, I did, and I saw your mother there also. She's been working with us to protect you."

"I think that Chloe needs to know everything," Frank said, looking directly at Edith.

However, there was one thing that Frank was not willing to share with his daughter nor with the other two women, and that was Joan's back-up plan. Now more than ever, Frank secretly hoped that Joan would be able to successfully carry out her plan. Frank knew that his daughter would never be safe if Joan failed.

Holding Chloe's hand, Edith quietly asked, "Chloe, did you read the letters in the cabin?"

Chloe nodded. "I have the letters in my purse. That's why I wanted my purse."

Edith continued, "Good. Your mother put them in the cabin for you to find. Luckily, both your mother and I had held onto the letters we wrote each other back then. So, I'll skip the beginning of the family saga then.

"When I arrived in Wisconsin about twelve years ago, I reached out to Gladys about the possibility of doing an exorcism on your grandmother. I also discussed the option with your grandmother, and she was absolutely against the idea. No surprise there, of course. However, Gladys needed to meet your grandmother and assess the situation before committing to an exorcism. I don't know how, but Joan tricked your grandmother into driving out to the fishing cabin that afternoon."

Edith stopped talking for a moment and then said, "I'm sorry, but I don't know if I should say Joan or your mother. Or, for that matter, if I should say Harriet or your grandmother."

"Please don't worry about which names to use. I just want to know the whole story," Chloe said. "So Grandma Harriet knew nothing about what was planned at the cabin?"

"No, she thought only Joan would be here. She wasn't very happy to find out that Gladys and I were also waiting for her there," Edith said. "However, your school called early into the assessment, saying that you were ill, and your mother left to pick you up. After she left, Gladys continued to talk with your grandmother at length. At a certain point, Gladys also left, saying that she would let me know her decision."

"If I had thought that the situation would get as far out of hand as it did, I wouldn't have left," Gladys interjected. "When I talked with Harriet, I asked about things like family issues, childhood traumas, drug and alcohol addiction, mental illness, and so on. I never jump to the conclusion of possession. Harriet seemed irritated but nothing more serious than that when I left."

"Unfortunately, your grandmother grew increasingly angry afterwards," Edith said. "To say the least, Harriet wasn't happy that your mother had tricked her. She was also not happy about the topic of exorcism. I couldn't calm Harriet down and phoned Joan, asking for help."

Chloe nodded, relieved to be finally hearing the whole story.

Edith squeezed Chloe's hand and continued, "When Joan returned, you and your puppy were in the car. I was worried that you would get underfoot, but Joan assured me that you were asleep in the backseat."

"Were you also at the cabin, Dad?"

"No, but I wish now that I took all of this more seriously back then," Frank admitted. "Your mother and your grandmother had been arguing in the weeks leading up to this. That alone was unusual, but I never imagined it would lead to what happened. The demon stuff seemed crazy to me. I still don't know if I believe that, actually. Anyhow, I left for an out-of-town conference without a second thought."

"Don't blame yourself, Dad," Chloe softly consoled her father. "No one would have believed that."

Edith continued, "Your grandmother was furious at Joan, screaming at her and calling her a traitor. I got angry and slapped your grandmother, telling her to shut up. That was a mistake, of course. It only made Harriet angrier. Your mother asked me to leave at that point as she wanted to talk to Harriet alone. I initially refused to do so. I was worried that something awful would happen. However, your mother insisted and promised that she would leave shortly also. I really wished that I had stayed."

Edith inhaled deeply, trying to find the courage to continue telling her story. She looked over at Frank and after gaining his approval, Edith explained, "I'm not sure what happened after I left, but your grandmother appeared a few hours later at my motel. She wasn't making a lot of sense. Joan had apparently left right after me but had returned later."

Edith went silent for a few seconds and then quietly said, "This was hard for me to hear at the time, and it'll be even harder for you to hear, Chloe. Your grandmother told me that she had shot and killed Joan, dragged her body out into the woods, and buried her."

"What?" Chloe asked, "Buried Mom? But Mom is alive."

"Yes, she's alive, but no one knew it back then," Edith explained. "Your grandmother was confused and rambling, and it took a while for me to understand what she was saying. I finally figured out that she was trying to tell me that she killed Joan. I was dumbfounded. Shocked might be a better word. I asked about you, Chloe, and your grandmother assured me that she didn't harm you."

"Mom had taken me home and helped me into bed and then left again. That's probably when she returned to the cabin. I didn't see her again until today," Chloe quietly explained.

"I don't really know why I tried to cover up what I believed was the murder of your mother," Edith said. "I should have called the police as soon as Harriet appeared at my motel door. But instead, I made the decision to protect her. I felt so guilty for not trying to protect her when we were kids. Poor Harriet was so severely abused back then. But I was too afraid as a kid to help her."

Edith paused and then added, "I also believed then, as I still do, that it was the demon Abigail who had pulled the trigger, not Harriet. I drove Harriet back to her house, and I had her change into fresh clothes. I used Harriet's key to your house and went to check if you were truly okay. Thankfully, I found you safe and asleep. I then went back to Harriet's, and we waited to hear some news. We knew eventually that either the police or your father would show up. There was no way that your mother's disappearance would go unnoticed."

After a deep sigh, Edith continued, "Your father called early in the morning and told us that Joan's car was found submerged in the Mississippi River. The authorities believed that she had skidded off the icy road. The river was at flood stage, and per the authorities, the currents were too strong for even a good swimmer. As a result, the authorities assumed that Joan had drowned."

Edith looked at Chloe, who seemed overly quiet. She hoped that Chloe was not overwhelmed by the onslaught of information that she was suddenly learning.

"Are you okay, Chloe?" Edith asked. "Do you need a break?"

"No, please continue."

Edith continued once again, "I was relieved to hear about the drowning because it meant that Harriet hadn't killed Joan. It's a strange feeling to be relieved that someone had drowned as opposed to being shot. Although your father asked several questions about what had happened when he was out of town, I didn't provide many details to him. I only told him that Joan had argued with Harriet on the previous day. I also briefly mentioned that an exorcism had been discussed but not done. I didn't, of course, mention Harriet's confession of murder. I felt that it was better that he didn't know."

"Edith had also mentioned that the argument between your mother and grandmother had taken place at the cabin," Frank said. "Later that day, I drove out there, and I found the cabin in disarray—furniture was turned over and whatnot. I also noticed some blood droplets. I felt that whatever had happened at the cabin between your mother and grandmother was bad."

In a quiet, sad voice, Chloe said, "What happened was so awful."

"Yes, you're right," Frank agreed. "But since I thought that your mother had drowned in the Mississippi, I decided to just tidy up the cabin and forget what I saw there. I also never went there again. It was too painful of an option for me. It had been your mother's favorite place. Because of that, I also could never bring myself to sell it."

Frank cleared his voice before finishing. "Unfortunately, I never informed the police about the condition of the cabin nor the fight between your mother and grandmother. I knew that your mother was upset and anxious about your grandmother.

And I figured that her anxiety contributed to the car accident. To be honest, I also didn't want anyone to find out about the demon stuff. It would've tarnished your mother's memory, and people would have gossiped about our family. I know that it shouldn't have mattered, but it did. I'm so sorry for that."

"I understand, Dad. But does anyone know why Mom was by the Mississippi River?"

"I don't know, not then and not now," Edith said. "The authorities had called your father a couple of hours earlier, and he had rushed home. He was upset, of course, and he didn't understand why Joan was in that location either. That's something hopefully your mother will explain someday."

After another deep sigh, Edith continued her story, "Your father stopped over later in the morning. However, Harriet was almost catatonic by then and didn't respond to any of his questions. In the days that followed, Harriet didn't get any better. Your father mistook this for grief, which was partially correct. However, I believe that it was more guilt than grief. I don't think she understood that Joan had drowned. She always believed that Joan was buried near the cabin. Your grandmother cared about your mother in her own way. She had built her life around her."

"If Grandma Harriet is really possessed by a demon, why would she feel guilty?" Chloe asked. "When I was with Grandma Harriet on our road trip, I felt uneasy sometimes. But at other times, I really enjoyed being with her."

"I can explain that," Gladys said. "It was the demonic entity that made you feel uneasy. Despite what it might seem, the demon and your grandmother are *two* separate beings. And a demonic possession can fluctuate. A demon will drift into the background on occasion or even leave and then return. So very likely, your grandmother's true nature broke through at times."

"I know that Grandma Harriet did horrible things, but I feel sorry for her and for you also, Aunt Edith. Both of you had such an awful childhood." Chloe reached over and held Edith's hand briefly.

"You feel that way because you're a good person. I'm proud of the young woman that you have become, and your mother would be too," Frank said.

Edith agreed with that sentiment then returned to her story. "It was clear back then that you and your father were deeply heartbroken by your mother's death. I offered to take Harriet back to Albuquerque with me, and your father agreed. He certainly didn't want to deal with a heartbroken mother-in-law. However, I remember the frightened look on your face when I brought your grandmother over to say goodbye. I was never sure what you had seen that night, but I felt that you needed to be spared the worst of it."

Chloe quietly said, "The truth is always better."

"Yes, now that you are an adult, you are probably right. But I still believe you needed to be spared the truth back then. You were only a kid," Edith answered. "Once we arrived in Albuquerque, your grandmother agreed to be committed to a mental institution. She was at the institution for the last twelve years."

"That must have been expensive," Frank said.

"Yes, it was. Harriet allowed me to sell her house and liquidate her other assets, which covered the costs for a couple of years. But I handled the rest of it. I could afford it, and I willingly paid for her care. Harriet was my sister, after all," Edith explained, failing to hold back tears.

Edith quickly rubbed her eyes, wiping the tears away. "However, she never really recovered. She remained largely uncommunicative and locked within herself. It's true that Harriet wasn't a great parent, but I think that Joan was the only person in the world who mattered to her."

Taking a sip of her beer, Edith added, "Beer was a good choice, Frank."

Frank laughed and said, "Beer's always a good choice. This is Wisconsin, after all."

Edith laughed, took another sip, and restarted her story. "Early on, I decided to tell your father that Harriet had died of a heart attack. It seemed the simplest way to prevent you from finding out the awful truth. I don't mean just the truth about what happened here twelve years ago but also the truth about our family's gruesome history. It was just too horrible of a story to share with a child. I was very relieved that your father never asked any questions about your grandmother's estate."

"I just didn't care. I was glad to be rid of Harriet," Frank honestly answered.

"So why did my grandmother come back now?" Chloe asked, looking directly at Edith.

"Harriet found out that your mother was alive, and this must have triggered something in her. She left the institution and headed back here," Edith answered. "And your mother and I followed to ensure that you weren't in any danger. I had kept in touch with Gladys over the years and asked Gladys for her help as well."

Looking over at her father, Chloe asked, "Did you know that Mom was alive?"

"Yes, your mother and Edith came here a few days ago," Frank said in a voice barely louder than a whisper. "But I want to be completely honest. A while back, I thought that I saw your mother when I was in Colorado at a conference. I was pretty sure it was her but not completely. I never knew how to tell you. I believed she didn't want to be part of our lives, not your life nor my life. And that was too painful to talk about."

Chloe wasn't sure how to respond. So instead of speaking, Chloe got up, limped around the table, and gave her father a long hug before returning to her chair.

"Chloe, I think that your mother does love you," Edith softly

Never Tell Chloe

said. "Although she isn't damaged in the same way that Harriet and I were, your mother is also a damaged soul. I have talked to her a great deal over the recent days, and she desperately needed to find peace and to heal. She was very unhappy and lost back in those days. Joan never felt loved growing up. I don't think that your grandmother understood how to show motherly love. She never had a loving mother to emulate."

"But you didn't turn out to be a crazed madwoman like my grandmother. I don't understand how Grandma Harriet became so horrible and not you."

"I can only say that your grandmother welcomed the darkness into her soul. She gave it a home. I didn't," Edith answered. "However, I didn't escape my childhood with a clean slate. I have issues with alcohol, and I have trust issues. I avoided long-term romantic relationships and also avoided having children. I avoided a lot in life. I also spent a lot of money and time at my shrink's office. I worked hard to avoid becoming a crazed madwoman, as you say."

"I'm so sorry, Aunt Edith."

"It is what it is," Edith said. "I asked my shrink the same question that you just did. She didn't know why one child in a family can recover from abuse, and another is permanently broken. It might be due to a difference in the severity of the abuse suffered; it might be genetics. Or, in my case, it might be the loving foster home I had."

"Oh," Chloe responded—her thoughts too many to be expressed more fully.

"Chloe, please understand, your mother didn't leave because she didn't care about your father or you. She left to avoid repeating her own mother's mistakes with you," Edith quietly said.

"Looking back now as an adult, I realize that my mother was suffering from depression," Chloe said. "However, she was *not* an unloving mother. I felt loved during my childhood by both of my parents. Some of my best memories are those with Mom, especially our nature hikes together. She was so fun to be with on those hikes."

"Maybe someday, you'll be able to tell her that," Frank said. "And maybe someday, I'll be able to tell her that I'm sorry that I didn't recognize her unhappiness. I'm very sorry for that."

"I'm still trying, however, to come to terms with the fact that she was gone for twelve years," Chloe said, her voice so soft that it could barely be heard. "I can understand why she left. But I don't understand why she was gone for twelve years. That's a long time for a kid not to have a mother. I honestly still love Mom—or at least the mother that I remember. But why didn't she at least call? I'm not sure if or when I can forgive that."

"That's understandable, Chloe," Frank said. "But I know that your mother loves you, and the process of forgiveness doesn't involve an exact time frame. You'll be ready when you're ready."

Chloe looked around the table and then asked, "What do you think is going to happen between my mother and Grandma Harriet? Will Grandma Harriet hurt Mom?"

No one answered. Finally, Gladys spoke, "To put it mildly, the mother-daughter connection between the two of them is frayed. I'm hoping that Joan will get through to Harriet. She may be the only one that can. Harriet has the power to reject the demon herself. A demon has no power over you unless you freely give it. I'll pray for both of them."

"But will Mom be okay?"

Again, no one answered right away.

"Chloe, I don't believe that any of us know the answer to that. I know that your mother is determined to keep you safe. But I'm not sure how she intends to do that," Edith said.

Chloe looked down but didn't respond.

"If your mother fails in her efforts, then the demon will only grow bolder," Glady warned. "If something evil feels that it can get away with whatever it wants, then it will surely do so."

"Can we try to help Mom?"

"I've tried to phone her several times, but my calls go straight to voicemail," Edith said. "I don't think that your mother wants anyone else involved. We can only pray and hope that she succeeds."

Frank looked down at the table, still not sharing his wife's plan to kill her mother. He wanted Joan to succeed. He wanted his daughter to be safe.

"Just one more question, Aunt Edith. Do I resemble your mother?"

"No, you do not," Edith lied.

Chapter 13

Joan drove non-stop until she reached South Dakota. The truck was deadly silent; Joan nor her mother had spoken a word since leaving Wisconsin. Just east of Sioux Falls, Joan stopped briefly to fill her gas tank and to give the dog a chance to stretch her legs and such. Once the dog jumped back into the truck, Joan continued to drive further into South Dakota, avoiding the main highways.

Her mother's silence surprised Joan, and she sensed that her mother was resigned to her probable fate and perhaps hoping for a swift end to her torturous life. Or at least, that's what Joan hoped.

After an hour or so, Joan veered off the paved road onto a little-used dirt road and drove another hour into the wilderness. Upon reaching what most would describe as the middle of nowhere, Joan stopped the truck and once again pointed the handgun at her mother, ordering her to get out.

"Are you going to kill me?" Harriet quietly asked as she obeyed.

With the dog at her side, Joan stood in front of her mother, looking directly in her eyes. After a few seconds, she answered, "I don't know yet."

Harriet cocked an eyebrow but said nothing.

"Head over there," Joan ordered. Her gun remained pointed at her mother. "There's a path that leads up the hill."

"Why do you want to go up there?"

"At the top, there's a waterfall. It's stunning."

"How do you know that?"

"After you left me for dead twelve years ago, this was the first place that Molly and I camped after I fled Wisconsin. I found it by chance."

"This is a very isolated, rugged area."

"That's very true. I've been here many times since then. Watching the water rush down the rocky bluff is mesmerizing—almost spiritual. The waterfall actually sparkles on its way down. It's a stunning sight."

"Sounds nice, I guess."

"Yes, and it's hard to hate when you see such stunning natural beauty."

Harriet started toward the path, saying nothing in response to her daughter's last comment.

The hour-long hike over the treacherous rocky terrain and up to the top of the hill took well over an hour. The dog was panting heavily as they reached the top, and Joan knelt down to pet her. The hike had been difficult for the old dog, and Joan was concerned. She was unconcerned, however, about her mother's labored breathing.

The dog's panting soon returned to normal, and Joan stood up. Pointing toward the waterfall, she said, "Stunning. And listen to its roar. It almost seems alive. Some say that waterfalls have mystical powers, and that might be true. They always seem to calm me, helping me to see things clearer. Isn't the waterfall beautiful, Mother?"

Harriet stared at her daughter. She neither spoke nor looked at the waterfall.

Joan watched the waterfall as it tumbled over the jagged ledge and noisily plunged into a small, rocky lake at the bottom. A swirling mist marked where the two became one.

After several minutes, Harriet finally spoke. "I'm so sorry for everything. I know that I wasn't a good parent. But you need to understand that I didn't know how to be. My parents were vile. However, I *tried* to make a good life for us, a perfect life."

"I know that you tried."

Joan walked closer to her mother, noticing how old and worn out she now seemed. She wondered if the demon had departed. Joan's resolve softened slightly, and she cringed thinking about her mother's horrific childhood.

However, Joan believed that her mother was guilty of much evil herself. She also believed the evil in her family had flowed from one generation to the next—from her grandparents to her mother and then to her. Joan was determined to permanently stop the evil. It was the only way to keep her daughter safe, she believed.

"Mother, would you have really killed Chloe?"

"No, I only wanted to get to know her."

"The sky's so blue today—no clouds hiding its beauty. It's a good day for the truth, Mother."

Harriet gazed up at the sky only briefly. *The truth had never served me well*, she thought.

"Over the years, did you kill any of the young girls that you picked up and beat?"

"No, never. I needed to vent my rage at times, though. Rage always built up inside me—over my job, my lovers, my neighbors—even sometimes, just over traffic. But I was determined not to turn my rage against you. I didn't want to be like my parents.

So I picked up a wayward teen from time to time and slapped them around a bit. That must make me sound like a monster, but it was my way of keeping you safe."

Harriet looked at her daughter, trying to gauge the effect of her confession.

Joan walked over to a nearby large rock and waved her mother over. The two women sat on the rock, and Joan embraced her mother, dropping her gun on the ground.

Harriet quietly whispered to her daughter, "Is there any way that you can forgive me?"

Joan hugged her mother again and said, "I forgive you."

Joan rose, turned, and walked over to the dog. The dog's eyes locked on Harriet.

"My dear, dear daughter," Harriet said, now standing and pointing the gun at Joan's back.

Joan turned around, unsurprised by the sight of her mother holding the gun.

"I lied." Harriet's voice and demeanor were eerily calm.

"About what?"

"About everything. Confessing or not confessing my sins won't save me. I'm not asking for absolution. Oh, dear Joan, I had worked so hard to create a perfect life for you—something that I never had. Your murder was my only sin that truly horrified me. It destroyed me."

Joan stared at her mother but said nothing.

"I tried to pay my penance for it. I lived in an ugly room in a mental institution for twelve years. But you were *not* really dead, my dear. Oh boy, what a surprise that was to me. How the hell are you alive?"

Joan didn't answer.

Harriet glared at her daughter for a moment before continuing her rant. "You let me think for twelve years that I had murdered you! And you know what was even worse? Your audacity to show up at the mental institution and offer your forgiveness to me. Oh please, you should have asked for my forgiveness. So, sweetie pie, I'll get my revenge. After I kill you and that damn dog, I'm going kill your sweet Chloe. She looks too damn much like my mother anyhow."

Joan remained silent.

"I had planned to let you and Edith live with the pain of Chloe's death, with the pain of knowing that you failed to protect her. Oh well, plans don't always work out. But you'll die knowing that your dear Chloe is next. That might be even better!"

Laughing, Harriet pulled the trigger, and then she pulled the trigger again and again. But nothing happened; no bullets discharged. Confused, Harriet looked down at the handgun and then up at her daughter, quickly realizing that she had been tricked. Her anger was evident as she threw the gun to the ground and walked toward Joan.

The dog took a few steps toward Harriet and growled. It was a low, guttural growl, and it brought Harriet to a stop. She took several steps backward until her feet were on the very edge of the rocky cliff.

Joan inched over to a thicket of trees. As she held onto a tree branch with one hand, she held her other hand out to her mother. "Mother, you're too close to the edge. Take my hand before you fall."

Harriet did not reach for it.

"The ground looks unstable there, Mother. Please take my hand."

"Why are you trying to save me?"

"I've already told you. There's no room for hate out here amongst such beauty."

"Bullshit. Hate is everywhere."

"Only if you choose to hate. Mother, please grab my hand."

Joan continued to hold her hand out. But Harriet only

laughed. Suddenly, the ground crumbled under her feet, and she plunged down the steep 60-foot cliff, crashing on the jagged boulders below.

Joan screamed. Holding tightly onto the branch, she cautiously peered over the edge, knowing that her mother could *not* have survived such a plunge. She muffled another scream as she saw her mother's lifeless body lying twisted among the boulders that lined the edge of the lake below.

As she watched, a ghostly silhouette rose from her mother's body and drifted silently into the mist. It was her mother's soul—of this, she was sure. Stunned by what she witnessed, Joan said a silent prayer, hoping that the waterfall's mystical powers could cleanse the evil from her mother's soul.

Joan picked up the handgun, and with the dog following, she hiked down the hill to the pickup truck. They drove off, unsure of their next destination and unaware that a shadowy figure had emerged from the mist.

Two days later, Joan and the dog were sitting on the sandy shore of a lake somewhere in Minnesota. Much to Joan's surprise, the old man she had met a while back in Oregon sat down next to her. His fishing cap was still covered in silver fishing lure, and the lures jingled and shimmered in the sunlight.

"It looks like a good day for fishing," he said.

"My soon-to-be ex-husband, Frank, would have said that any day is a good day for fishing."

The old man laughed. "He sounds like a smart guy."

"We met once before. It was a while back in Oregon. You gave me some advice."

"I hope that the advice worked out for you."

Joan looked over at him, trying to decide if the advice had worked out for her.

"It did somewhat, I suppose. You said that I needed to finish one chapter in my life before starting the next. I've tied up some loose ends, so to speak, but I still don't seem able to start the next chapter in my life. I feel stuck. I don't know how to move on."

"Maybe there's more to take care of."

"What do you mean?"

"Give me an example of when you ended something and successfully started over?"

"Okay, what pops into my mind is that when I was first married, I had an awful job as a secretary. Although the actual work wasn't horrible, my boss was. She was very Machiavellian. If advantageous to her, she didn't hesitate to sink her manicured fingernails into someone's back."

"Please explain a little more."

The old man's voice was gentle, and Joan was surprised at how comfortable she felt talking with this shimmering old man. Or was it just that his fishing cap shimmered, Joan wondered.

"To be blunt, my boss was unscrupulous and dishonest. She spoke in this sweet, phony voice. It was so annoying. Anyhow, she never let the rules, or for that matter legality, get in her way. At a certain point, I could no longer exist in such a toxic environment, and I walked out one day. I never regretted my decision to quit. I didn't realize it until years later, but my boss reminded me of my mother."

Joan was quiet for a couple of seconds and then added, "The only thing that worried me at the time was money. My husband was just starting out after law school, and we didn't have a lot of money. But he was wonderful and told me not to worry about money. We managed okay, and eventually, I found another job."

"What's different this time?"

"I have some regrets."

"Why?"

"Because this time, I deeply hurt the people that I care about. I left without any sort of explanation, and that's unforgivable."

"Most things are forgivable."

"I hope so."

"You need to ask for forgiveness, Joan. That's the only way you'll be able to move on."

"Yes, you're probably right."

Joan looked closely at the old man next to her. "Are you a shrink? I'm opening up to you, and I don't easily do that."

The old man laughed. "No, I'm not a shrink. I was a pastor in Wisconsin at one time . . . and also a cook. My pastor gig paid almost nothing. So, I ran a small local diner. Not to brag, but my diner offered the best Friday night fish fry in the area."

This time, it was Joan's turn to laugh.

"That's saying a lot because Wisconsinites love their Friday night fish fries. My husband would have loved to try your fish fry. He was the real cook in our family. I could make a decent meal, I guess. But he could *really* cook."

Joan sighed deeply as she thought back to earlier times. "Frank said that he learned how to cook from his Ma, as he called her. I thought that was so cute. He called his folks Ma and Pa. Whereas I always called my mother, well, Mother. I think that my mother was jealous of how normal and happy my in-laws were."

"What were your in-laws like?"

"My mother-in-law was a great cook. She only needed salt and pepper, potatoes, and a chicken to create the best Sunday dinner in the world. My father-in-law was a quiet man but the salt of the earth. My husband, Frank, would say that his Pa didn't need words to say *I love you*. He said it through his actions. Oh, and the cookie jar was always full when the grandkids visited."

"They sound like good people."

"Yes, absolutely. My in-laws were good, decent family people. I really cared about them. They loved their kids and grandkids. Frank said that he could always count on his folks."

Joan went quiet. She felt guilty. She had deserted her family, something her in-laws would never have done.

Sensing her pain, the old man tried to change the subject. "It's too bad that my diner is closed now. It's been closed for about twelve years."

"That's really sad. Food brings people together. My in-laws had a sign in their kitchen that said something like: Cook, Sing, Laugh."

"Good advice."

"My in-laws are no longer alive. I always wished that my daughter had known them. But they died before she was born."

"How did they die?"

"They died from carbon monoxide poisoning. They had a gas furnace, and apparently, the vent or flue or something was damaged. Frank was surprised because his father was usually very meticulous about such things."

Joan's mouth dropped open. A sudden thought came to her. "My god, Mother, you murdered them."

"What?" The old man was distracted for a moment as he noticed a dark, shadowy figure forming on the other side of the lake.

"Do you think that God forgives everyone?"

"Yes, Joan, I believe that God forgives. But one must still atone for their sins. I don't mean fire and brimstone but at least an acknowledgement. Admitting one's sins allows healing to begin, and healing is available to all of God's children—whether it's in this life, in Heaven, or in future lives. If a soul wishes, it's always possible to be forgiven, to heal, and to evolve into a more enlightened self."

"That's a nice thought." Joan hoped that her mother would seek forgiveness and healing on the other side.

The old man turned his attention again to the other side of the lake.

Joan shivered suddenly and said, "I should probably hit the road again. I feel a little nervous for some reason. However, it was nice running into you—for the second time."

"Okay, but this is the third time that we met, not the second. Don't you remember the first time?"

"Where was the first time?"

"At the Mississippi River."

Trying to remember, Joan looked down at the sand. When she looked back up, the old man was gone. Joan stood up to get a better view of the area; however, he was nowhere to be seen.

Joan had remembered their first meeting and was sorry that he disappeared. She wanted to thank him. She closed her eyes, and much like watching a movie, her first meeting with him played in her memory.

~

Parked next to the Mississippi River, Joan thought about how everything had gone horribly that day. The exorcism hadn't happened, and of course, her mother had tried to kill her. Horrible was an understatement, she knew.

But now, an hour or so after her near death, Joan's earlier rage was gone. Instead, she felt an overwhelming sense of hopelessness. And she felt empty, dead inside. She wanted to escape her life—permanently.

So in the darkness of the night, Joan made a sudden decision. She drove her car into the roaring, fierce Mississippi River. Its banks were overflowing from the recent, heavy rains. No turning back now, she thought.

But the puppy was still with her, and it kept looking at her with a puzzled look.

"Oh crap!" Joan said to the puppy. "I can't let you die."

Joan forced the car door open, and she swam out of the car, taking the puppy with her. But Joan struggled against the fierce, raging currents. Despite being a good swimmer, the currents were too much for her. Joan quickly panicked and yelled, "God, please help!"

Out of nowhere, Joan saw an old man running toward the river. The silver lures on his fishing cap bounced about as he ran, and Joan was strangely comforted by the jingling, shimmering lures.

"Hold on there," he yelled. "I'm coming to help."

He had a rope with him, which he hurriedly tied around a nearby tree. Holding onto the end of the rope, he leaped into the cold river. Effortlessly swimming over to Joan and the puppy, he said, "Take the rope and pull yourself to safety. I'll be right behind you with the pup."

Joan obeyed, and soon she was safe on the river's edge. The man was only moments behind her, and he quickly joined Joan with the pup as promised, holding her soaked but intact purse as well.

"Thank you," Joan said as she hugged him.

"Not a problem, dear. Are you okay?"

"Yes. I'm so lucky that you came to my rescue. This is the second time tonight that I've been rescued. I guess God doesn't want me yet, eh?"

"Nope." The old man laughed and handed the puppy and purse over to Joan.

"I'm Joan, and the pup is Molly. What's your name?"

"They call me Pastor Bob. I'm the pastor at a small church north of Rhinelander."

"Thank you so much again for saving us," Joan said. She then inexplicably confessed, "I had planned to kill myself, but I just couldn't take the pup with me. It wasn't right."

"I know, dear. Please promise me that you'll drive up to my church sometime. I think that you'll like it."

"I promise," Joan said, not meaning it.

"Now head over to the road. You'll need to catch a ride. Unfortunately, I can't give you a lift."

Joan was confused by that statement, but she obeyed again and walked to the road. She looked back at the river, but Pastor Bob was nowhere to be seen.

∼

Joan looked at her dog and asked, "Do you think there's a reason that I keep bumping into Pastor Bob?" The dog gave a soft bark in response.

"Should we go find his church, Molly?" The dog barked again, wagged his tail, and ran toward Joan's truck.

Before driving out of Minnesota, Joan stopped at a local post office and mailed a large envelope via overnight delivery. She then called Edith.

Chapter 14

After yet another day of questioning by the police, Frank was finally home. He was worn out, and although he hadn't seen Chloe or the other two women since the previous day, Frank assumed that they had been questioned again as well. Each had answered more questions than they could fathom over the last few days.

However, there were only two questions that the police kept re-asking: Who was the person buried under the lilac bushes? And why did Harriet want to harm her own granddaughter?

With regard to the body under the lilac bushes, all truthfully and repeatedly answered that they didn't know. Edith, however, shared Joan's childhood memory with the police, allowing them to narrow down the general timeframe of the homicide. Although the police were running through old missing person cases, they hadn't yet identified the victim.

However, concerning the other often-asked question, the answers provided to the police were less forthright. As they sat at Frank's table, sipped beer, and talked on that first morning after the incident at the cabin, Frank shared an opinion. Namely,

Never Tell Chloe

the police would *not* accept a demon named Abigail as a likely suspect. He suggested that it was best to avoid the topic entirely. Each agreed to stick with a simpler answer: *Harriet was crazy*.

Frank's second suggestion to the three women on that first morning was briefer: Don't out and out lie to the police—but don't volunteer any details. They all agreed not to mention that Joan had also been at the cabin.

Frank's third and final suggestion on that morning was the briefest: Don't panic. Frank assured the others that the police would, most likely, consider them victims and not suspects.

And this proved true. The police had since provided Frank and the others with two pieces of information. First, Chloe's young neighbor had recovered sufficiently at the hospital to identify Harriet as her sole assailant. Chloe was cleared of any involvement.

Second, the coroner confirmed that the body buried under the lilac bushes had died several decades prior. Since Harriet owned the house during that timeframe, she was the main suspect in the homicide. Fortunately, the police seemed more interested in identifying the body than the person who tried digging it up.

The police's efforts now seemed primarily focused on locating Harriet, and this worried Frank. He clung to the hope that Joan had *disposed of* her mother by now.

Frank stopped at his mailbox as he entered his condo building, discovering that he had received a large envelope. He noticed that the envelope had a Minnesota postmark on it but no return address. Once inside, Frank sat at his kitchen table and opened the envelope. Inside were three items: signed divorce papers, a short letter, and a news clipping.

Dear Frank:

I'm truly sorry for the pain that I have caused you and Chloe.

I've enclosed a signed set of divorce papers. However, I hired an attorney to revise the papers that you gave me. The settlement agreement you drew up was much too generous. I shouldn't get half of everything. It's not right. After all, I abandoned you and Chloe.

I only want a small divorce settlement—just enough to buy a little house or cabin somewhere for Molly and me. She deserves a quieter life now that she is getting older. She has earned it. Without this sweet dog at my side, I wouldn't have made it through these last twelve years. I honestly feel that Molly is an angel who was sent to help me.

But the most important thing to know is this: Mother is dead. I've enclosed a news article that relates to this. I have also called Aunt Edith and explained what happened. If you decide that you want to know the details, I've asked her to share them with you. It's a tough subject for me to talk about. Despite everything, she was still my mother. So please forgive me, but I simply cannot describe the events a second time.

Will you please, however, let Chloe know that I'm not a monster like her grandmother?

If you're wondering, I never actually fired the gun that you saw in my truck. In fact, I have since disassembled it and tossed the pieces into several different lakes. No one else will ever be tempted by it.

Once I find a place to settle, I'll let you and Chloe know.

And if the two of you are willing, I would like to meet and explain some things.

On that awful night twelve years ago, I gained my freedom. But it came at a cost, and that cost was paid by you and Chloe.

I'm so very, very sorry.
I only wish the best for you and Chloe.

Joan

~

BODY OF ELDERLY WOMAN FOUND BY HIKER

The body of an unknown elderly woman was found yesterday by a local hiker. The hiker informed authorities that while he was hiking, he heard a laugh and looked up. At the top of a nearby cliff, he saw a woman standing. He next heard a scream and saw the woman fall. The hiker stated that it took him roughly 30 minutes to reach the woman. Upon reaching the body, it was apparent to him that the elderly woman had not survived the fall. Due to the lack of cellphone reception in the area, the hiker walked several hours before he could call the authorities. The hiker also stated that he did not see anyone else on the cliff and that the woman appeared to be alone. Pending a final determination by the coroner, the police are treating the death as accidental. If anyone knows the identity of the elderly woman, please contact the authorities.

~

Frank read the news article several times.

"Chloe's finally safe," he said out loud, cracking a smile.

Frank felt that it shouldn't take the South Dakota authorities very long to match up their unidentified body to the all-points police bulletin issued on Harriet. And as soon as the police in Wisconsin were notified that their sole suspect was dead, Frank felt that the investigation would be wrapped up quickly.

However, as a long-time attorney, Frank understood police procedures. He realized that the police's first step would involve comparing Harriet's fingerprints and DNA against the evidence found at the various crime scenes, including that found with the body under the lilac bushes. But Frank knew that this step would confirm Harriet as the only possible suspect, bringing the investigation to an end.

After all, he thought—*you can't arrest someone who's dead.*

Chapter 15

Joan pointed her truck in the general direction of Rhinelander, certain that she would somehow be guided to the church. After several hours of driving, Joan turned into the parking lot of an old, historic church just north of Rhinelander. It sat on the edge of a quaint little village, whose welcome sign listed the population not by a numerical count but only as *Happy*. Joan had smiled at the sign as she drove by it.

Joan and the dog exited the pickup truck, taking in the peaceful scenery. The dog happily pranced around the edge of the parking lot, finding just the perfect spot to water the grass, as one might say.

"Yoo-hoo," an elderly woman yelled from the church's doorway.

Joan walked closer to the elderly woman and said, "Hello, I hope that you can help me. I'm looking for Pastor Bob's church."

"You've found it, dear."

"Oh, that's wonderful. Pastor Bob suggested that I visit his church. My name's Joan."

"My name is Lizzie. Did Pastor Bob mention me? I've been

telling people that you would be coming, but everyone thinks that I'm senile."

"I don't understand. Did Pastor Bob phone you today?"

"Oh no, of course not. Pastor Bob has been dead for about twelve years now. He was at a religious conference in La Crosse a little more than twelve years ago. Sadly, he had a heart attack there and passed away. We all really miss him. He was a very special person."

"Pastor Bob is dead? If that's true, how did you know that I was coming?" Joan felt that Lizzie might be as confused as apparently *everyone* thought.

Seeing Joan's confusion, Lizzie pulled a photo out of her billfold and handed it to Joan. She then asked, "This is Pastor Bob. Is this who you met?"

Joan looked closely at the photo, realizing that it was indeed a photo of the nice old man with whom she had talked several times. She handed the photo back to Lizzie and calmly answered, "Yes."

"Pastor Bob pops into my dreams from time to time, and he has been assuring me that one day we would have a new pastor. It's so very hard to attract pastors to these little out-of-the-way churches, you know."

"I'm sorry, but I'm not a pastor."

"Pastor Bob said that a woman with a friendly dog would show up one day, and she would make a wonderful pastor. He said to watch for the woman driving a pickup truck."

"I'm very sorry to hear that you can't recruit a pastor. This looks like a really charming church, but I'm not a pastor."

"Pastor Bob would never lie."

"Hopefully, you'll find a pastor soon. Is there a motel around here?"

"No, but you're welcomed to spend the night in the church."

"Are you sure that's okay?"

"Of course, it's okay. After all, I am the chairwoman of the church's governing board. What I say pretty much goes."

"Thank you."

"The keys are in the kitchen on the lower level. Please lock up the church after I leave. It's very sad, but we need to lock the church up at sundown these days. We get a lot of tourists in the Northwoods, and some seem intent on vandalizing old churches. There's a room with a bed next to the kitchen. Pastor Bob used to let wayward souls stay at the church from time to time."

"Wow, that was a kind thing for him to do."

"Oh, and there's some food left over from our Sunday potluck yesterday in the icebox. Sorry, I mean refrigerator. Old habits, you know. I have to go now. I need to get supper on the table for my husband. He should be home from fishing by now. Don't forget to lock up."

"I won't."

"It's nice to have you here. I'll bring some of the others around to meet you tomorrow."

Joan watched Lizzie drive off. "Okay, Molly, let's get our stuff from the truck so we can lock up and settle in for the night. We need to get some rest before *the meet and greet* tomorrow."

After carrying in a rucksack stuffed with their necessities, Joan discovered a container of leftover hamburger and macaroni hotdish in the *icebox*. After sharing the hotdish with the dog, Joan was ready to sleep. As she settled in bed, Joan jumped at the sound of her cell phone ringing.

It was her divorce attorney, and Joan was pleased to find out the hearing to finalize the divorce could be scheduled sooner than expected. The judge had surprisingly waived the mandatory 90-day waiting period. And as if by divine luck, the judge had an opening on his calendar in just a few days.

After ending the call, Joan quietly said out loud, "Thank

goodness. Once the divorce is over, I can finally start the next chapter in my life."

Suddenly, the lights in the church started to flicker on and off.

"If that's you, Pastor Bob, I have *not* forgotten about explaining things to Frank and Chloe and asking for their forgiveness."

The lights stopped flickering.

"However, Pastor Bob, I don't understand this pastor thing. What is that all about?"

No answer was forthcoming. The lights didn't flicker. Pastor Bob didn't appear. Joan shook her head and said, "Okay, if you don't want to answer, that's fine. I'm going to sleep now."

True to her word, the next morning, Lizzie stopped by the church with three other members of the church board—Gus, Cora, and Mildred. Although none of the board members appeared under sixty years old to Joan, all seemed energetic and happy. After Lizzie made the introductions, she led the way to a small conference room, which contained a long, lunchroom-style table and several folding chairs.

After everyone sat, the interrogation started. Or at least, that was what it felt like to Joan.

"Joan, did you really talk to Pastor Bob?" Gus asked.

"Yes, I actually met him three times."

"You realized that Pastor Bob has passed over, correct?" Cora asked.

"Yes, I do."

"Are you saying that Pastor Bob sent you here to be our new pastor?" Mildred asked.

"No, I'm not. I'm not a pastor. As I have told Lizzie, Pastor Bob only suggested that I visit his church."

"I have told them that," Lizzie pointedly said. "But how can you explain that both you and I have been contacted by Pastor Bob."

"I cannot explain it, but I think that Pastor Bob has been trying to help me. The first time that I met him was about twelve years ago. He jumped into the Mississippi River and saved us from drowning. That is, he saved my dog and me from drowning."

Everyone was quiet for a moment, and then Joan quietly added, "I had tried to kill myself. If not for Pastor Bob, I would have died. The other two times that I encountered Pastor Bob were more recent."

"Jumping in to save you sounds like something that Pastor Bob would do," Gus said. "And I can understand why he would have sent you here. Pastor Bob always said that our quaint little church is like a magnet for lost souls. He preached that God loves everyone—regardless of the baggage that they carry around. Pastor Bob said that there are times when people just need a quiet place to think and shed some of their worries."

"I agree," Cora added. "Pastor Bob would help anyone, but there's a problem, however. Pastor Bob couldn't swim."

"Oh, that's right," Mildred said. "When did you say that he saved you?"

"He saved me from drowning about twelve years ago. It was early spring."

"Hmm, Pastor Bob died just before Valentine's Day twelve years ago," Lizzie said. "I remember that because the church was planning a Valentine's Day party for the young folks."

"Yes, that's true. Pastor Bob would have already died when he saved you," Gus said. "That's very interesting."

"Since Pastor Bob sent you here, then you're welcome to stay as long as you want," Cora said. "Isn't that right, everyone?"

"Of course," all of the board members said in unison.

"Thank you, but I have a question. All of you accept that Pastor Bob, your deceased pastor, sent me here?"

"I do," Gus said.

Cora and Mildred nodded their heads in agreement with Gus.

"As do I," Lizzie added. "I've been telling them for a long time about my dreams. Although they thought that I was a little crazy, the fact that you have finally arrived proves that Pastor Bob has been visiting me. And, of course, you are exactly like I described."

"But I'm not a pastor."

"That's true, I guess. But if Pastor Bob said that a pastor will show up, then one will," Lizzie said. "I believed in God and in Pastor Bob."

"Thank you again. I'm going to take you up on the kind offer and stay a little while longer in the church. However, I have an appointment in Madison on Friday. If it's okay, I would like to come back up here afterwards to attend the Sunday service."

"That would be wonderful," Lizzie said, genuinely happy to hear Joan's plan to return.

"Oh, you'll need to bring a dish to pass," Mildred said. "We always have a potluck after the service."

"I'll be happy to bring a dish." Joan smiled, feeling strangely drawn to this small group of churchy folks as well as to the church itself.

A few minutes after the others left, Joan decided to take the dog on a walk. She wanted to see more of the village. But after only a block or so, the dog stopped suddenly and growled.

Joan scanned the area but noticed nothing of a concerning nature. Despite an uneasy feeling, Joan and the dog continued on their walk. Her uneasiness was quickly eased by the calming effect of the quaint village. At the far end of the village, Joan stopped at an empty lot.

"Hi, there," Gus said, walking up behind Joan. She jumped at the unexpected sound of his voice.

"Hi, Gus. I didn't hear you approach."

Never Tell Chloe

"I didn't mean to scare you, but I wanted to talk to you alone."

"Really? Why?"

"This empty lot was where Pastor Bob's diner stood. It burned down on the night that he left."

"I'm sorry to hear that. Pastor Bob bragged that he served the best Friday night fish fry in the area."

"Oh, that wasn't bragging, Joan. It was the truth."

"What did you want to talk to me about? I'm not a pastor, you know."

"I understand, but before Pastor Bob left here twelve years ago, he stopped by my house. It was late, and he had just closed up the diner. You see, Pastor Bob and I were good friends. I thought that I knew him pretty well. However, he shared something with me that night. Something that I never knew or could have guessed. It's something that I have never repeated."

"I'm not sure why you are telling me this, Gus."

"Let's sit over there on the bench, and I will explain why."

"Why is there a bench in an empty lot?"

"Our church just started to transform this lot into a park. It will be named after Pastor Bob. Since he virtually had no assets when he died, the bank took ownership of the lot to cover his outstanding loan. It took quite a while to raise funds to buy it back from the bank."

"Wow, that's a nice thing to do. He must have been really loved by everyone."

"He was," Gus agreed as they sat. "Pastor Bob helped most of us in one way or another. Quite a few of us church members have checkered pasts, I guess. When I met Pastor Bob, I was an alcoholic. Lizzie, believe it or not, was a battered wife—very meek. However, one day she shot her first husband in self-defense and fled. She found her way here quite by accident. Her first husband, thankfully, was only very slightly injured. Pastor

Bob sorted out the legal issues, and Lizzie has been here ever since. Cora was a drug addict, and Mildred had served time for embezzlement. Pastor Bob saved all of us in one way or another. He saved a lot of other folks as well. Some stayed here; some moved on."

"Pastor Bob sounds like a saint."

"We thought so, and he was in a way. But Pastor Bob always said that everyone has regrets and secrets and that he was no exception."

"What were his regrets and secrets?"

"Pastor Bob wasn't at a convention twelve years ago. It was a cover story that he told everyone. On the night that he left, Pastor Bob told me that he had a child."

"Really?"

"Yes, many years ago, he was in the Navy and stationed in Maine. Apparently, that was when he became involved with a woman. He described the woman as beautiful, wild, and a little scary. However, she became pregnant, and much to his regret, Pastor Bob asked her to get an abortion."

"Wow, that surprises me."

"It surprised me too. But Pastor Bob regretted suggesting an abortion at once and returned to the young woman's apartment a few days later. Although he didn't plan to marry her, Bob wanted to pay child support and be a part of his baby's life. However, the woman had vanished, and he had no way to contact her. Unfortunately, he didn't see nor hear from the woman for well over a year. Then one day, a photo of her and the baby came in the mail."

"What happened? Did he do right by the baby?"

"He wasn't able to do so. The envelope didn't have a return address. It only had a postmark from Madison, Wisconsin. When Pastor Bob completed his tour of duty in the Navy a few months later, he came to Wisconsin. He hoped against all odds that he could find his child."

"Did he find her?"

"I will get to that. As luck had it, Bob ended up sitting in one of our church pews, praying for help. At the time, the church had an elderly pastor by the name of Ralph. Oh, I should have mentioned that Bob wasn't a pastor yet. In fact, it wasn't even a career field that he considered up to that point in his life."

Still confused as to why she was being told this story, Joan looked closely at Gus. She was surprised that Gus was looking just as closely at her.

"Pastor Ralph asked Bob to help out at the church. One thing led to another, and after Pastor Ralph retired, Bob took over as pastor. I believe the reason that Pastor Bob could connect with lost souls because he was one himself."

"Pastor Bob was a lost soul?"

"Well, that's how Pastor Bob described himself to me that night. He had a lifelong regret—a lifelong secret. A hole in his heart, I guess. He had always wished and prayed that he could meet his daughter. However, although he tried, he never found her. His best guess was that the woman had assumed a new name, making it impossible to find her."

"I'm so sorry to hear that he never found his daughter."

"He was going to fix things. That's what he said that night. You see, Pastor Bob had started having dreams about his daughter. He believed that she was in danger and needed him."

"Based on his dreams only?"

"Yes, and I tried to reason with him, telling him that they were only dreams. However, Pastor Bob insisted that he couldn't let his daughter down again. So that night, he drove off. A few hours after he left, someone saw flames from his diner. Apparently, he had forgotten to turn off one of the burners on the stove. As a result, a pan overheated, and the diner burned to the ground."

"Wow, that's awful. Was Pastor Bob able to find his daughter?"

"I don't know. I tried calling him several times after the fire, but I only got his voice mail. I didn't understand why he failed to call back until a few days later when I received a call from the police. They had found him in his car next to the Mississippi River. Bob had died from a heart attack."

"That's so sad. I hope that Pastor Bob was able to find his daughter before he died."

"I can't shake the feeling that you might be his daughter. Why else would his spirit hang around the Mississippi River after he died—if not to save his daughter? You sort of look like him also; you have his smile. I hope that I don't sound crazy. Do you know who your father is?"

"No, I don't. My mother refused to tell me." *And I was too afraid of her to ask more than once,* Joan thought.

"Bob was my friend, and I planned to keep his secret for the rest of my life until I heard your story and your name."

Gus eyed Joan closely again, and in a quiet voice, he said, "I volunteered to bring him home after his death, and I found a photo of the woman and the baby in his belongings."

Gus pulled the photo out of his shirt pocket and handed it to Joan. "I think that you should have it." Joan stared at the photo but said nothing.

Gus got up, but before walking away, he said, "If you decide to stay, there's a small house for sale right down the street. The owner is moving to be near her grandchildren. The price is cheap, and although the house is old, it's livable. I'm the real estate agent, and I can handle things for you."

As she watched Gus walk away, Joan struggled to breathe for a few moments. The photo was of her mother and a baby. On the back of the photo were two sentences—*This is Joan, your daughter. You will never find her.*

After regaining her composure, Joan and the dog started walking back to the church. Midway, a cold wind rushed past them. Despite the summer heat, Joan shivered, and the dog growled again. What Gladys had warned about suddenly rushed back to her: *The possessed can be killed but not the demon.*

"Oh crap, Abigail is back." With her dog following, Joan hurried to the church.

Not knowing how to deal with the story of Pastor Bob nor the return of Abigail, she avoided thinking of either. Instead, Joan spent the next several days hiking in the woods, chatting with the locals, and enjoying a few days in denial. However, Joan made one very important decision during her period of denial. Joan felt at peace in this little village, and she decided to buy the old house. She was staying.

Chapter 16

The hearing at the courthouse was at nine o'clock on Friday morning, and Joan was determined not to be late for it. So, with an abundance of caution in mind, Joan decided to leave for Madison on Thursday afternoon rather than early Friday morning.

Since Gus had agreed to take care of the dog while she was gone, Joan was alone in her pickup truck and alone with her thoughts. She thought about the last twelve years—about how she had healed and about who she had hurt. Joan wanted to mend fences with Chloe and Frank.

She also wanted to finally start the next chapter of her life. Before that could happen, however, she knew that there were three things left to do: finalize the divorce, ask for forgiveness, and get rid of Abigail—permanently.

It took her roughly four hours to reach Madison, and as soon as she did, Joan checked into a downtown hotel near the courthouse. She set her alarm clock and tried to sleep. But she was too anxious to do so. She couldn't escape thinking about three things: Tomorrow, her marriage would officially end.

Tomorrow, she would speak with Frank and Chloe. Tomorrow, she would ask for their forgiveness.

Joan also felt an ominous darkness hovering close by. As it had over the last several days, the darkness called out to her, shrouding its wickedness behind whispered words of comfort. Joan ignored the whispers of the darkness, refusing to give it power over her and silently vowing to force it back to hell. As the sun rose, Joan was grateful that the morning light drove the darkness back into the shadows, freeing her to face events of the new day.

She checked out of the hotel early and walked over to the courthouse. After the divorce hearing ended, Joan ran down the courthouse steps to catch up with Frank.

"Frank," Joan yelled.

"Yes, Joan?" Frank stopped on the steps.

"I want to thank you for the generous settlement. You gave me much more than I asked for."

"Like I said to the judge, I now understand why you needed to leave. I'm sorry that I didn't recognize your unhappiness back then. I was so wrapped up in my career that I ignored my family. I even failed to recognize the danger that my family was in back then."

"Frank, you were a wonderful husband. You don't need to apologize. Like they say, it wasn't you—it was me. I would like to talk with you and Chloe. I want to explain some stuff and to ask for your forgiveness."

"Joan, I forgive you without hesitation. You don't need to explain anything more to me. After everything that I've learned about and experienced lately, I understand why you left. Yes, I wish that you had let us know that you weren't dead. However, I also understand why that was difficult for you to do. And frankly, I owe you a huge debt of gratitude. You came back to protect our daughter. At the end of the day, that's all that matters to me."

Joan was finding it difficult to hold back her tears.

"Please forgive yourself, Joan."

"I had hoped that Chloe would be here also." Joan raised her eyebrows, silently asking where she was.

"Chloe loves you but isn't ready to meet with you yet. A lot has happened, to say the least."

Joan glanced away to hide her tears.

"Take care of yourself, Joan," Frank said as he walked away.

Although disappointed that Chloe hadn't shown, Joan was relieved as well. She had feared that she wouldn't find the right words to use and worried that the conversation would never rise above small talk. She still sensed, however, that it was important to reach out to her daughter in some way.

She dried her tears and stepped into a nearby drug store to purchase a pad of paper, envelopes, and postage stamps. Joan then walked over to a coffee shop, ordered a strong cup of coffee, and wrote a letter to her daughter. On paper, Joan felt unshackled from the limitations of nervous chatter.

Dear Chloe,

Your father said that you need time before meeting with me. I understand and will respect your wishes about if or when you want to meet.

However, I feel that it is as important for you to know my story as it is for me to share it.

I know that Aunt Edith shared the events of twelve years ago with you. However, some of my story was too painful for me to share with Aunt Edith. But I want to be fully honest with you, and this letter is my way of doing that. To do so, I need to start with that awful night twelve years ago.

After I dropped you off at home, I returned to the cabin. I still had the puppy with me. That silly puppy refused to get out of the car and go into the house with you. I had no choice but to take her along. She had stuck close to me all day. Molly somehow knew that I needed her. I strongly believe that animals are gifted with a sixth sense of some sort.

It must have been a shock when you saw me (and the dog) at the cabin the other week. The dog, by the way, is Molly. She's still the sweetest dog that one could ever hope to find.

But getting back to my story, when I returned to the cabin, Mother and I continued to fight. We screamed ugly things at each other. I don't remember most of what was said, but everything said that night was full of hate and rage. What I do remember vividly is that Mother screamed over and over that she had sacrificed her entire life for me—that I owed her.

I never knew who my father was until recently. But that's a story for another time.

I was so angry at Mother that night. However, it was really more than that. All of my pent-up rage just poured out. I blamed her for my own unhappiness. I was sick of trying to be the perfect daughter in the fantasy world that she had created.

I could only wear what she deemed acceptable, only have friends that she picked out, and so on. All of my words, thoughts, dreams, and activities were carefully controlled by my mother. She even picked out who I dated—right up to your father.

Please don't think that I'm saying anything negative about your father. He is and always was a wonderful man. But although I cared for him, I never truly loved your father.

Some would say that she was just being a good mother, but it was darker than that. There was something evil in the air when I grew up. I didn't understand it as a child, but I sensed it regardless. Although she never beat me, Mother still completely controlled me, ruling my life like a wicked queen in a scary fairy tale. I was as much of a prisoner in my childhood home as my mother was in hers.

Throughout my life, I played the part of the perfect daughter, the perfect wife, and the perfect mother—forever under the watchful eyes of my mother. I was my mother's empty, lifeless puppet.

However, despite my mother's controlling influence, I have very fond memories of my life with your father and you, especially during our times at the cabin. I loved being out there. Things always seemed so peaceful and happy at the cabin.

Unfortunately, Mother started coming to the cabin at a certain point, perching herself on the porch, knitting and watching—always watching. After that, I just gave up on happiness. I functioned only as a walking imitation of a person. My words and actions seemed lifeless even to myself.

On that awful night twelve years ago, things went from bad to worse. It was as if the only feelings that I had were ugly and evil. If I had a gun in my hand that night, I would have killed Mother without a second thought. It's strange how quickly hate and evil took over me. I wholeheartedly believe that evil is contagious. Once it's out in the open, evil spreads quickly. It's like a plague that is hard to cure.

Mother became so enraged that she brutally beat me, hitting me with her bare fists and then with some type of heavy object. To this day, I only remember some of what happened next.

I remember the horrific pain, and I remember curling up in a ball on the floor, trying to shield myself from her rage. Eventually, she stopped and sat in a chair, telling me over and over that it was my fault that she had to beat me. Or rather, it was my fault that Abigail had to beat me.

I crawled outside of the cabin, and she followed me with a gun. And she then shot me. Fortunately, the bullet failed to cause any real damage. In old-time cowboy movies, they would say the bullet just grazed me. But let me tell you, there was still a lot of pain and blood.

Unfortunately, I passed out. When I started to regain consciousness, Mother was dragging me by my feet through the woods. Although I was barely conscious, I clearly remember my head bouncing along on the ground. It hurt like hell.

I also remember Mother's heavy panting. I always thought that it was due to her exertion, but I'm not sure anymore. The panting was more beast-like than human. It was a frightening sound.

The ground was only starting to thaw after the long winter. But Mother somehow dug a shallow grave, rolled me into it, and threw dirt over me. I cannot explain what it feels like to be buried and left for dead. For years, I woke up screaming.

I would have died that night except for Molly. Somehow, that silly puppy knew to quietly follow, wait until Mother left, and then quickly dig the dirt off of my face. I've never understood how a puppy knew to do this. However, I'm forever in Molly's debt. She's my angel.

But as I took my first gulp of air and spit the dirt out of my mouth, I didn't feel grateful to be alive. I didn't actually feel anything; I was numb. As you might guess, everything was out of focus to me that night.

So why didn't I just come forward back then and tell the police what had happened? I can't really answer this—maybe shock?

I got into the car with Molly, and I just drove away. I was only vaguely aware of where I was heading. Eventually, I got to the Mississippi River.

I sat there, staring at the raging river. I felt so hopeless, so drained. Any spark of life I had seemed to fade away, and I just drove into the freezing, raging river. As the car was filling up with water, Molly kept looking at me. She never made a sound and never panicked. I'm convinced that Molly knew that I wouldn't go through with it. I couldn't let her die.

I somehow forced the car door open and swam out of the car with the puppy under one arm. However, it was raining heavily, and the river currents were too strong for me. We would have drowned if not for an old man who jumped in and saved us. Strangely, he also thought to save my purse. His name was Pastor Bob.

Once back on solid land, I walked away with Molly and my soaked purse.

Eventually, a woman saw us as she was driving by, and she picked us up. She asked who I was, but I didn't answer. Assuming that I was a battered wife, she drove us to a woman's shelter, and I stayed there for a few days.

I had always kept a wad of money stashed in my purse. The money was a secret, a just-in-case sort of thing. It was the money that I would use whenever, or if ever, I found the courage to run away. I guess being buried and left for death has a way of giving you courage.

Basically, my story is this: I ran away.

I used part of the money to buy an old pickup truck with a camper on the back. Before I hit the road, however, I made sure you were safe. I hope that your father shared that with you.

I sold my paintings here or there and took odd jobs for cash. I felt free for the first time in my life.

Molly and I hiked the mountain trails in Vermont and jogged on the beaches of California. We camped all over the country. We breathed the fresh air, and slowly I started to heal. I went from being an empty caricature to an actual living person.

However, during all of the years that I was gone, I never forgot you nor your father. Both of you were in my thoughts every day. I did and still do love you, Chloe. I just didn't know how to be a mother.

You're probably wondering why I never called your father to let him know that I was alive. The simple truth is that I didn't know what to say. How could I explain that I had always desperately wanted to leave, that I was finally happy, and that I wasn't planning on returning?

I realize that sounds horrible, but the truth is I was too much of a coward to call.

A couple of weeks ago, I found myself in Albuquerque, and I walked into my Aunt Edith's art gallery. She didn't recognize me at first. However, to be fair, a reporter was there doing a news story on the gallery, and Aunt Edith was distracted. And in my blue jeans and t-shirt, I no longer looked like the preppy housewife that she had met years prior. The reporter clicked some pictures, and I did my best to stay out of the shots.

After the reporter left, I walked up to Aunt Edith and told her who I was. She almost fainted, but she was also happy to know that I was alive. Over the next couple of days, I told her about my journey of healing and that I wanted to let Mother know that I forgave her. Aunt Edith supported my decision.

And so I went to the mental institution where Mother was a patient. When I sat down in front of her, I could hardly breathe. Everything from that night came rushing back to me, and I almost got up and left. Somehow, I managed to tell her that I forgave her. I sat there for a long time, but Mother never said a word to me.

The next day, Aunt Edith received a phone call from the institution, saying that Mother had discharged herself. Edith was beside herself with fear, and she was right to be. I was also afraid.

My gut told me that you were in danger and needed to be protected from your grandmother. I had learned over these *many years to listen to my gut—to my intuition. If your gut tells you something, it's probably true.*

I took off in my pickup truck and headed straight to Wisconsin. However, once I got here, I wasn't sure what to do. I found your apartment, and I stood in the darkness, watching and praying that Mother would never come.

I was too scared to actually knock on your door. I didn't want to tell you that your grandmother planned to kill you, and I didn't want to explain why I was gone for twelve years. I was more afraid of knocking on your door than facing your grandmother.

Aunt Edith flew into Madison a few days later, and both of us decided to contact your father. He needed to know the truth about what happened twelve years ago, and he needed to know that you were in danger.

We wanted to spare you the ugly truth of what had happened back then. We all agreed that you shouldn't know that your grandmother had tried to kill me—or that she wanted to kill you. We also all agreed that you should never know any of my family's sordid history. We assumed that you would be better off not knowing anything.

However, we were wrong. It's always better to know the truth than to live with a lie. At some level, our souls recognize a lie.

Over these last weeks, you have proven yourself to be a brave and strong young woman. I wish that I had been as brave at your age. Back then, I never had the guts to stand up to my mother.

Unfortunately, I also never had the guts to just take a jump into the unknown and find my own path in life. I made the mistake of doing what was expected of me and not what I really wanted.

Please remember that it's your life to live. Find and walk your own path. Don't be afraid of failing. If plan A doesn't work out, try Plan B, and then Plan C.

I have one more thing to say before this letter gets any longer.

I was told once that forgiveness is a necessary part of healing. It's healing for the person who asks for forgiveness, and it's healing for the person who forgives.

So Chloe, I'm asking for your forgiveness. Whether you grant me this or not, please know that I love you.

With Love,
Mom

P.S. I have enclosed my new address and phone number. You will always be welcome.

Chapter 17

After mailing the letter, Joan had one more thing to handle, and that was Abigail. Hoping for advice, Joan called her Aunt Edith, discovering that both she and Gladys were at a resort in Arizona for the next two weeks. Not wanting to spoil their much-earned vacation, Joan kept the call short, assuring them that all was well.

Joan started aimlessly walking. She soon caught sight of her reflection in a shop window and stopped to look closely at herself, slowly realizing that what she saw was a strong, formidable woman. Joan envisioned the strong women of bygone eras, who helped their families survive through all types of hard times— the Great Depression, world wars, global pandemics, and more. Joan knew she needed to stand firm in the face of her foe as well.

However, Joan knew that even the most formidable women needed to be armed with a plan. Slipping into a small New Age store, Joan discovered an array of merchandise, including crystals, incense, sage, smudging supplies, and candles. She walked around the shop, studying each item. Still unsure of what was needed for her task, Joan asked the shopkeeper for advice. Eventually, Joan left the shop with a bagful of merchandise and a lot of advice.

Exhausted by the day's events, Joan sat on a nearby bench to rest. A short while later, a woman, who was accompanied by a dog, sat on the bench directly across from her. The woman appeared to be roughly the same age as Joan and was dressed in a simple, conservative black dress. Joan returned the other woman's smile, feeling a connection that she couldn't explain.

"Do I know you? My name's Joan."

"My name is Amy, but I don't think that I know you. I saw you in the New Age store, however. You sure bought a lot of stuff."

"Yup, I sure did. I have a situation that I need to take care of."

"Yes, I overheard you. I didn't mean to eavesdrop, but it's a small store."

"Yes, it's small but packed with lots of interesting stuff." Joan slowly stood up. Her thoughts were focused on her upcoming battle with Abigail.

"Before you leave, can I ask something? I'm a pastor. Is there something that I can help you with?"

Sitting back down, Joan calmly said, "Well, my mother died recently, and the demon that had possessed her is now lingering around me. Is that something you can help with?"

"Maybe. I would have to research it. I've never handled a situation such as that."

"Most conventional pastors would dismiss what I just said as crazy and refer me to a shrink."

"I don't get the feeling that you are crazy. And according to my last two churches, I'm a little unorthodox. I guess that's why I am between churches, as they say."

"That's interesting. I know an unorthodox church in need

of a pastor. The church is roughly four hours north of here, however. Do you want their phone number?"

"Why not? I might give them a call."

"Are you sure that we have never met? You look so familiar to me. Do you have a sister maybe?" Joan studied the woman sitting across from her.

"I had a sister once; however, she's no longer with us."

"I'm sorry for your loss."

After what seemed like too long of a silence, Joan decided to change the subject. "I don't remember seeing your dog in the store."

"Oh, I didn't have her in the store. I had left her at a nearby doggie daycare earlier today. She loves to play with the other dogs."

"What type of dog is she?"

"She's part beagle, but I'm not really sure what else. She's a rescue mutt but very friendly. Her name is Ziggy."

"That's a cute name. I have a dog too. Her name is Molly. Well, it was nice meeting you."

Joan got up again and started to walk away.

"Wait," Amy called.

Joan returned to the bench and sat.

"About twenty minutes ago, an older gentleman stopped me as I exited the Sheriff's office," Amy said. "At first, I thought that he was lost. He really didn't look like he belonged in downtown Madison. In fact, he looked more like he should be fishing on a lake somewhere. He asked me to walk with him. I don't really know why, but I obeyed him. A few minutes later, he pointed you out to me."

"Really?"

"Yes, and he said that I should talk to you about lilac bushes." Amy looked down, feeling foolish for saying it.

Joan was stunned. She now realized who Amy resembled.

"Was he wearing a fishing cap with silver lures?"

"Yes, he was. The lures sparkled in the sunlight, actually. I got a strange vibe off him—sort of spiritual. I know that sounds odd."

"No, it's not odd. It's a long story, but he's a ghost."

Amy stared at Joan, trying to decide if Joan was, indeed, crazy. She then asked, "You met him also?"

"Yes, I have. He saved my life."

"Since I am a pastor, it goes without saying that I believe in angels. I'm not sure about ghosts, however."

"Most people don't believe in ghosts, I suppose. Why were you at the Sheriff's office?"

"They wanted my DNA to test against a body, or rather bones, that were found. I wasn't given much info, except that they had contacted the families of several missing persons who had disappeared during a specific timeframe. My sister is a missing person and has been for many years. Since my parents have both passed, and I'm the only sibling, I came as requested."

Joan was silent, unsure of how to explain the significance of the lilac bushes to Amy. However, she assumed that Pastor Bob wanted her to bring closure to Amy.

"I have long believed that my older sister was dead. It was just something that I felt in my bones. She was five years older than me, and we were polar opposites. She was very wild, and I was, well, not wild. I was shy and followed the rules. But despite everything, we were close. However, when she was sixteen, my sister ran away. She was never seen again."

Joan reached over and held Amy's hands, whispering, "I need to tell you something."

After the story was told, both women embraced. As their tears flowed, both ignored the stares of those walking by. After a while, Amy broke free of the embrace, stopped crying, and stated firmly, "Obviously, I need to help you banish this dark energy or demon—or whatever it is. Its evil has unspeakably harmed both of our families. We're connected by our tragedies."

"Thank you, but I only wanted you to know the truth. I don't want you to get involved with this darkness. It's dangerous, but I'm not afraid to deal with it alone."

"I appreciate your concern, but there's safety in numbers. I'm joining this fight."

"Okay, thank you," Joan said, secretly grateful for the assistance. "I'm heading back home right now. I live in the same village as the unorthodox church that I mentioned. I mean that I decided to live there. I put a small down payment on a house a couple of days ago. Since the current owner has already moved, she has kindly allowed me to stay in the house while the sale is finalized. I feel that this needs to be done there—in my new home."

"Please give me your address. I'll grab a few things at home, and Ziggy and I will get on the road as soon as possible."

~

As Joan arrived back in the peaceful little village, daylight was giving way to night. She stopped by Gus's house to pick up her dog. The dog quickly ran over to the truck and jumped in, and Joan waved a thank you to Gus. As she pulled away, Joan watched Gus in her rearview mirror, noting a concerned look on his face.

In the driveway of her new home, Joan sat quietly for a few minutes, looking at the house. The small blue house was weathered, and she felt that the yard required a touch of love, maybe a few flowers and a little garden gnome or two. Joan smiled at the thought of mischievous gnome statutes perched on her lawn—an image so different from the evil that she was about to battle. Joan hurried into the house, carrying the bagful of supplies from the New Age store.

Joan looked around at the furniture left behind by the owner, including a plaid couch, a rocking chair, a dinette set, mismatched chairs, beds, and assorted other items. Although everything showed wear, Joan was grateful for it. Decorating would need to wait. She had other things to handle at the moment.

"Molly," Joan said. "I missed you, sweetheart. I bought you a new toy."

Rather than run over to get the new toy, the dog slowly marched to the patio door and stared into the backyard. Joan stared into the backyard as well. As the sun set, the shadows became long and many. Seeing nothing but aware that the evil was lurking in the shadows, Joan whispered to the dog, "Molly, one more battle and then we'll be free."

Joan unpacked her bag and placed lemon-scented candles around the small house. Next, she placed an array of crystals throughout the house. Finally, as advised, she placed selenite crystals by each window as she opened them, allowing the fresh night air in and creating a pathway for the negative to depart. She then found an empty glass bowl and placed the white sage inside, setting a lighter next to it.

Joan stood still for a moment, trying to remember everything that she'd been told earlier at the store. Suddenly the doorbell rang, and Joan jumped slightly in surprise. It was an unfamiliar sound to her, and for a second, she wasn't sure what it was. "Oh geez, it's the doorbell."

Opening the door, Joan said, "Amy, you got here awfully fast."

"I probably set a speed record on the highway," Amy laughed. "I didn't know that my old pickup truck could go that fast. And thank goodness for GPS. This place is a little out of the way."

"Where's your dog?"

"She's in the truck. Can I bring her in? Ziggy isn't going to be happy if I leave her in there too long."

"Yes, of course. My dog, Molly, gets along with almost every dog that she meets."

Amy brought her dog inside, and after Ziggy and Molly sniffed each other, they trotted off to explore the house.

Amy glanced around the house. "I see that you have things set up. I have a few more items that might be helpful tonight. I brought a couple of crosses to hang above your doorways. I also brought a cross that you should wear around your neck."

"Thank you." Joan slipped on the necklace with the cross.

As she hammered nails in the walls to hang the crosses, Amy said, "I also have my Bible, of course, and I stopped at my old church for holy water. I think that we should sprinkle the holy water around the house as part of the purification process."

The doorbell rang again, but this time Joan didn't jump. As Gus stood in the dim light of the doorway, Joan was taken back by his appearance. Although a sixty-something man, he had projected a youthful energy. But now, the dark circles under his eyes and the intense wrinkling of his forehead projected a much different type of energy—a type of heavy energy that drains away the spark of life, leaving only gloominess and emptiness behind. Joan feared that the evil was trying to take hold of him as well.

"Sorry to bother you," Gus mumbled. "But I can't shake a feeling that you might be in danger. I have been worrying about you the last couple of days. Is there anything that you need help with? I think that Pastor Bob would want me to help you. I feel that there's something really, really wrong."

Joan was silent as she wondered how to respond.

"Hello, Gus," Amy said, walking over to the door. "I'm Pastor Amy. I'm here to help Joan banish a dark presence that has affected both her family as well as my own."

Gus took a step or two into the house and saw the candles and crystals. He nodded and said, "I understand now. Pastor Bob told me once that darkness will sneak up and attach itself to whoever it can. From time to time, he helped people dispel the darkness that had found its way into their souls."

"Pastor Bob did exorcisms?" Amy asked.

"Oh, I don't think that he ever called it that," Gus said. "But Pastor Bob said that he was called not only to take care of the good folks of the church but also those whose souls needed a little cleansing. Is there anything that I can do?"

"Actually, yes. It just hit me," Joan said. "It's not a good idea to have the dogs here. I don't want to risk them being traumatized or harm in any way by what is about to happen. I also remember being told once that demons can possess animals as well. Would you please take Molly and Ziggy for the night?"

"Of course," Gus said. "I hope they like bratwursts. I have a couple left over."

Amy's eyebrows shot up at the thought of Ziggy eating bratwursts, but she didn't share her concern.

Joan knelt down by Molly and whispered, "Molly, please watch over them tonight. I know that you understand what's happening."

Molly barked, wagged her tail, and trotted off with Gus and Ziggy.

"I was told once that hate, evil, darkness, or whatever you want to call it spreads if it's not stopped," Joan said, watching Gus and the dogs walk away.

Amy was silent.

"If we don't stop the evil, Amy, it will engulf this whole village. I'm not going to let that happen."

"I agree with you. Evil cannot be allowed to spread."

"Do you know how we should start, Amy?"

"Not really, Joan. I didn't have time to research the subject in depth. However, I honestly feel that it's important to just call upon God and tell the dark presence, or demon, or whatever it is, to leave."

"I sure hope it's that simple." Joan's voice quivered, revealing her uneasiness and fear. She sensed the darkness; the demon was very near.

Despite her desire to help, Amy felt unsettled by the recent discovery of her long-dead sister, and she said in a surprisingly flat voice, "Turn off all of the lights in the house."

"Should I light the candles?"

"No, Joan. We can light them later."

As Amy remained in the foyer, Joan walked throughout the house, turning off the lights.

"Okay, all of the lights are off, Amy. But I think we need to light the candles. It's pretty dark in here."

No response came from Amy.

Joan's eyes adjusted to the darkened house, and she rounded the corner, entering the foyer. As she did so, Amy stood deadly still. Standing within inches of each other, Joan tensed, feeling anger mixed with a touch of evil in Amy's stillness.

"Are you okay?" Joan quietly asked.

"No. As I drove up here, I started to think about my parents, and I became angrier and angrier with each mile. Do you understand how much my parents suffered, wondering about what happened to their daughter? I then thought about how each of them, first my father and then my mother, went to their graves like two shattered, broken old people."

"I'm so sorry for the pain that your parents felt."

"Are you, Joan?"

Stunned by the question, Joan didn't respond.

With her anger apparent in each word that she spoke, Amy

continued, "It would have been so much better to know the truth. Do you have any idea how many hours and days and years my parents suffered, imagining the worst but hoping for the best? Was my sister living on the streets? Was she addicted to drugs? In trouble? In need of help? Was my sister dead or alive?"

"It must have been horrible for your whole family. I'm so sorry."

Amy took a step forward and slapped Joan across the face. "Why the hell didn't you call the police that night?"

The force of the slap caused Joan to lose her balance. As she steadied herself, Joan whispered again, "I'm so sorry."

"Stop saying how sorry you are! You watched as my sister was being murdered. And you knew where your mother buried her. Why didn't you call the police?"

"I was only a kid. I blocked the whole thing out of my mind."

"You haven't been a kid for thirty-some years, Joanie, my dear. You could have let someone know where my sister was a whole lot sooner than you did! That makes you almost as guilty as your mother and almost as evil."

Amy suddenly pushed Joan to the floor. Joan flinched as she felt the first of Amy's kicks and then flinched again as she felt the next kick and then the next. Amy dropped to her knees, and with her hands bent into hard, angry fists, she repeatedly struck Joan. Joan offered no defense. With each kick and blow, Joan painfully recalled how years of pent-up anger can turn into violence. Then just as suddenly as the violence started, it ended.

Joan now felt a familiar evil presence nearby. Crawling into the living room, she could see a dark form lurking in the shadows, becoming more and more empowered as it fed on Amy's anger. Reaching for the lighter, Joan lit a candle and saw that Amy was now curled up in a fetal position, silently sobbing.

Joan crawled back over to Amy, and she wrapped her arms

around Amy, much like a mother comforting a frightened baby. "Ssshhh," Joan whispered. "I understand."

"I don't know what happened. I just snapped. I'm so sorry."

"I understand, Amy. I really do. Please believe me."

Amy looked into Joan's eyes and saw the understanding.

"The darkness, the demon, is here. We need to fight it. Can you do that, Amy?"

"Yes," Amy whispered, taking a deep breath and standing.

Joan also stood, lighting more candles until their glow filled the house. As the refreshing scent of lemon drifted through the house, Joan lit the sage, placing it back into the glass bowl. Amy retrieved her Bible, the holy water, and a large wooden cross from her purse.

"Ready?" Joan asked, and Amy silently mouthed that she was.

Joan walked from room to room, waving the smoke from the sage in clockwise circles. Amy followed close behind, holding her Bible and cross, loudly praying, "We pray to Archangel Michael and all his angels and ask for protection as we battle the forces of evil. We pray to Archangel Michael for help in casting out the demon, the darkness, and the evil that has attached itself to Joan and has entered this home. We pray to Almighty God and the Archangels to cast out this demon and all of the dark entities that lurk in this house, as well as those trying to invade this village. We pray to Almighty God and the Archangels to send all of them back to hell."

As they continued to move through the house, Amy sprinkled holy water. And Joan began to loudly proclaim, "Demon, hear me, I do *not* give you permission to be here nor do I give you power over me. I reject you. You must leave my house, my family, my village, and my friends, Amy and Gus."

The two women trembled as they watched the dark, lurking shadowy form appear, disappear, and then reappear again and again. They jumped as the windows rattled; they froze at the sound of growling; they cringed as they heard eerie laughter; they endured waves of nausea, but they remained fearless.

As the candles burned down and their flames flickered out, the morning sun rose, filling the house with natural light. The two women finally sat, exhausted from a night of prayers and rituals.

"I think that the evil is gone. Do you agree, Amy?"

"Yes, Joan. It feels so much more peaceful here."

"Thank God, Amy."

"Yes, I will."

"I hope that it stays gone."

"Me too, Joan."

"I read once that the only way to ensure that darkness stays away is to live a happy life, to live in the light. I want to turn this house into an actual home—a happy place. I want to fill it with the smells of cooking and the sound of laughter. I want flesh flowers growing outside. Do you think that will keep the darkness away from me, Amy?"

"Yes. I can't believe a demon would ever dare to enter such a home."

Both women smiled.

"Amy, do you want to attend church tomorrow with me? You never know—maybe you will want to stay and be their new pastor."

"After last night, I don't think that I should try to be a pastor in any church. I snapped and attacked you. I never realized how much anger was inside of me. I'm going back to Madison and bury my sister. Didn't you say that you hit the road for a while to find some sort of peace? Maybe I should do that? What was it like being on the road?"

"Lonely but healing."

"You were on the road a long time, right? Are you truly ready to stay in one place and make this your home?"

"Yes. Awhile back, I sat next to a worn-out-looking woman at a laundromat in a little town in the Mojave Desert. We were both waiting for our clothes to dry, and she said something that stuck with me. *You need to live through a drought before you can really appreciate a cold glass of water.*"

Amy laughed and said, "I have to agree with her!"

"I think that you would love being the pastor here. The people are very welcoming. Lizzie, who heads up the church board, told me earlier this week that Pastor Bob was a great pastor because of his pain. She believes that unless someone has felt pain themselves, they cannot fully understand the pain of others."

Amy nodded in understanding.

"However, I can understand that you need to find closure. But if you run across a preacher in need of a church, mention us. I'll call Gus and let him know that you are on the way."

∼

Amy had expected her dog to be upset after spending the night without her. However, as Amy drove up to Gus's house, her dog ran over to greet her with her tail wagging. After a few *kisses* from her dog, Amy laughed, "Wow, Ziggy, I'm so happy that you aren't mad."

Amy thanked Gus, and with Ziggy in tow, she drove away. After about an hour, she reached Rhinelander and pulled off the road. She sat in an empty parking lot, petting her dog and thinking about the emotional roller coaster she and her parents had endured. They lived in a state of worry for so many years, shifting between hope and hopelessness.

Amy painfully remembered the loneliness that she felt after

her sister disappeared. It wasn't just that Amy missed her sister. It was also that Amy no longer felt a part of her family. She was pushed into the background as her parents searched for her sister, and then again, as her parents gradually accepted that her sister would never return. There seemed little room for Amy in her parents' world of grief.

Amy also felt alone in her school and among her friends. None seemed truly capable of understanding what she was feeling. She had long wished to feel a part of something—to escape her sense of isolation. That was a large part of why she chose to be a pastor. However, she never found a church in which she truly felt she belonged.

Lonely—that was how Joan had described life on the road. Such a life seemed very, well, lonely to Amy. She wanted to live among people, to belong somewhere. She no longer wanted to feel lonely. Amy thought about the little unorthodox church that needed a pastor.

"Should I turn around and check out the church, Ziggy?"

The dog barked and popped her head out of the window, waiting for the truck to roar down the highway again and the wind to blow in her face. Amy pulled out of the parking lot and drove back to the little village with the unorthodox church.

It was still very early in the morning, and Lizzie was just unlocking the church door. As Amy got out of her truck, her friendly dog ran ahead to meet Lizzie.

As Amy approached Lizzie, she said, "Hello, I'm Pastor Amy, and I was told that you were looking for a pastor."

Lizzie looked first at the pickup truck, then at Ziggy, and finally at Amy, and said, "Yes, we have been waiting for you."

Chapter 18

A car slowly pulled into Joan's driveway. It was unnoticed by Joan, whose focus was fixed on her task—setting a tulip bulb gently into the hole she had dug, refilling the hole with dirt, and then scooting over roughly six inches and repeating the process.

However, Amy was nearby, raking the fallen autumn leaves. She watched the car pulled into the driveway, and a young woman get out. "Can I help you?"

"I'm looking for my mother."

"Joan, there's someone here to see you."

Amy's raised voice drew Joan's attention away from the tulip bulbs. Standing up, Joan brushed the dirt off of her pants and walked over to her daughter. They stood, facing each other, but neither spoke.

Breaking the silence, Amy said, "It's nice to meet you, Chloe. I've heard a lot about you. I'm the pastor at the local church here, and my name is Amy."

"It's nice to meet you," Chloe politely answered, still facing her mother.

"I think that I'll get the dogs from the backyard and take

them for a walk," Amy said, leaving mother and daughter standing alone.

"Do you want to come inside?"

"Yes, thank you."

Once inside the house, Chloe and Joan again stood in awkward silence until the little bird inside of a vintage cuckoo clock popped out, announcing it was noon.

Chloe jumped slightly and laughed. "Oh my god, that surprised me!"

"It took me a while to get used to it too. The clock belongs to Amy. It originally belonged to her parents and has a lot of sentimental value to her."

"She lives here?"

"Yes, the church pays almost nothing. I offered to let her live here, and she agreed. There's a story behind how we met, and maybe I can share that with you someday if you want. But it's nice to have a roommate. I was alone for a long."

"Yes, twelve years to be exact." Chloe regretted both her words and her tone, and she decided to quickly change the subject.

"Mom, did you know that I spent a night here during my road trip? We slept outside of the church."

"Yes, Aunt Edith recently told me."

"I met an old man at the church that morning, and he said that they didn't have a pastor."

"Amy has only recently become their pastor."

"I'm happy that they found someone for the gig."

"Why don't we sit?" Joan walked over to an old plaid couch and sat. Chloe followed and sat on a rocking chair across from her.

"Interesting furniture."

"Yes, it was left behind by the prior owner, but I kind of like it. It's old but homey. How was your drive up here?"

"It was okay, less traffic than during the summer."

"That's very true. The majority of the vacationers have left. Now the locals can enjoy the area. It's theirs again—at least for a while. Though some vacationers still venture up here to enjoy the autumn colors."

"I love autumn, Mom. It's my favorite season."

"Mine too. Like mother, like daughter." Joan smiled; Chloe didn't.

"Did you get my letter?" Joan asked, trying to turn the conversation away from idle chit-chat.

"Yes, I read it many times. I understand why you left. But twelve years is a long time."

"Yes, it is, and I'm sorry."

Chloe noticed several photos that hung on the wall and asked, "Where did you get those?"

"I asked for some photos of you, and your father mailed a bunch to me. He's a good man."

"Yes, absolutely. Did you know that he closed down his law office and is opening up a small diner in town? Dad loves to cook, and he wants to do something that brings him joy."

"No, I didn't know that, but I'm happy for him. He's one of those people who are genuinely decent. I think God put people like your father on earth for a reason—so the rest of us can see what decent looks like."

"That's a nice thing to say about Dad. I'll have to tell him that."

Chloe noticed a small framed photo sitting on a nearby side table. "That's the man that I met at the church. Do you know him?"

"Yes, that's Pastor Bob. I mentioned him in my letter to you. He was previously the pastor at the local church."

"Really? He never mentioned that he was a pastor. Is he retired?"

"No, he's not. He passed away about twelve years ago."

"Passed away? Twelve years ago?"

"Yes, that's right. Do you believe in things like ghosts and angels?"

"After this summer, Mom, it would be hard not to. Actually, I always sort of believed. It's odd that we both met Paster Bob's ghost, though."

"Not as odd as you think. I would really like to talk to you about Paster Bob at some point, but it can wait. I know that you didn't come here to talk about him."

"No, I didn't. I came because I needed to say something to you."

Joan braced herself, unsure of what her daughter felt toward her.

"I have to be honest, Mom. I've been feeling a range of emotions since you returned. I'm relieved that you're alive and thankful that you protected me. But the fact that you stayed away for so long still hurts."

"Chloe, I never stopped loving you."

"I know, and I love you too. I also understand why you had to leave. I've been trying to be philosophical about all of this. I honestly believe we're all here on earth to learn lessons during our lifetime."

"What lessons have you learned?" Joan asked, surprised by her daughter's philosophical nature.

"I learned that facing your fears is the only way to defeat them."

"I learned that also, Chloe."

"I also *relearned* that I love the outdoors."

"I'm happy to hear that. But your dad mentioned that you decided to go to law school."

"Yes, I had been trying to figure out what I wanted to do with my life and had been wishy-washy on the idea of becoming an attorney. But I've decided to pursue a law degree after all and focus on environmental law. I feel a true calling to protect what's left of nature, and laws are one of the best ways to do that."

"I'm so happy that you have found something that you truly want to do."

"I've also learned, or to be more precise, decided something else. I've decided that I can't judge you. I've never walked in your shoes. I can't know for sure what I would have done under similar circumstances."

Joan silently cried, relieved to hear her daughter's words.

Chloe crossed over to the couch, sat close to her mother, and hugged her. "I forgive you, Mom."

"Oh Chloe, I love you."

Molly burst through the door, excitingly jumping up on the couch and wedging herself between mother and daughter. Her wagging tail confirmed what all felt. They were happy to be back together again.

Acknowledgment

Most, if not all, first-time authors learn that writing a book is not easy. It takes time—lots of time. You sit endlessly at a keyboard and bang out a bunch of words that you hope someday will become a book. Finally, you have a bunch of pages filled with a bunch of words. It's at this point that you turn to others to help turn those words into a book, and I want to thank the following people who helped me do just that.

I want to thank Valerie Biel, Lost Lake Press, for her editing skills, insight, and suggestions. Her suggestions were spot-on and helped to point me in the right direction.

I also want to thank Saundra Norton, Norton Editing, for her proofreading, edits, and comments. I appreciated her comments/suggestions just as much as her expertise in proofreading.

Next, I want to thank Christine Keleny, CKBooks Publishing, for her help in turning my manuscript into an actual book. Without her skill in print and ebook design/formatting, my book might have remained just another unpublished manuscript.

About the Author

Diana L. Forsberg is a proud Wisconsinite. She currently lives in a small Wisconsin community nestled between a lake and rolling farm fields. After working too many years in the world of office memos and spreadsheets, she decided to leave the safety of an office cubicle to write. Combining her life-long interest in the paranormal and her desire to write, she hit the keyboard and wrote her first novel, *Never Tell Chloe*.